ACTS OF VIOLETS

A FLOWER SHOP MYSTERY

ACTS OF VIOLETS

KATE COLLINS

THORNDIKE
CHIVERS

This Large Print edition is published by Thorndike Press, Waterville, Maine, USA and by BBC Audiobooks Ltd, Bath, England.

Thorndike Press is an imprint of Thomson Gale, a part of The Thomson Corporation.

Thorndike is a trademark and used herein under license.

The text of this Large Print edition is unabridged.

Other aspects of the book may vary from the original edition.

Set in 16 pt. Plantin.

LIBRARY OF CONGRESS CATALOGING-IN-PUBLICATION DATA

Collins, Kate, 1951–
    Acts of violets : a flower shop mystery / by Kate Collins.
      p. cm. — (Thorndike Press large print mystery)
    ISBN-13: 978-0-7862-9616-3 (alk. paper)
    ISBN-10: 0-7862-9616-X (alk. paper)
    1. Knight, Abby (Fictitious character) — Fiction. 2. Florists — Fiction.
    3. Large type books. I. Title.
    PS3603.O4543A63 2007
    813'.6—dc22
                             2007011595

BRITISH LIBRARY CATALOGUING-IN-PUBLICATION DATA AVAILABLE

Published in 2007 in the U.S. by arrangement with NAL Signet, a member of Penguin Group (USA) Inc.
Published in 2007 in the U.K. by arrangement with the author.
U.K. Hardcover: 978 1 405 64178 4 (Chivers Large Print)
U.K. Softcover: 978 1 405 64179 1 (Camden Large Print)

Printed in the United States of America on permanent paper
10 9 8 7 6 5 4 3 2 1

ACKNOWLEDGMENTS

Authors never write entirely alone; don't let anyone tell you otherwise. There are always editors and agents and husbands and mothers and fathers and children standing silently (or not) in the background. Also those pesky little voices in our heads.

To that end I would be remiss if I didn't thank my husband for providing a shoulder to whine on, as well as his legal expertise (*the* best lawyer in Indiana — not that I'm prejudiced or anything); my sister, Nancy, and best friend, Barb (more shoulders for whining; how do they stand me?); "My Kids: The Entire Collection"; my editor, Ellen Edwards; my agent, Karen Solem; the terrific artist who designed the Flower Shop Mystery covers (absolutely the coolest!); my stepmom, Bonnie (the American version of Grace); and of course the clowns Jocko and Bimbo, who were the true inspiration for this book, not to mention for Abby's night-mares. The voices and I thank you all.

This book is dedicated to the memory of Joseph Eberhardt, a man who endured unbelievable hardships yet never lost his enthusiasm for life. His ready smile and generous heart will always be an inspiration to those of us who loved him. God bless you, Joe.

CHAPTER ONE

"You think that was funny? You think I don't know you did that on purpose? Well, I've got your number, shorty, so let me tell you something: Paybacks are murder."

Paybacks? Murder? Shorty! Hugging my purse to my chest, I gaped at the bad-tempered buffoon as he gathered his cucumbers, climbed onto his unicycle, and rode off to join his troupe. You wouldn't expect that kind of behavior from a clown named Snuggles.

Was it my fault he ran over my purse and fell off his tall perch? No, it was the bozo's behind me — pardon the clown pun — who was too busy stuffing his face with a bratwurst to notice the short redhead with an even shorter fuse standing in front of him. This was a small parade. He was a big guy. Did he have to be in the front row? And who eats brats at ten o'clock in the morning?

I turned my attention back to Snuggles, who was once again juggling cukes from his seat-in-the-sky as he pedaled up the street. My policy was to stand up to bullies — and that snarled threat was certainly bullying behavior — but before I could give him a piece of my mind (I was thinking along the lines of recommending a place to store those cucumbers) I was yanked back onto the sidewalk by my best friend and roommate, Nikki Hiduke, an X-ray tech at the county hospital, who had shared many childhood adventures with me and lived to tell about it.

"Abby, are you all right? You look dazed."

"Nikki, that clown threatened me! As if I elbowed myself off the sidewalk." I cast a glare over my shoulder at Mr. Oblivious, who had finished his bratwurst and was slurping mustard off his fingers. I was amazed he wasn't also talking on a mobile phone. Oh, wait. Yes, he was. He had on an earpiece.

"Snuggles the Clown threatened you?" Nikki stared after the troupe — three acrobats, two unicyclists, one stilt walker, and the last (my favorite because of the huge purple lily atop a long green stem waving from her bonnet), a baby-doll clown peddling a giant purple tricycle. "But he looks so harmless."

"Don't let that goofy smile fool you." I scrubbed the black tread mark off the tan leather purse that I'd almost gone into hock for. "Beneath that greasepaint is a nasty temper and a voice that would make a polar bear shiver."

"Abby, you have mustard on your shoulder."

Wonderful. I took a tissue from my tire-engraved purse and blotted the yellow stain on my white shirt. Why had I even bothered to come? It was a sunny Saturday morning, and although my flower shop, Bloomers, was open on Saturdays, this was my one weekend a month to sleep in. But no. Attending the Annual Pickle Fest Parade was a family tradition, and to break that tradition was to incur the wrath of my mom, Maureen "Mad Mo" Knight.

Speaking of whom, where was she? I'd never known her to miss the start of the parade, when Peter Piper led his merry band of Pickled Peppers up Lincoln Avenue to the strains of a John Philip Sousa march.

I scanned the crowd lining both sides of the street. Today was the start of New Chapel, Indiana's, fall Pickle Festival — a weeklong celebration of brine-soaked vegetables attended by thousands of people from all over the state, some from as far away as Chicago, giving the local newspaper, the *New Chapel News,* fodder for headlines such as VISITORS RELISH THE PICKLE FEST. I had a hunch it wasn't so much the pickled produce as it was *getting* pickled that was the actual draw.

All four streets around the courthouse square had been blocked off to accommodate the huge crowds. Restaurant owners set up tables in front of their establishments to sell beer, hot dogs, bratwurst, dills, pickled beets, pickled tomatoes, pickled watermelon, and, yes, pickled peppers to the hungry visitors. For the truly desperate, pickled herring and pickled pig's feet were also available. Shoe shops, gift boutiques, and clothing stores put out their wares, and even Bloomers had a display of mums, roses, asters, and greenery for sale.

Then there were the ever-popular arts and crafts booths that dotted the huge lawn around the big limestone courthouse in the middle of the square. Beneath the shady maples and elms, brightly colored canvas tents housed ceramics, watercolors, oils, clay sculpture, silver jewelry, quilts, pottery, toys, metal sculpture, and even marble birdbaths.

My mother would have her work on display somewhere in that mix. In addition to being a kindergarten teacher, Mom now fancied herself an artist, having received a pottery wheel for Christmas last year. Before she grew bored with clay, she had produced a variety of weird sculptures such as the infamous *Dancing Male Monkeys Table* and the *Human Footstool.* She had since moved on to mirrored tiles, with which she'd covered nearly every object in her house, making a washroom visit a truly frightening experience. I didn't know what craft she was into this week. My father would only say, "It's a tickler."

"Do you see my family?" I asked Nikki. Being a head taller (even more if you added her spiky blonde hair), she had a sight advantage. She also had a body advantage — slender, long legged, and small breasted, something I had aspired to from the age of thirteen. My brothers, both doctors, insisted that people stopped growing when they reached puberty, but they were only half right; I hadn't gone beyond my five-foot-two-inch frame since junior high, but I had gone *way* beyond my training bra.

"I don't see any of them," Nikki said, holding up her hand to shield her eyes.

Normally, they weren't hard to pick out, since Jonathan and Jordan had the same flame red hair and freckled skin that my dad and I had. My mother's hair was a soft brown, lucky woman, and my sisters-in-law — Portia and Kathy — had also escaped the curse of the red.

"There's Marco," Nikki shouted in my ear as the New Chapel High School marching band passed by. She pointed between green-coated band members to the opposite side of the street, but I had already spotted him. How could anyone miss a dark-haired, virile-bodied, extremely hot hunk like Marco Salvare, a former Army Ranger and ex-cop who now owned the Down the Hatch Bar and Grill — as well as my heart?

"Who's that woman talking to him?" Nikki asked.

I eyed the attractive girl beside him. "I don't know. She's pretty, isn't she?"

"*Pffft.* No way. Ew. And would you look at those split ends?"

"Nikki, you can't see split ends from here, and besides, it's okay to agree with me. I don't feel threatened by the woman. I'm not the jealous type."

She burst out laughing.

Ignoring her, I narrowed my eyes at the pair, watching as Marco tilted his head toward the woman to catch something she said. She couldn't have been a day over twenty-five, and had an oval face with delicate features framed by long, thick black hair topping off a perfectly proportioned body. She was talking animatedly and pointing to something or someone up the street. The Pickled Peppers? The clown troupe? Someone in the marching band?

"Abigail, there you are!" my mother called. I turned to find her parting the crowd so the humongous feathered hat on her head could fit through. Normally, she wasn't one to wear hats, let alone feathers, but she did have a way of surprising me. "We've been looking all over for you. Why aren't you in front of Bloomers?"

"Because we always meet here, by the Clothes Loft. Where are Dad and the gang?"

"By your shop, which is where I thought you'd be."

"It's hard to see the parade from Bloomers, Mom. You know it doesn't go down Franklin. Besides, we always meet here. If you wanted to meet elsewhere, you should have told me."

"I would have told you if I thought there was a need to tell you. But since you're a shop owner now, I really didn't see the need."

I started to argue that my being a shop owner had nothing to do with it, but Nikki nudged me and coughed. That was the signal we used when one of us was expecting a family member to be rational.

"Shall we go get everyone and bring them back here?" Mom looked at me from under the wide, feathered brim of her hat, her eyes scouring me for signs of illness or distress. Like a hawk, she instantly homed in on the yellow splotch on my shoulder. "How did you spill mustard on your shirt?"

"Ask him," I said, hitching a thumb toward Mr. Oblivious, who was now giving a running commentary to whomever was on the other end of his phone line. "He pushed me into the path of a clown."

"Well, thank heavens it was *only* a clown. It could have been that team of horses." She pointed toward the two grays hauling a nineteenth-century fire wagon. Seated on a bench beside the driver was a giant inflatable cucumber dressed in an old-fashioned red fire hat and yellow slicker. Every entry in the parade had to incorporate something pickled, which could have gotten racy except that entrants also had to go before a review panel of six somber senior citizens.

"But *this* clown threatened me, Mom."

"A clown threatened you?" asked a familiar, husky male voice from behind me.

My heart skipped a beat as I turned to see the owner of the voice, Marco (minus the pretty woman), looking extremely macho in his tan Down the Hatch T-shirt, slim-fitting blue jeans, and dusty brown boots. He'd managed to cross the street between floats and was now holding a strawberry ice cream cone, unaware that he was being ogled by every woman within a ten-yard radius.

Marco wasn't handsome in the movie-star sense of the word. He didn't have a straight nose, or baby blue eyes, or a wide, perfectly even smile. What he *did* have were deep, dark, bedroom eyes, a masculine nose, a firm mouth that curved devilishly at the corners when he was amused, and an olive complexion that was rarely without a five-o'clock shadow. He was tough and quick-witted, but amazingly sensitive to my moods and feelings. Maybe that was why he brought me the cone.

He held it out and I took it. Ordinarily, I don't eat ice cream before lunch, but after being shoved and threatened and stained with mustard, I felt a strong need to soak my irritated nerves in butterfat. Once they were thoroughly saturated, I'd ask him about the woman.

"Morning, Nikki," he said with a little nod in her direction. "Mrs. Knight, new hat?"

"Yes. Thank you for noticing, Marco." Throwing me a *shame on you for not notic-*

ing look, Mom gave him a hug. She gave everyone hugs. It was part of being a kindergarten teacher.

"Tell me about the clown," Marco said, regarding me with that intense expression cops get when interrogating a witness. I knew that because my father had been a cop, and throughout my high school years my dates had been subjected to both the expression and the interrogation.

"He was just your standard, bulbous-nosed, orange-haired, cucumber-juggling unicyclist with an attitude problem," I said between licks, "who mistakenly believed I threw my purse in front of him to knock him off his cycle. Who then went on to snarl something about paybacks being murder, as if he wanted to get even with me for tripping him. Go figure."

Marco rubbed his jaw, staring up the street after the departing fire wagon. "Not your typical clown behavior."

"His name is Snuggles," Nikki put in helpfully. "It's on the back of his costume."

"Snuggles," Marco repeated, as though storing it away for future reference.

My mother gazed at me sadly. "I'm sorry, honey. You've always liked clowns."

I swallowed a big glob of ice cream. "I've *never* liked clowns. I've had a fear of them since I was five years old, when a clown with bad teeth tried to toss me into a burning building. You have to remember that."

"We were at the circus and it was part of their act," she assured me. "If there had been any danger involved, your father would never have let your brothers volunteer you."

"They volunteered me?" I sputtered.

She handed me a tissue to wipe the ice cream off my mouth. "When Abby was little," Mom explained to Marco and to anyone else who cared to listen, "she had imaginary friends who were clowns."

"They weren't my friends, Mom." I rolled my eyes at Marco.

"Then why did you play with little Jocko and Bimbo? Hmm?" To Marco she whispered, "That's what she named them. Jocko and Bimbo."

"I played with them because I'm a firm believer in the keep-your-friends-close-and-your-enemies-closer philosophy. It was purely self-protective."

"You were such a cute girl," she said, tucking a lock of hair behind my ear. Mothers were forever tucking and straightening and — even worse — licking their palms to flatten hair that wouldn't lie down. "Mom-spit," my brothers called it. I'd long ago made a vow to never inflict that kind of torture on my kids — if I ever had the urge to have any.

"Well," she said with a sigh, "shall we go? Marco, you're coming with us, aren't you?"

Of course he was coming with us. He'd promised to watch the parade with my family, and then he and I were going to hang out together for the rest of the day and enjoy the festivities.

"Thanks, but I have some business to take care of first." He put his mouth close to my ear and said huskily, "I'll catch up with you later."

I started to complain, but he was staring past me with a perturbed frown — the same frown he'd worn the time he'd cautioned me not to attempt the rescue of a young, captive Chinese woman, which I did anyway, then was nearly drowned in a hot tub. Or the time he warned me not to go back for the funeral rose I'd delivered to a dragon of a law professor, which ultimately led to me being the prime suspect in a murder case. It made me wonder what kind of business he was talking about now.

"Marco, you wouldn't be going after that clown, would you?"

"Nah."

"He didn't hurt me, you know. No harm done."

"I know that. I'll be back soon." He nodded a quick good-bye to Nikki and Mom, then slipped into the crowd.

Oh, yeah. He was going after the clown.

CHAPTER TWO

"Abby, where are you going?" my mother called as I started after Marco.

"On an errand. I'll meet you and Dad back here in ten minutes." I turned and ran into a trash can. Luckily, I needed to find one anyway to dispose of the sticky ice cream cone wrapper in my hand.

"I'm coming with you," Nikki said, dodging people — and the trash can — to catch up with me. "You're following Marco, aren't you?"

"Why would I follow Marco?"

We wove through a gaggle of teens and veered around a young mom pushing a stroller.

"To see if he meets up with that woman. I mean, come on. You have to be a tiny bit curious."

A *tiny bit* curious? Was she kidding? Great. Now I had two missions instead of one. "I think he's just looking for Snuggles, Nikki."

"To do what? Rough him up? He didn't take the clown's remark seriously, did he? I mean, he's a *clown*."

"Maybe he knows something about Snuggles. Maybe the man beneath the white paint and rubber nose is someone Marco has had run-ins with before. Otherwise, there wouldn't be a point in going after him. It's not like there's a need to defend my honor, and Marco isn't the type to browbeat someone for making an idle threat."

"Which takes me back to my original conclusion. He's looking for that woman." Nikki lifted an eyebrow.

"Fine. If that's what you want to believe, then he's looking for that woman, but if that's true, then it must be for a private investigation he's working on."

Or so I hoped. Although I'd known Marco for four months, dated him for three, and had even tracked down several killers with him, he was still very much a mystery to me. In fact, what I knew about him could fit into a single paragraph.

He'd been an Army Ranger, went to College on the GI Bill, joined the New Chapel police force, then abruptly quit a few years later to buy the bar and do some private eye work on the side. He'd grown up in the next county, had a mother (whom I'd never met) who had recently moved to Ohio, a father who was deceased, two brothers and a sister scattered across the country, and a younger sister nearby who had a little boy named Christopher.

Everything else I knew about Marco I'd gleaned from watching him and, trust me, he was a pleasure to watch — broad of shoulder, narrow of hip, with well-developed muscles and a sexy swagger that melted my mascara. But that wasn't all there was to him. He was also fearless, bright, and fun, and had more integrity in his little toe than most people had in their entire bodies — a rarity in a world where good qualities were in short supply. He was also perfect husband material, if either one of us ever felt inclined to get hitched.

But right now Marco seemed to enjoy his bachelor life. Although I didn't mind being single and *relatively* carefree, either — no one could be totally carefree if they were mortgaged to the eyeballs — one day I hoped we'd both be ready for the whole white-picket-fence and baby-diapers scene. For now, I was happy just to hang out with him whenever our schedules allowed. Today was supposed to be one of those days, but right now it wasn't looking promising.

Plowing through a crowd, ninety-five

percent of which was taller than me, I quickly lost sight of Marco and had to rely on Nikki. One block later, she came to a sudden halt and I smacked into her. "Let's go back," she said, turning me by the shoulders and giving me a forward push.

"Why?"

"Don't ask questions. Just go."

"Don't ask questions? And you've known me how long? Tell me what you saw."

"You don't want to know."

"Nikki, if you don't tell me this minute I'll start singing the national anthem right here in the middle of the crowd."

She gave a violent shudder. She had been in the seventh-grade glee club with me. "It's Marco," she said regretfully. "And he's with that woman." She hitched a thumb over her shoulder.

I leaned to the right to peer around her. "Where?"

"Standing in the doorway of Pipsqueaks."

I shifted my gaze to the front of the children's clothing store and found them. "Damn."

"Okay, maybe it's not as bad as it looks. Maybe it *is* just PI business."

Considering that Marco had his hands on either side of her face and was gazing intently into her eyes, I had my doubts.

Marco said something to her, then turned and rejoined the crowd, while the woman watched him go with naked longing. Her shoulders moved up and down with a heavy sigh. Then she headed in our direction.

I was just about to step in front of her and ask what her business was with Marco when Nikki blocked my path. "Let's go meet your parents and watch the rest of the parade."

That was her gentle way of telling me to knock it off, and I knew she was right. Marco and I didn't have an exclusive agreement. If he wanted to see someone else, then he was free to do so. And I was going to become an astronaut and fly to Saturn.

"Let's just see where the woman goes, Nikki. Also, what kind of car she drives and what her license plate number is."

"Seriously, Abby, your mother will send out a search party if we don't get back there."

"You're right. Let's go." Because I just couldn't help it, I peered around Nikki again, but the woman was gone.

A big cheer went up as the 1967 Cadillac convertible carrying the Cucumber King and Queen came into view. Dressed in a dill green gown, with a silver tiara on her head,

Ms. Cuke waved enthusiastically, while Mr. Cuke, in a red pepper–patterned jacket, tossed out wrapped candy and gold foil chocolate coins. I dodged a coin with barely an eye blink, my thoughts still on Marco.

"What's the matter, Abby?" my dad asked, gazing up at me from his wheelchair. "You're usually fighting for those chocolate coins."

"It's that nasty clown incident, Jeff," my mom said. "Abigail, why don't you ask your father to speak to one of his friends on the force about it?"

"Abby is twenty-six years old, Mo," my dad said. "She doesn't want me fighting her battles."

"Thanks, Dad." I patted his shoulder. "Mom, it was just a rude comment. Trust me. I've already forgotten about the clown."

My father, Jeffrey Knight, had been a sergeant on the New Chapel police force until three years ago, when a felon's bullet hit his leg and surgery to remove the bullet had caused a stroke that put him in a wheelchair. For a man who was used to being independent and in charge — and a terrific dancer, I might add — it had been a terrible blow. But, as he did with everything else he encountered, he dealt with it. I tried to model myself after him, but it didn't always work, such as now, when I couldn't get the sight of Marco tenderly stroking another woman's face out of my mind.

At least my brothers and their wives hadn't joined us. I wasn't keen on having Jon and Jordan tease me mercilessly about bringing down a cucumber juggler. I could just imagine the kind of cracks it would spawn. *"Was he workin' his gherkin, Abs?"*

When the last float had passed — a giant jar with people inside dressed to look like dill slices, sponsored by the New Chapel Savings and Loan and bearing the slogan, DON'T GET YOURSELF INTO A PICKLE. COME SEE US FOR A LOAN — we crossed the street and headed toward Bloomers, located directly across from the old limestone courthouse.

On the four streets surrounding the courthouse were the typical assortment of family-owned shops, banks, law offices, and restaurants. Five blocks east of the square marked the western edge of the campus of New Chapel University, a small private college where I would have graduated from law school if I hadn't flunked out. It had something to do with the law professors not liking the way my brain functioned — *when* it functioned. Apparently, I was supposed to use things like legal precedence, not common sense.

With Nikki forging a path through the crowd and my mother pushing Dad's wheelchair, we made our way up the crowded sidewalk on Franklin, past the Down the Hatch Bar and Grill — Marco's place. At a table outside, two of Marco's waitstaff were selling grilled bratwurst, hot dogs, and beer by the plastic cupful. Through the big picture window I could see Chris, the head bartender, standing behind the long, polished walnut counter, chatting with a row of customers as he worked the taps.

Two doors down was Bloomers, with its two bay windows and its old-fashioned yellow framed door with beveled glass center. Bloomers occupied the first floor of a deep, three-story, redbrick building. On the right side was our Victorian-inspired coffee and tea parlor, complete with white wrought-iron tables and chairs, and china cups and saucers in an old-fashioned rose pattern — a great find at the antique mall.

On the other side was the sales floor, where customers could browse the glass-fronted display cooler for fresh flowers; or the shelves of old bookcases and an antique armoire for silk floral arrangements and small gift items; or even the walls, draped with swags and wreaths and decorative mirrors. For me, though, the real delight lay behind a curtained doorway in the back — my own little slice of paradise, the work-room.

It was a tropical garden–like space filled with fresh blossoms, dried flowers, heavenly aromas, and glass vases and pottery containers of all sizes. It was in that room that I could open up my soul and let it sing. Holding those dewy petals in my fingers, smelling the sweet fragrance of the beautiful blossoms, I was lifted away from the everyday problems and stresses of life and transported into a zone of tranquility.

I had always loved the old redbrick building on the square, but I never dreamed I would own a business in it. After my disastrous year at law school and my breakup with my fiancé, Pryce Osborne II, I didn't think I had any dreams left. Then my former employer, Lottie Dombowski, made a startling suggestion: buy her flower shop.

She hadn't really wanted to sell the quaint little shop, but her husband's enormous medical bills had wiped out her cash reserves. I wanted to help her out — I had worked as her assistant, delivering flowes and helping with arrangements — but what did I know about running a business? Nothing. Still, the only things I'd ever had luck with were plants, so six months ago I used the rest of the trust fund my grandfather had left me to secure a mortgage; then I immediately hired Lottie as my assistant. It had worked out beautifully for both of us.

When we reached Bloomers, Lottie was out front assembling a bouquet for a waiting customer, while Grace was inside, handling the shop and coffee parlor. Business was usually dead on the festival's opening day, so we used the table outside to lure customers from the arts and crafts fair across the street.

While Mom took Dad inside for a cup of Grace's famed chamomile tea, and Nikki went along for a cup of espresso, I stayed to chat with Lottie.

"How's business?" I asked quietly.

"Starting to pick up now that the parade is over." She handed the wrapped arrangement to the customer, then glanced at me. "All right," she said, folding her arms over her bounteous bosom, "you want to tell me what's causing that wrinkle in your forehead?"

I tried to erase the crease with my index finger — as if there was a way to hide anything from the mother of seventeen-year-old quadruplet boys. "I'm just feeling a little bummed."

31

"Abby saw Marco with another woman," Nikki said, standing in the doorway with a cup and saucer in her hands.

"A *pretty* woman," I corrected her.

"She had split ends," Nikki whispered to Lottie, who merely clucked her tongue at me.

"Sweetie, if you're gonna get your nose bent out of shape every time you see your man jawin' with a female, you'd better sign up for some plastic surgery."

That was one of the things I loved about Lottie. She didn't mince words. She had a generous amount of what she called "Kentucky horse sense," even if she did wear a bright pink satin barrette in the brassy curls above her left ear. Her philosophy on life was "Stuff happens, so suck it up."

"Now, *there's* the guy you should go for." Lottie pointed across the street to where deputy prosecutor Greg Morgan was giving an interview to a reporter and posing for the TV cameraman from WWIN, the local cable television station. "My, my. Isn't he a looker?" Lottie heaved a wistful sigh.

"And doesn't he know it," Nikki said with a snort.

Lottie belived Greg Morgan was the handsomest man she'd ever seen, and that he and I were made for each other, even though I'd explained to her many times that Morgan gave new meaning to the term *stuck on himself.* In high school he'd kept a hand mirror, hair spray, and dental floss in his locker and had joined as many clubs as he could squeeze into his schedule so he could get his photo in the yearbook more times than anyone else.

"Sweetie, all men are just big lumps of clay that you gotta mold into an acceptable form," Lottie had once opined. "So why not start out with his form and see where it takes you?"

"The only place it would take me," I'd retorted, "is into therapy."

As if he could sense us watching, Morgan glanced over and waved. Lottie waved back, while Nikki ducked into the shop and I pretended not to see him. Naturally, he came striding over, flashing the hundred-watt smile that highlighted the blond glints in his chestnut hair and the sparkle in his angelic blue eyes.

Morgan wasn't tall — or all that smart — but he was always well dressed, which was probably why Lottie admired him so. If any of her boys were to show up wearing something other than ripped, baggy jeans, an old T-shirt, and laceless shoes, their hair sticking out at every angle, she would have called a press conference.

Today Morgan was sporting a light blue denim shirt tucked into a pair of dark blue jeans with a crease carefully ironed into them. "Are you ladies enjoying the festival?"

"We are now," Lottie boomed in her big voice, nudging me. At that moment, three women came up to ask her advice on flowers, so she turned to wait on them, leaving me to handle The Ego alone.

"Abby, I'm glad you spotted me," he said. "How about being my date for the charity luncheon in the pickle tent? Proceeds are going to Haven for the Homeless, which I organized, FYI."

Ordinarily, a free lunch would be right up my alley, but I'd endured enough meals with Morgan to know that it was an experience I suffered if and when I needed information that only he could provide. Otherwise, I'd rather have an enormous water balloon fall on my head. Repeatedly.

"Thanks, Greg," I said, trying to look both admiring and regretful, "but my parents came downtown for the festival and I'd hate to abandon them. They've been looking forward to spending some quality time with me."

At that moment, my mother breezed through the open doorway, pushing my dad, and called, "We're off to the booths, Abigail. See you later."

Feeling Morgan's gaze on my face, I blinked rapidly, trying to fire my brain cells into action, because the only thing I could think to do now was run away, and I was a little too old for that. I glanced at Lottie for help, but she was still talking to the three women.

"Coffee break is over, Abs," Nikki said, stepping through the doorway. "Let's go pig out on elephant ears. Oh, sorry. Hello, Greg. Did I interrupt something?"

That was Nikki's attempt to rescue me.

"We were just making lunch plans," Morgan replied. "Want to join us?" That was Morgan's attempt to surround himself with women; the more the merrier.

"Sorry, I'm on a diet," Nikki replied instantly; then, realizing she'd contradicted herself, she added, "The elephant ear diet." She glanced at me with a shrug, as if to say, *Hey, I tried.*

Suddenly, a police car sped up Indiana Street, behind the courthouse, and screeched to a stop in front of the police station. The cops hopped out, opened the rear door on the passenger side, and pulled out a snarling clown with orange hair, a red nose, and an armful of cucumbers.

"Hey, that's Snuggles," Nikki exclaimed, causing Lottie and her customers to crane their necks for a look.

It seemed there *was* justice in this world, after all.

CHAPTER THREE

"Is Snuggles a friend of yours?" Morgan asked Nikki with a snicker.

She gave him a glance that was at once sultry and withering. "I'm not into evil clowns this week, *Greg.* For your information, Snuggles threatened Abby this morning during the parade."

Morgan's blue eyes widened as he — and Lottie's customers — turned to stare at me. "He threatened you? Why?"

"Because I was bumped off the curb into his path, knocking him off his unicycle," I explained.

"What did he say to you?" Morgan asked.

"That he knew I did it on purpose, that he had my number, and that paybacks are murder." I left out the part about Snuggles calling me shorty. It was a sore spot.

Morgan's shocked expression gave me a possible way to escape having lunch with him — the pity party. "Yes," I said, heaving a tremulous sigh, "the whole scene was upsetting, which is why I don't have much of an appetite, so maybe we can do lun—"

Throwing back his shoulders to look important, Morgan strode toward the police station, calling over his shoulder, "I'll find out what happened and be right back; then we can grab some food."

"Great. You do that." I stepped into the shop and motioned for Nikki to follow. "When Morgan comes back, get the scoop for me."

"Where will you be?" she asked as I started toward the curtain to the workroom.

"Hiding."

"So I'm your sacrificial lamb? No way. If you don't want to have lunch with Morgan, just tell him straight out."

"I can't do that. Morgan is my contact at the courthouse. If I tick him off, the next time I need information I'll be out of luck. Besides, I want to phone Marco. I have a feeling he was somehow involved in Snuggles's arrest. Just get the story from Morgan, then tell him I had to go to the . . ." What could I use as an excuse? The bathroom? He'd wait. The ER for a broken ankle? Hard to pull that off unless I wore a cast for the next six weeks.

I glanced over to the doorway of the coffee parlor to see my other assistant, Grace Bingham, watching me with the sage expression and statesmanlike pose that signaled she was on the verge of delivering a lecture, which usually began with a quotation. Grace was a trim, active, sixty-year-old widowed Brit who'd had many careers, including librarian and legal secretary. She spoke with a lovely, crisp accent and operated under the assumption that she could mold me into the perfect human being by bombarding me with insightful sayings. So far, it hadn't helped, but she wasn't the type to give up without a fight.

Working with Grace was one of the joys of owning Bloomers. How lucky for me that just when I'd needed someone to run the coffee and tea parlor, Grace had retired from her job as legal secretary for Dave Hammond (the lawyer for whom I had clerked one summer) and was looking for something to do. Since she was an expert tea brewer, a whiz on the coffee machines, and a top-notch scone baker, it had been a perfect fit. In Grace and Lottie, I had the best assistants in town.

"Abby, dear," she began, "I realize Mr. Morgan is not your favorite person, but do bear in mind Sir Walter Scott's immortal words, 'Oh, what a tangled web we weave /

When first we practice to deceive.' "

"You tell her, Grace," Nikki said.

"If I may say something in my own defense," I replied, trying to sound astute, "sometimes telling a tiny cobweb of a lie is the kindest thing to do. Otherwise, Morgan would want to know why I don't want to have lunch with him, and I'd have to say it's because he's an egotistical jerk, and then his feelings would be hurt. *You* try getting information from him after that."

Grace pondered it a moment. "You do have a valid argument. Heaven knows you're not the most politic person in the world. So perhaps it would be best if you departed by the back door and left Mr. Morgan to me. I'll get the *scoop,* as you phrase it, then ring your mobile."

"Works for me," Nikki said, heading for the curtain.

"I'm right behind you, Nikki. Just one more thing, Grace. When you said I wasn't the most politic person in the world, did you mean —"

"Come on, Abby!" Nikki latched onto my arm and dragged me through the curtain.

"I think Grace just accused me of being tactless."

Nikki and I dashed through the curtain into the workroom, sidestepping the long slate-covered worktable in the center, passing the stainless steel walk-in cooler on the right, and my desk and long counter space on the left. We hurried through the tiny kitchen and out the back door into the alley, where I put in a call to Marco.

"Come on, Marco. Pick up," I muttered as we hurried toward the street. But the phone continued to ring. "Where are you? Why aren't you answering?" I finally got his voice mail and left a message for him to contact me. As soon as I put my phone back in my purse, it rang.

"There he is," Nikki said with as much relief as I felt.

My relief lasted until I heard my mother's voice on the line. "Bring Nikki and come across the street to booth twenty-four. I have a surprise for you."

I relayed the message to Nikki, and she groaned. Anyone close to my mother knew the word *surprise* was the term she used for her latest artistic endeavor. Unfortunately, this kind of surprise wasn't the pleasant feeling you got when you ripped open a brightly wrapped gift and found your favorite perfume inside. It was more like *expecting* to find your favorite perfume and getting an onion.

"Mom, I'm kind of lying low for the time

being, so . . . Hold on. I'm being beeped."

"*There's* Marco," Nikki said.

Wrong again. It was Grace. "Mr. Morgan just rang to say he wouldn't be able to make it after all. He sends his apologies and says he will phone in a bit to let you know about Snuggles."

"Thank you, Grace. That's great news. See? No webs woven."

"Don't jump for joy just yet. Your mother phoned here and it appears that she has art to show you."

"She found me. I guess we'll head that way now."

"Stiff upper lip, dear," Grace said.

I put away the phone and we continued up the alley. But as we passed Down the Hatch's back door I came to a quick stop. "Let's see if Marco is back."

Nikki sucked in her breath as if I'd just belched loudly in public. "Are you sure you want to do that? You've already left a message. You don't want him to think you're worried."

"I *am* worried."

"But you don't want him to know it. It makes you look — I don't know — controlling."

"Will it look controlling if I simply ask if Marco is there — or has been there — or has at least phoned in to say where the *hell* he is?"

"Yes."

"I'll just have to live with that."

But after checking in with Chris and learning that Marco hadn't been seen or heard from since the start of the parade, I wasn't worried about appearing controlling, I was just worried.

As Nikki and I wandered the booth aisles, hoping to delay the moment when I would have to come face-to-face with my mother's latest creation, I kept a sharp eye out for Marco. Despite Nikki's warning, I'd called his cell phone twice more, but he hadn't picked up. It simply wasn't like him to ignore his phone message or to stay away from his bar without contacting someone.

Normally, I would have been too busy myself to fret about Marco's silence, but this hadn't been a normal day. I tried to assure myself that it was nothing more than a phone glitch and that he would show up at any moment. But as more time passed, that excuse stopped working.

"Would you quit checking your phone?" Nikki asked, growing impatient with my fretting, which, by the way, was a trait I inherited from my mother, so it wasn't like I could get over it. She pointed to a blue striped canopy just ahead. "There's number twenty-four, but I don't see your parents . . . Wait. Is that your mom's hat?"

We came to a halt in front of the booth and stood openmouthed. "It propagated," Nikki said in awe.

Hanging from hooks on a pegboard on the right side were rows of big feathered hats in an assortment of styles — wide brimmed, panama, fedora, derby, and even beret — in colors such as frightening fuchsia and garish lime green. On a narrow shelf below the hats stood similarly hued feathered fans and picture frames. By contrast, sedate, hand-loomed capes and scarves by an artist named Claire from Fond du Lac, Wisconsin, filled the other walls.

Nikki immediately grabbed a bubblegum pink sun hat and tried it on in front of a mirror, tilting her head at a rakish angle for effect. "What do you think? Kind of cool, huh?"

"Yes, if you're a pink flamingo."

Throwing me a scowl, she put the hat back on its hook.

"May I help you?" a woman asked us.

"We were just admiring these hats," Nikki replied, ever the diplomat.

"Aren't they unique? A local artist did them."

"Really?" Nikki asked, trying to look serious. "What's her name?"

"Nikki, stop teasing poor Claire," my mom said, stepping into the booth behind us. She introduced us to Claire, a heavyset woman well into her sixties who had long gray braids that draped over the shouldes of a blue, green, and white plaid cape. Then Mom turned to me with a smile. "How do you like my new art project?"

A small crowd had gathered behind us, gawkers who were pointing to the hats and elbowing each other with snickers. No way was I going to let them make fun of my mother. I was the only one allowed to do that.

"Mom, these hats are going to be sellouts," I gushed loudly, snatching one for my own head. "Everyone in town is going to want a Maureen Knight original. It'll be the new status symbol. I mean, look at them. They're so breezy, so joyous, and the colors — wow."

"Take it off," Nikki whispered frantically. "The hat. Take. It. Off."

I checked my reflection in the mirror and saw the reason for her panic. The orange and yellow derby had settled on my head in such a fashion as to make my red hair stick out beneath it like a clown's wig. Certainly not a strong selling point. Luckily, the crowd had moved on.

"Didn't I tell you her new project was a tickler?" My dad chuckled at his joke as he wheeled himself into the now-deserted booth. He held up one of the small, wax-coated bags of baby dills sold all over the square. "Pickle?"

Ick. Too sour to eat alone. I took a pass and so did Nikki. "Ready to go, Abs?"

"Ready. Good luck with sales, Mom."

"Whatever doesn't sell here at the booth I'll bring to Bloomers," she told me.

Yay? Dad held out the bag and I stuffed a gherkin in my mouth.

"By the way," Mom said. "Your father and I saw Sean Reilly earlier, so I mentioned to him what happened to you at the parade. Oddly enough, he didn't seem shocked."

Considering that Reilly thought I was a walking trouble magnet, no, he wouldn't be shocked. As a young rookie, Sgt. Reilly had worked with my dad, then years later had helped train Marco, forging a friendship that endured to this day, which was how I'd met him. Now Reilly and I were friends, too, sort of, except when I poked my nose into police business, or put myself in danger, or put myself in danger *because* I'd poked my nose into police business. Then he wasn't so friendly.

"Mom, I told you it was no big deal. You didn't have to bother Reilly with that."

"It *is* a big deal, Abigail, at least to some of us. Did you know Snuggles was arrested?"

"We saw the cops take him in," Nikki said.

"And do you know why? Because after the parade was over, he got into a fistfight with a bystander."

"A clown in a fist fight?" Claire looked appalled.

"Never trust a clown," I told her. "They'll toss you into a burning building without giving it a second thought."

Mom turned me to face her. "Abigail, the bystander was Marco."

My jaw dropped. Marco and Snuggles? Oh, no. Was it because of what Snuggles said to me? I was horrified. I was also secretly flattered. More than that, although it was hard to admit, I was relieved that Marco's absence hadn't been because of the woman. "Is he all right?"

"The police arrived before any harm was done," Dad said.

So my gut feeling had been right after all. Marco *had* gone after the clown.

As soon as we'd hunted down an elephant

ear for Nikki, we agreed that checking in with the crew at Down the Hatch, to see whether Marco had shown up yet, was a good idea. Unfortunately, as my eyes adjusted to the dim light inside the bar, I saw in one sweep that he wasn't there.

The bar had been the town's local watering hole for at least fifty years and still retained the original decor despite Marco's promise to rehab it. Carrying a corny fishing theme too far, the original owners had mounted a huge fake carp on a wooden plaque above the highly polished walnut bar. There was also a bright blue plastic anchor on the dark paneling above the booths that lined the wall, a big brass bell near the old-fashioned cash register, and a fisherman's net strung across the beamed ceiling, all of which needed to go. But in the six months that Marco had owned the place, that had yet to happen. I had a feeling he was afraid of a citizen revolt if he dared to disturb anything.

"Has Marco checked in?" I asked Chris.

"He called about ten minutes ago. He said he had business to take care of and would be in later this evening. He also said to tell you that he got all of your messages and you didn't need to leave any more."

Two of the waitresses pretended to cough,

but I knew they were covering laughs.

"Let's go watch the acts on the main stage," Nikki suggested, ushering me through the crowd.

As we walked outside I whispered, "Is it my imagination, or were they laughing at me?"

"It wasn't your imagination."

"They think I should stop checking on Marco so much, don't they?"

"That'd be my guess."

"If I start to call him again, will you smack me?"

"Absolutely."

"You don't have to sound so happy about it."

"Sorry."

"Then stop smiling. It's annoying."

A stage had been erected on the west side of the square, in front of the New Chapel Savings and Loan, with rows of bleachers facing the stage. People had taken seats on the bleachers, the stone steps in front of the building, as well as on the west side of the courthouse lawn. We stopped at one of the food stands to buy sodas, then found a spot on the end of the second row of bleachers just as the Irish step dancers were finishing their routine. Next up were the three acrobats from the clown troupe, followed by the stilt walker and one of the unicyclists, who tossed bowling pins back and forth to each other.

"Look, Nikki," I whispered. "No Snuggles. The cops must have jailed him."

"You know who else is missing? The clown on the tricycle."

Sure enough, the girl with the big lily on her hat was nowhere in sight. "Maybe she doesn't juggle or do acrobatics."

"Then why would she be in the troupe?"

"You're asking me like I'm a clown expert."

After the clowns came the rock group Peck's Bad Boyz, with a preview of their evening concert, the one Marco and I were supposed to attend. All at once, a pair of hands covered my shoulders and a deep voice said in my ear, "Hello, Sunshine."

"Marco!" I swiveled around, ready to throw my arms around his neck and hug him in relief — then pester him for details. But I stopped myself. I'd learned from experience that Marco would tell me everything in good time. Taking a breath, I forced myself to say calmly, "What's up?"

"Not much."

Not much? I nearly shredded my tongue. Okay, so he wasn't ready to tell me about the fight with Snuggles. I could wait . . .

about thirty seconds, then gray matter would start to leak from my ears.

He came around and squeezed onto the bleacher beside me, his thigh resting against mine, setting off all kinds of delicious tingles that threatened to melt me right onto that wooden bench. So maybe I'd give him *sixty* seconds to spill his guts.

"Are you all right, Marco?" Nikki exclaimed, leaning around me to gaze at him wide-eyed. "We heard you got into it with Snuggles."

This was another reason that Nikki and I were best friends. When one of us hesitated, the other stepped up to bat.

In a very nonchalant tone he said, "It was nothing. Don't worry about it. He's just got a short fuse." Then he shifted his gaze to the band.

A short fuse? That was it? I wanted cold facts, hard figures, relevant data, but as Marco wasn't being forthcoming I dropped the subject. Maybe he was embarrassed because the cops had been called. Maybe he didn't want me to know he'd gone after Snuggles to defend my honor. Like most males, he hated to be quizzed, so I'd have to be patient. He'd talk when he was ready and not before, whether I was leaking gray matter or not.

"Good show?" he asked me.

The show, his spicy scent, the heat from his body, the low timber of his voice — oh, yeah, it was good, like a slow, sensual massage. I leaned my shoulder into his and he responded with a hand on my knee, turning it to pudding.

"Sorry I didn't get back to you right away," he said, his lips against my ear producing tingles of excitement. "It couldn't be helped."

So many questions and still no answers. Trying to act unconcerned, I asked, "Are we on for the concert tonight?"

There was a long pause. So long that I turned to gaze at him. "Marco, did you forget we made plans for this evening?"

He put an arm around my shoulders and said quietly, "I'll have to take a rain check."

I hid my disappointment behind a light shrug. "Sure. No problem. Do you have to be at the bar tonight?"

"No, I have to do some investigative work."

"Must be a big case, then. I know you wouldn't cancel our date unless it was really important."

Marco merely gave my shoulder a gentle squeeze, which meant that he appreciated my understanding and was done talking about it. Naturally, being a female, *I* wasn't done talking about it. I hadn't even *begun* to talk about it, and his silence served only to make me want to talk about it *more.*

"So," I leaned close to ask, twirling a lock of hair, "does this case have anything to do with that woman at the parade this morning, the one you spoke to right before you brought me the ice cream cone? The one with" — I knew I was going to hate myself for saying so, but I just couldn't help it — "split ends?"

"Her name is Trina Vasquez. She's a close friend of my kid sister, and yes, it does involve her. She asked me to look into something for her."

What kind of something would take precedence over our date? A number of scenarios ran through my mind, but I couldn't very well ask him to reveal his client's information. In the PI business, the client had to be assured of confidentiality. So I crossed my arms and forced my attention back to the rock group on stage, who, by the way, wouldn't have made it beyond their first appearance on *America's Got Talent.*

Marco sat through the end of the song, then glanced at his watch and patted my knee. "I have to get going. I'll be in touch when I can." He gave Nikki a nod, then slipped off the end of the bench and was gone.

"What's up with him?" Nikki whispered.

"He's working on a PI case."

"Don't tell me. For that dark-haired woman we saw him with at the parade?"

"That's the one."

At Nikki's raised eyebrows I said, "It's okay. She's a friend of his sister."

"Oh, right. The *friend-of-his-sister* excuse." She rolled her eyes, as if to say, *Sucker!* I pretended not to notice. Marco didn't make excuses. He just did what he had to do.

"This music is giving me a headache," she whispered. "Let's get some food. I'm so in the mood for pickled pig's feet."

I scooted off the bench and waited for her to join me. "Since when do you like pickled pig's feet?"

She pushed my shoulder as we headed across the lawn. "You are *so* gullible."

"Thanks a lot. By the way, don't trip on your left shoe lace. Your sneaker is untied."

Nikki stopped short, glanced down, then remembered she had on sandals. I just kept walking so she wouldn't see the big smile on my face. Gullible girl.

CHAPTER FOUR

After a long, busy weekend, a best friend could be such a comfort, knowing just the right words to soothe your jangled nerves, ease your stress, or make you laugh. I especially needed it that Monday morning, because my internal radar had beeped all night long, robbing me of sleep to nag me that something was wrong. And not only was something wrong, but also it involved Marco.

So when Nikki showed up in the kitchen that morning desperately seeking caffeine, I mentioned my concern, hoping for some reassurance. She listened quietly, took a sip of the java I'd made, then scrunched up her mouth. "This coffee tastes bitter."

On the other hand, a best friend could also be a pain in the neck. It hadn't helped the situation any that we'd spent Saturday together at the Pickle Fest, then most of Sunday painting the walls of our apartment.

There *was* such a thing as too much girl time.

Unaware of my simmering irritation, she dumped the allegedly bitter coffee down the drain. "What kind of bean did you use?"

"Jelly," I muttered, slathering orange marmalade on my toast and stuffing a bite in my mouth before I said something I regretted.

"Sarcasm doesn't work on me. You know that."

"Look, I'm really sorry you have to work the day shift, Nikki, and get up early like the rest of the world, but you don't have to criticize my coffee, too."

Pressing her lips together, Nikki marched out.

"Hey, wait," I called. "You're right. The coffee *is* bad this morning. I made it too strong because I wasn't paying attention to what I was doing."

"It must be the paint fumes. They can affect your brain, you know. Let's open the windows."

"It's not the fumes that are affecting me, Nik. I can't shake this gut feeling that something bad happened to Marco. Besides, it's chilly outside. Summer is over."

"So we'll bundle up. The cool air will help clear your thoughts so you'll be able to see how pointless it is to worry about a man who was an *Army Ranger.*" She emphasized the last two words, in case I missed the irony. "Marco invaded countries, for God's sake. I think he can look after himself."

No missing that irony. "I'd feel better if he called, that's all."

"Why don't you call him?"

"I did. His voice mail picked up."

"Then the ball is in his court."

We took our cups up the short hallway to the living room to open a window and admire our handiwork — walls in a soft ivy green shade (my second favorite color) and a ceiling in a pale violet shade (Nikki's favorite color). Blame it on the home-decorating shows on TV. We'd spent hours with paint brushes and drop cloths and blue masking tape, and had the splattered sweat-shirts to prove it.

"That hallway is next on the list," I told her, pointing to the hall to my right that led to a roomy bathroom and our two bed-rooms. "How about if we stencil ivy vines on a pale purple background? We can start this evening."

Nikki sipped her coffee, leaning against the bookcase. "Let's think about why you're suddenly in the mood to redecorate."

"I don't have to think about it. White walls

are boring, blah, bland."

"Really? According to a psychology article I read last weekend, your apartment represents your psyche, the inner Abby, so to speak. So what you're really saying is that *you* are boring, blah, and bland. Am I right?"

"Where did you read this article?"

"In a magazine at the dentist's office."

Snickering, I turned around and went back to the kitchen to finish my toast. Nikki was way off base. First of all, my inner Abby was just as lively as my outer Abby, only not as curvy. Second, I wasn't trying to color my psyche; I was trying to divert my thoughts from Marco. The logical part of my brain disagreed with my concerns, of course, by presenting me with a list of reasons that he hadn't contacted me.

1. He could be out of town. *Without access to a phone? He'd have to be on the moon.*

2. He lost his cell phone. *And couldn't find a pay phone? Had he ever heard of a toll call?*

3. He was still angry about his leather jacket. (A little mishap involving his coat and my leaky pen.). *Nuh-uh. I'd promised to have it professionally*

cleaned.

4. He was on a stakeout and couldn't contact anyone. *Most likely reason.*

"You know what?" I said to Nikki, returning to the living room. "You're right. I'm spending way too much energy worrying. Marco is an experienced PI and a grown man who can take care of himself."

"Well, there's news," she said with a cynical sniff.

"I need encouragement here, Nikki."

"How's this for encouragement? It's almost eight o'clock. Time for work."

I ran for the toothpaste, brushed my teeth, grabbed my purse, and was out the door in five minutes. (It didn't look right when the boss was late.) I slid into my beloved refurbished 1960 Corvette convertible, put the top down, and took off for Bloomers, ready to enjoy the sun on my face and the wind in my hair, even if it was technically too cold for a topless ride.

My Vette was one of those once-in-a-lifetime finds that had been buried in a farmer's barn for decades and, because of its condition, sold cheaply; otherwise, I wouldn't have been able to afford the steering wheel. Lottie's nephew had repaired the top, mended the fiberglass body, and repainted the dingy white to my favorite color, bright yellow, which looked pretty snazzy with the black leather interior, though it was cracked and worn from wear.

But even after the breezy drive into town I couldn't shake that nagging feeling that something was wrong. Fighting a knot in my stomach that was threatening to become a major source of distress, I parked in a public lot a block east of the town square, put the top up, and hoofed it to my shop.

I always looked forward to going to work, today more than ever, knowing that when I stepped beyond that yellow door I'd be transported to a serene place where I could lose myself in masses of fragrant blossoms, moist greenery, and heavenly aromas, and where two of my most favorite people awaited to offer me cheer and support. With a sigh of relief I unlocked the door — we didn't open until nine o'clock — and went inside, singing out, "Good morning, ladies."

I could hear raised voices behind the curtain, so I peeked in to see what was going on.

"Beans!" Lottie said in disgust, folding her arms across her chest, which today was clad in a bright aqua satin blouse. She sported matching barrettes in her hair.

Grace gave an elegant lift of her silver-haired head. "What's wrong with my beans?"

Oh, no. Not the coffee bean thing here, too.

"It's grits or nothing," Lottie retorted.

In the coffee?

Grace held the lapels of her crisp, tan linen blazer, assuming her lecture pose. "As the fine British writer Mary Wortley Montagu wrote, 'Be plain in dress and sober in your diet.' Now, I ask you, what could be more sobering than beans?"

"Is that the British way of saying gassy? 'Cause that's what you'd be all day if you ate beans first thing in the morning."

I parted the curtain and stuck my head through. "Good morning, ladies."

"Abby, would you eat beans with your eggs?" Lottie asked as I stepped into the workroom.

"What she should be asking," Grace said to me, "is, Why would you *not* eat beans with your eggs? They're full of protein and fiber and other nutrients."

I tossed my purse on the desk. "Why are we having this discussion?"

"Grace brought in mashed beans as a side dish."

I clapped my hands to my face. "Oh, no! I ate breakfast!" Another sign of how distracted I was. Monday breakfast was a tradi-

61

tion at Bloomers, with Lottie's fabulous scrambled eggs and crisp toast and Grace's fresh-brewed gourmet coffee. My contribution was an appetite.

"It's okay, sweetie," Lottie said, throwing a generous arm around my shoulders. "We sure do understand how you could have forgotten today."

"Quite understandable," Grace added, "considering."

Bewildered, I looked from one to the other.

"She hasn't seen the newspaper," Lottie said to Grace, shaking her head and reaching for the front-page section on the worktable. I took it from her and read the big black headline across the top: EX-COP QUESTIONED IN MAN'S DEATH.

My gaze jumped to the photo of the victim, a man I'd never seen before. He appeared to be in his late thirties, with a shaved and tattooed head, multipierced earlobes, a flattened, crooked nose, and a thick neck. The caption beneath the photo read, "Dennis Ryson outside the motorcycle shop where he worked."

Still not understanding their concern, I read the article that followed.

"A New Chapel man was found dead

yesterday evening after neighbors heard a disturbance at his residence and phoned police. Dennis Ryson, 34, a mechanic at Wheel and Deal Motorcycles, died after suffering apparent head trauma. Witnesses identified the man they saw exiting the house as Marco Salvare, owner of the Down the Hatch Bar and Grill. Salvare is being held for questioning."

I put down the paper and braced my hands on the table, feeling suddenly sick to my stomach. My gut had been right after all.

"She needs food and coffee," Lottie said to Grace, and at once I found myself ushered through the workroom into the tiny kitchen in back, where Lottie served up a mound of buttery yellow scrambled eggs on a plate at the tiny counter. "Eat up, sweetie. It'll do you good."

I picked up a fork and put it down again. Even if I hadn't already had breakfast, I couldn't have swallowed a bite. What I needed to do was talk to Marco to make sure he was all right. My mind wouldn't think beyond that point. "Maybe later. I don't think my stomach would hold anything right now. I need to make a call."

I dashed to my desk and phoned Down

the Hatch first, then his mobile number, where I left another message for him to call ASAP. Then I drummed my fingers on the desk, wondering whom else I could tap to find out what was going on.

"Here, dear," Grace said, setting a cup of coffee in front of me.

I took a sip of the fragrant, mellow brew and thought hard. Sgt. Reilly. That's who I could call. I had his private cell phone number that I used in emergencies. I used it now.

"Hey, Reilly, it's me, your favorite redhead. How's the world's best sergeant?"

"You can lay off the compliments, Abby. I can't tell you anything about Marco."

"Come on, Reilly. I just read the newspaper and I'm going crazy with worry. All I want to know is if he's okay."

There was a pause, then a weary sigh. If Reilly had learned anything about me over the past several months, it was that I was persistent. He called it badgering, but that was splitting hairs. "I'll tell you this much. Marco had better get a good lawyer because he's in trouble up to his eye sockets."

My whole body shuddered. "Has he been charged with anything? Are you holding him in jail?"

"He'll be out soon. That's all I'm going to

say, so don't ask me anything else."

"Okay, Reilly, thanks for being so chatty."

As I hung up with him, I heard my cell phone chirping in my purse. I dug it out, saw Marco's name on the screen, and hurriedly flipped it open, practically shouting my hello.

"Sunshine," Marco said tensely, "I need your help."

CHAPTER FIVE

I was so relieved to hear his voice that I jumped out of my chair. "Marco, I just read the newspaper. Who is this Ryson character? Why were you at his house? Were you hurt? Have you been charged with anything?"

"Whoa. Calm down. I'm not hurt and I'll fill you in on the details later. Can you meet me at the bar at noon?"

"Of course. What else can I do? Do you want me to call Dave Hammond?"

"I've already done that. Just be at the bar at noon."

I hung up and glanced at the clock. Three and a half hours. A whole bunch of worry would fit into that amount of time. Luckily, Monday mornings were busy at Bloomers, so it wouldn't be too difficult to fill. There were inventories to take, supplies to order, wire orders to process, a calendar to update, the display case to stock, customers to wait on, and questions to answer. The questions came from Lottie and Grace, who wanted to know everything that had happened during the parade and after. It took a while, since the story had to be told in bits and pieces between business over the course of the morning, but I managed.

"What do you think he wants you to do for him?" Lottie asked after she'd had a chance to digest the whole story.

"That's simple enough to answer." Grace came through the curtain from the shop side bringing a pot of freshly brewed mint tea with honey and two cups on a cherry wood tray. Somehow she always managed to overhear what went on behind the curtain, even when she was in the coffee parlor. Either she had the ears of a bat or the workroom had been bugged. "He wants Abby to clear his name."

As if I needed more to worry about. "Trust me, Marco would *not* put such a crucial task in my amateur hands. He's the pro. If he needs something done, he'll do it himself."

Lottie took a cup from Grace, then paused to inhale the mint vapors, which Grace swore cleared the sinuses. "Well, sweetie, that may be true, but what would you do if he *did* ask you to clear him?"

"I know my limits and so does Marco. I'm

a great assistant, but I'm not even a good detective."

"You're not giving yourself enough credit, dear. You uncovered Professor Reed's murderer."

"That was more of a stumbling into than an uncovering."

Grace was not to be deterred. "What about the chap who did away with your cousin's best man?"

I rubbed my nose. "He found me before I found him."

"And the jack-in-the-pulpit killer?" Lottie asked.

"Came *looking* for me."

"Then perhaps you're right, dear." Grace picked up her tray and headed for the curtain. "Marco should do it himself."

By the end of the morning my stomach was in a major knot and my neck was sore from turning to glance at the clock on the wall so often. With five minutes to go, I rolled on some lip gloss, grabbed my purse, and dashed out the door, arriving breathlessly at Down the Hatch with one minute to spare. If nothing else, I was punctual.

Chris gave me a grim look and nodded toward the back. "Marco's in his office."

I made my way through the busy bar, calling greetings to some of the regular customers as I went. I paused outside Marco's office door to rap lightly, waiting for the okay to enter. When I got it, I opened the door onto a room that was a complete contrast to the old-fashioned bar in front. It was sleek and modern, with dove gray walls, silver miniblinds, and black leather furniture. The desk was black and chrome, and there was a black TV mounted in the opposite corner. It was a spare, masculine room and it fit Marco to a T. If only he'd do the rest of the bar in a similar style.

Today he had the miniblinds shut tight against the sun and no lights on except for a green glass lamp on his desk. His head was bent as he scribbled on a piece of paper, and all he said was, "Have a seat. Do you want something to eat or drink?"

He sounded so casual, like it was no big deal to make the headlines in a murder investigation. "Marco, I've been worried sick about you. First you disappear for two days; then you don't answer your phone or return my messages; then I'm reading about you in the newspaper; and then I get your phone call asking for help. Will you please tell me what the hell is going on?"

With a heavy sigh, he pushed back his chair and stood up, giving me a full view of his face. Even though the light was dim, I couldn't help but gasp. He had a purple bruise on his right cheekbone, a butterfly bandage over his left eyebrow, and a damaged left ear. He also had a day's growth of beard and looked haggard, as though he hadn't slept in a week. And yet my heart still beat faster when I saw him. Bruises or not, he was the sexiest guy on earth.

I was around the desk before he could ease himself back into his chair. "Oh, my God, Marco! How did this happen?"

"Go easy," he said, holding up his hands to fend off my probing. "I've had a rough night. Why don't you sit down and I'll tell you about it. You sure you don't want something to eat?"

"I couldn't swallow a bite. I've been a wreck ever since I saw the newspaper article this morning."

"Sorry I wasn't able to call you sooner. I spent a long night at the police station with Darnell and Corbison."

That was bad news. Detective Al Corbison was a paunchy, middle-aged, bald man with a bad temper and no sense of humor. Chief Prosecuting Attorney Melvin Darnell prided himself on being the good guy who put the bad guys behind bars. I'd tangled with both men when I was the prime suspect in the murder of my former law professor and I knew how single-minded and ruthless they could be.

I returned to the sling-back chair but sat on the edge, too wired to relax. "Who is this Dennis Ryson character and why are they questioning you for his murder?"

Marco tilted his chair back, scraping his fingers through his hair and shaking his head, as though he still couldn't believe what had happened. "They questioned me because Ryson and I" — he paused to choose the right words — "had an altercation."

"So you got into a fight?"

"No, I defended myself. I don't know if the guy was drunk or doped up or what, but he went ballistic on me and I reacted. What really pisses me off is that I should have seen it coming. I let my guard down for one second. That's never happened before."

"How *much* did you defend yourself?"

"Enough to stop him. But when I left him he wasn't dead or even close to it, and I've been through enough to tell the difference."

I sat back with a sigh of relief. "Then it was just a matter of self-defense."

"That's what I've been telling you."

"You're probably going to say this is silly,

but when I saw the headline in the paper this morning, my first thought was that you'd gone after Snuggles."

Marco fingered the bandage over his eyebrow. "Snuggles and Ryson are the same guy, Abby."

My brain stalled. "What? Wait a minute. That sneering guy on the front page of the paper is Snuggles? No way."

Marco peered at me from beneath lowered brows. "Take my word for it."

I slumped against the back of the chair, stunned. "Dennis Ryson, a motorcycle mechanic, was also a juggling, unicycle-riding, red-nosed clown? Wow. And people have the nerve to ridicule my fear of clowns."

Marco grunted.

"Where were you when he ambushed you?"

"In his house."

For ten seconds I simply gaped at him, dumbfounded. "You went to his *house?* Marco, that was totally unnecessary. I mean, what he said to me wasn't that big of a deal. I'm sorry I mentioned it."

"Abby."

"Still, I can't very well criticize you when you were protecting my honor. Not that I'm condoning that kind of behavior but, wow.

It just blows me away." I shook my head in amazement and knew there was a big, dopey grin on my face, but I couldn't help it. I felt like a princess whose handsome knight had just ridden up on a white charger.

Marco shifted in his chair, wincing as he rotated his right shoulder. "Abby, I didn't go after him for *you.*"

My grin faded, and I did my best not to look embarrassed. "Oh."

"I was working a case. Remember the woman you saw me talking to at the parade?"

I brushed a strand of hair off my face, trying to play it cool. "Hmm, let me think."

"The lady with the split ends." The corner of Marco's mouth twitched.

"Wait. It's coming back to me now. Trina, wasn't it?"

He knew I knew, but he played along, being the good sport that he was. "That's right. Trina Vasquez."

The image of the two of them in serious discussion at the parade flashed in my mind, and suddenly I realized who Trina had pointed out to Marco — Snuggles. But why? Maybe Snuggles had threatened Trina, too. Maybe she'd called first dibsies on having Marco defend her honor. Maybe she even had a thing for Marco. Maybe I didn't want to go there.

"So you were tailing Snuggles for Trina, the friend of your sister's."

"Right. She and my younger sister have been friends since grade school, like you and Nikki. Now she's a single mom raising a three-year-old boy and running a day-care center out of her home."

Marco's eyes grew distant, as though he was lost in memories. "Gina and Trina. They used to pass themselves off as twins. She was at our house so much I started thinking of her as my other kid sister."

I wondered whether he still felt that way. "What was her problem with Snuggles — or I guess I should say Ryson?"

"It started about two months ago, after Ryson moved in across the street and developed a thing for her. When she didn't reciprocate, he started to harass her. It got so bad that he even stalked her at the grocery store, to the point where she feared for the safety of the children."

"What a bully!" A stalking bully, to boot, uppermost on my list of despicable low-lifes. I didn't blame Trina for wanting to get rid of him.

"That's when my sister suggested she contact me."

I hated to sound as though I was questioning Trina's motives but — "Shouldn't Trina have called the cops?"

"She did call them and eventually got a restraining order, but you know how well those work. If someone is seriously determined, a piece of paper won't stop him. So Trina asked me to talk to him and that's what I tried to do."

"The newspaper story said Ryson died from trauma to the head. When did that happen?"

"I don't know. Look, let me tell you how it went down. I had Ryson under surveillance all day Saturday and Sunday so I could document his movements. Naturally, that would be the weekend he decided to lie low. Anyway, Sunday evening around seven o'clock, I went to Trina's house to talk to her about the situation. While we were sitting on her front stoop, Ryson came out of his house and started swearing at us, acting like a lunatic. We moved inside, thinking he'd stop, but he came across the street instead and stood on the sidewalk in front of her house, where he continued to curse up a storm. I'm sure the whole neighborhood heard him. So I went out to have a little talk with him. When h saw me, he beat a hasty retreat and started yelling at me through his window."

"What was he swearing about?"

"That I was trying to intimidate him, among other things. He wasn't sane, Abby."

"Why didn't you call the cops?"

"That wouldn't have put an end to the stalking. The cops would have thrown him in the slammer, he would have bonded out, and Trina's harassment would have begun again. Even if he did jail time, what were the odds that he'd leave Trina alone afterward? How many women are killed by stalkers every year? I wasn't about to let that happen to her."

"So you thought you could put an end to it by talking to him?"

Marco sighed. "I got caught up in the moment. Ryson was swearing his fool head off, Trina was upset, and her son was crying, so my instinct was to act. I had Trina pack an overnight bag and take her son to her mother's house for the night, just in case there were any repercussions; then I went back across the street. His door was open so I stepped inside to try to reason with him, and that's when I noticed he was sweating all over and his color was off, kind of gray. I reached into my pocket for my cell phone to call 911 and that's when he came at me. But I'm telling you, Abby, when I left his house, Ryson was subdued, but very much alive."

"Did you call the cops then?"

"No. I know I should have, but I had blood running into my eye and my ear hurt like the devil, so I drove myself to the ER for stitches. When I got home the cops were waiting to take me down to the station. Someone had called them after I left Ryson's house, but as usual, they wouldn't tell me anything."

"Have you been charged with anything?"

"No, but Corbison told me not to go anywhere."

"Do you know who else they've questioned?"

"No one else."

"There have to be other suspects, Marco. You can't be the only one."

"Would you like to tell that to the grand jury? They're convening a week from today."

No way. A grand jury was rarely used in our county except in cases where a police officer or prominent person was involved. "Are you telling me they have enough evidence to consider you their one and only suspect?"

Marco massaged his neck, wearing an expression I'd never seen before — worry. "Looks that way. They know I was in Ryson's house and they have eyewitnesses who saw me leaving — neighbors, no doubt. And then there are these." He indicated his wounds and bruises. "I tried to explain how it happened but no one was listening. Darnell has already made up his mind that I'm guilty."

Marco had reason to be concerned. As I knew from experience, once the prosecutor had decided on his prime suspect, the cops stopped looking for anyone else. "I don't get it. Someone obviously went into Ryson's house after you left. Why wouldn't they try to find that person?"

"Who are they supposed to be looking for? That's the problem. No one saw anyone there but me."

Marco reached for a glass of water on his desk, then held it in one hand, tilting it back and forth, making tiny waves inside, his thoughts far away. The inside of my stomach felt like those waves. I could only imagine what *he* felt like.

Marco's gaze lifted to mine, his soulful eyes reaching all the way into my heart. "My only way out of this mess is to track down the killer, Sunshine; otherwise, I'm toast."

"Tell me what I can do to help."

He put the glass down and sat forward on his chair, as though he'd been waiting to hear those words. "I need you to do what you do best. Snoop, pry, poke, eavesdrop, meddle — you know, make a nuisance of yourself."

"No problem. And while I'm making a nuisance of myself, what will you be doing?"

"Only thing I can do — run the bar."

"No, I mean what will you be doing to find the killer?"

He looked at me as if my gas tank was running on fumes. "I can't do anything, Abby. If the cops see me interviewing people, they could charge me with intimidation or witness tampering. I can't run that risk. All I need is to give them more reason to suspect me."

"So you're saying you want me to handle this investigation alone?"

"I'll guide you the best I can from here, but you're going to have to do the legwork."

I blinked several times — make that several dozen times — trying to think of a polite way out. I mean, prying was one thing. Clearing the man you're crazy about from a possible murder charge was another. "You've got friends on the force, Marco — Reilly, for one. Can't they help you find the killer?"

"Cops follow orders. They won't jeopardize their jobs or pensions by investigating this case on their own."

"What orders? Is someone ordering them not to investigate any other suspects? What cop would do that to you?"

Marco rubbed his jaw, as though debating how much to tell me. "Kellerman."

"Martin Kellerman?" As Lottie would say, *Whee doggies.* I'd been around cops long enough to know that if the chief of the Homicide Division wasn't in your corner, it was a very bad thing. "I don't understand. Why would he do that? What does he have against you?"

"I guess you could say we never saw eye to eye on things."

"That's it?"

According to the stories I'd heard about Kellerman from my father, not many cops did. Underneath Martin Kellerman's mild-mannered exterior lay a fifty-year-old control freak with all the emotions of a stone. When his only daughter was married at a church in town, he was too busy doing paperwork to attend. When his cocker spaniel was run over by a garbage truck, he had them toss the corpse in the back and haul it to the dump. If I were Mrs. Kellerman, I'd be watching over my shoulder for garbage trucks — and making my own funeral arrangements.

"So what if you didn't see eye to eye with the man, Marco? I'm guessing all the cops under him would say that."

"But not many can say that Kellerman would love nothing better than to see them behind bars."

"You must have really ticked the guy off."

He shrugged. "I didn't like to play by the rules. Kellerman had a hard time with that."

I'd always admired that maverick quality in Marco before. Now, not so much. So asking the cops to help him was out. That meant I had to find another exit strategy. "The thing is, as much as I love to snoop, I don't think Dave Hammond will be too pleased. He has this crazy notion that I invite trouble, and that's the last thing he'd want to happen while he's defending you."

"I hired Dave to represent *me*, Abby. I'm calling the shots. Besides, I'd think he'd be grateful for the extra help. If anyone knows how efficiently you meddle, it's Dave."

Damn. That hadn't worked either. "Okay, here's a thought. What if I meet with the chief of police and see what he can do to straighten this out? Chief Harrington is an old friend of my father's. I know he'd help."

Marco gave me one of those *you've got to be kidding* glances. "Right. Harrington would tell the prosecutor to stop investigating his prime suspect because he and your dad are friends."

Okay, dumb idea. Another example of why not to toss this hot potato into my lap.

With a sigh, I dropped my head into my hands. One week until the grand jury met. One week to find Ryson's killer with not one other suspect to investigate. There was no way on earth I could do that alone.

CHAPTER SIX

Marco had some nerve putting me on the spot like this. What was he thinking? I was a florist, not a licensed PI.

So now you're angry because he asked for your help? How many times have you asked Marco for help? How many times has he gotten you out of jams? Try four times, you ingrate. Now you're going to walk away and leave him in the lurch? Some friend/potential spouse you are.

Hateful conscience. I tried to block out that scolding voice, but I couldn't because once again it spoke the truth — and because it would never shut up if I didn't pay attention, which was one of the drawbacks of having a conscience. Was I going to leave Marco in the lurch? Not likely. As much as I wanted to run — not walk — from what was in reality my fear of failure, I would never turn my back on him when he needed me.

In all honesty, I was supremely flattered by Marco's confidence in me, but I was also scared witless. I'd failed miserably at law school. What if I failed Marco? Did I want his fate in my hands? What if he went to prison because I screwed up, which I was often wont to do?

"Abby, if it's too much, don't worry about it," he said, as though reading my thoughts. "I know you have a business to run. I'll hire a private investigator. It's not a problem."

I raised my head to gaze at him — that sincere, courageous, gorgeous hunk of a man who was trusting me with his life — and I quaked inside. "The problem isn't my flower shop, Marco."

"Then what's the problem?"

"Me."

With a wince of pain, he got out of his chair, came around the desk, and knelt before me, taking my hands in his. "How are you the problem?"

"I'm petrified that I'll let you down."

"I don't know if you understand how hard this is for me, Abby. I'm not used to asking for help. But I'm asking you now because I trust you. You'd be less than human if you didn't feel scared. You can do this. You won't let me down."

If only I knew that for sure. I studied those

84

dark, soulful eyes and mentally cringed at the hope I saw there. Marco wasn't a killer. The prosecutor was railroading him — probably at the suggestion of that jackass Kellerman. It was full-blown injustice, and there was nothing I hated more than injustice. I also knew that no one would try as hard as I would to prove Marco's innocence. But it would be the challenge of my life — and unfortunately Marco's hung on it.

You've never backed down from a challenge before, have you?

That chiding voice was right again. I'd never backed down before and I wasn't going to now. I put my hands over Marco's and forced out six of the most frightening words I'd ever uttered. "I'll give it my best shot."

In return, Marco gave me that heart-stopping grin that made my fears disappear in a wisp of smoke — for now, at least. Then he leaned forward and pressed his lips against mine for a full, blissful minute. I responded in my usual, low-key way — I threw my arms around his neck and peppered the unhurt side of his face with kisses.

"Ouch. Okay, Miss Marple. One more thing," he said, unwrapping my arms. "Let's keep this quiet. Only you, me, and Dave

Hammond will know you're involved, okay?"

"You've got it. Just you, Dave, and me. No one else."

He leaned back to give me that squinty-eyed cop look. "Do you want to finish that list or should I?"

He knew me so well it was scary. "Okay, Nikki, Lottie, and Grace, too. But that's it. Well, maybe Reilly — but only if I'm desperate."

"You've got to leave Reilly out. It's too risky for him."

"Fine. Reilly is out." (However, where Marco's life was concerned, if it came down to the wire, Reilly would be back on that list in a heartbeat. I just wouldn't tell Marco.)

"So, are you ready to get started?"

I dug in my purse for my little notepad and pen as he went back to his desk. "Ready."

"Okay. Talk to Dave Hammond first to let him know I asked you to help. Then, unless Dave has another idea, interview Ryson's neighbors. Find out what they saw and heard Sunday evening. Right now they're our only hope for solid leads, so talk to as many of them as you can. That should take you a couple of days."

A couple of days? When I only had a week? I glanced at my watch and saw I still had half an hour of lunchtime left. "Give me Ryson's address and I'll start canvassing the neighborhood right away."

"Atta girl. Check in with me this evening and I'll buy you dinner."

I knew exactly which neighbor I'd start with, too — Trina of the Split Ends. I needed to know her motives, and whether she actually did take her son to her mother's house that evening. Just because she'd asked Marco to handle the problem with Ryson didn't mean she couldn't have killed him.

I got up to leave, then paused at the door. "One more thing. My appetite came back. Can I get a turkey sandwich to go? On the house?"

There had to be a few perks with this job.

With the enticing aroma of honey-roasted turkey wafting from my purse, I took a quick jaunt around the square to Dave's law office, a one-man operation in a rented space over a restaurant. His entire staff was composed of two people: one secretary — the extremely capable and loyal Alice — and a part-time law clerk from the student ranks at New Chapel University law school.

A man of medium height and slightly soft

around the belly, Dave had a warm smile, a receding hairline, and lots of happy clients. He never tried to dazzle people with fancy legal terms, he got the job done right the first time, and he always returned their phone calls. His philosophy was that the client was paying him, not Alice, for his expertise, so why would he have Alice answer their questions? (Not that she couldn't have.) I was glad Marco had called him. There wasn't a lawyer in town I trusted more.

"Hey, Abby. Good to see you. Come in." He motioned for me to take a seat. As usual, he was slumped in a chair behind his old oak desk working on his computer.

"Sorry to drop in on you like this, Dave — Alice told me you have to get to court soon — but do you have five minutes so I can run something past you?"

He glanced at his watch. "That's about all I have, but you're welcome to them." He sniffed the air. "Why am I suddenly thinking about Thanksgiving?"

I patted my purse. "Because you smell my turkey sandwich. I have to eat on the run today. Anyway, Marco asked me to tell you that I'm going to investigate the Ryson murder —"

"Whoa. Hold it, Abby. You know I love

you like a daughter, but you're not a licensed investigator. I can't send you out to question people and hope to be able to use it in court. You know the law."

"Not to worry. I know how to get around the law."

He clapped his hands over his ears. "I can't hear this."

"Come on, Dave. I want to help."

"Do I really have to remind you that as a licensed attorney I can't have you going *around the law* to represent my office? In any way, shape, or form? Besides, I've already put in a call to Pete Peters to see if he's available."

"Pete Peters? You're not serious."

"What's wrong with Pete?"

"First of all, the guy moves at the speed of a turtle on Valium. He'd never uncover anything useful in a week."

"Pete has ten years of experience behind him. I think he knows what he's doing."

"Second," I said, ignoring Dave's feeble argument, "Pete isn't a people person. He's good at stakeouts, line tapping, and hiding in alleys. That's not what this case needs."

"Abby."

No way was he going to stop me now. I was on a roll. "And then there's his name — Peter — twice. What were his parents thinking? Do you have any idea what kind of heckling he must have endured in school because of that moniker? The guy has to have issues, Dave. Is it any wonder he enjoys sitting in a dark car for hours on end, drinking stale coffee and spying on people?"

Dave stared at me as if I'd sprouted Chia greens from my ears. "What does his name have to do with his ability to investigate this case?"

"I needed a third item because the list was thin. Look, I'm not thrilled that Marco asked me to find the killer. In fact, I'm scared out of my mind to have his fate in my hands. I know I don't have enough training or experience, or a license, but I do have one thing — determination. I care a lot about Marco. A. Lot. And someone has to find the real killer quickly. The police aren't going to do it, and Peter Peters, well, I've said enough about him. Whether you like it or not, Dave, Marco asked for my help and I'm going to give it to him." I folded my arms across my chest and lifted my chin defiantly. "Your turn, counselor."

He gazed at me for a long moment, his thumb and index finger plucking his lower lip as though he were preparing his cross-examination. "Is there any way I can talk you out of this?"

"Nope."

"So it would be a waste of breath to argue any further?"

"Yep."

He shook his head in bemusement. "What am I going to do with you?"

"Stand back and watch me go."

He heaved a sigh of resignation. "Okay, then — go find the killer, tiger. I suppose I'll just have to be the beneficiary of anything you find out."

That was *his* way of going around the law. Shrewd guy, that Dave.

He started packing files into his briefcase, preparing for court. "I *am* going to insist you follow some rules, though. Pay attention now because there'll be a quiz at the end. One: My name is never to be mentioned. Two: You are not working for me. Three: You can't claim any official standing of any kind. Four: Follow the first three rules. Got that?"

"I can't use your name and I'm not your employee or a licensed private investigator. Got it." I followed him out of his office, waved to Alice as we passed, and tagged after him down the steep staircase. "Have the police shared any information with you yet?"

"Not a lot. I should get more discovery

tomorrow — and, yes, I'll share it with you. But you should know that what I do have points directly to Marco."

Crap.

Dave opened the door for me and we stepped out onto the sidewalk. He put an arm around my shoulders and gave them a friendly squeeze. "You've got your work cut out for you, kid. Good luck."

I watched him head across the street toward the courthouse, his suit coat flapping in the breeze. Luck? With no attorney to back me up, no friendly cop to lean on, and no licensed PI to take the lead, I'd need a whole lot more than luck. I'd need a miracle.

CHAPTER SEVEN

Dennis Ryson lived on a block of homes built in the 1940s, a mix of narrow, old-fashioned, two-story frame homes and one-story bungalows. All the homes had detached garages at the rear of lots that were accessed from side driveways. There were no curbs, only narrow sidewalks that heaved and bulged like a roller coaster from the thick roots of the old maples and elms that lined the streets.

I parked in front of Ryson's house, balled up the paper wrapper that my sandwich had been in, checked my teeth in the rearview mirror, and got out of the car. His house was a dingy brown bungalow badly in need of a paint job, window screens to replace the ones that were ripped and dangling, and a big bag of grass seed, along with a heavy dose of weed killer for the ground that was supposed to be a lawn. The front door had yellow crime scene tape across it, and I suspected the back door did, as well. There was no point in even trying to get in until it was unsealed.

I turned to eye the house directly across the street, where Trina Vasquez lived. This, too, was a bungalow, but it was well cared for. The house and one-car garage were painted a soft blue with white trim. The yard was neatly mowed, and as I approached, I saw that the backyard had been fenced in. I stepped onto the stoop and rang the doorbell. It was answered shortly by the dark-haired woman I'd seen at the parade, carrying a sniffling child in blue pj's on one hip, with several more crowding around her to gawk at the visitor.

"Can I help you?" she asked.

"Trina Vasquez?"

"Yes," she said warily.

"Hi, I'm Abby Knight. I own Bloomers Flower Shop on the square. I'm working on the Ryson case and I have a few questions for you."

She tilted her head like a puzzled cat. "Abby Knight?"

"From Bloomers. I'm a friend of Marco's."

"Marco sent you here?"

"Yes." In a roundabout way. "Do you have a few minutes to answer some questions?"

Trina gave me a distrustful once-over. "Why didn't Marco come himself?"

"Because of some boring legal technicality that prevents him from working on his own case. You know how that goes."

"No, actually, I don't. Couldn't he phone me with the questions?"

"Um, well, no. He can't do that, either."

She still didn't seem convinced. "I'm going to have to call him before I agree to talk to you. I'm sorry, but I have kids to protect."

"I understand."

She shut the door and I heard the lock click into place. I glanced down at my outfit. Was I that dangerous-looking?

I turned around to study the houses across the street and caught a quick glimpse of a chalky, strange face peering out at me from a window of the house to the left of Ryson's. Instantly, the drape dropped back into place. I stared a moment longer, watching for it again, but then I heard the lock click open behind me so I turned back. "Did you reach him?"

"Yes. You can come in." Trina didn't sound pleased about it.

She stepped back, taking with her three toddlers in long-sleeved T-shirts and Pampers. She escorted me through an obstacle course of toys to the small kitchen in the back, where she had me sit at the kitchen table.

"Coffee?" She indicated the giant coffee machine on her counter, probably her lifeline to get through the day.

"Sure." I needed something to wash down the turkey sandwich anyway.

Trina put down a sniffling toddler who instantly began to cry. "Just a minute, pumpkin," she said in a soothing voice as she reached for a mug and poured some of the brew into it. "I'm going to get this pretty lady some coffee, okay?"

Now I felt bad for the derogatory comment about Trina's hair, which today was tied back at her neck. She had on jeans and a blue T-shirt that showed off her curves without being suggestive, which I thought was appropriate for a child-care worker. I glanced down at my own clothing — a white T-shirt with a stripe of flowers down each shoulder, freshly washed blue jeans, and a pair of Adidas walking shoes. Quite appropriate for a florist, but maybe not so much for a private investigator.

Trina handed me the coffee mug, put a plastic container of vanilla Coffe-mate on the table, then took a seat across from me and repositioned the sniffler on her lap. "Marco said to tell you about Dennis Ryson, but what exactly do you need to know?"

I reached for my purse on the floor beside the chair to pull out my notepad and pen, and found a kid digging through it. "Hey, that's not child proof." I grabbed the strap and found myself engaged in a tug-of-war with a tot.

"Chad, stop that," Trina said firmly. Chad ignored her.

"Then I guess it's corner time for you."

He dropped the strap and scooted backward, his eyes opened wide, as if a voice in his curly little head were screaming, *"Oh, no!* Anything *but the corner."*

I put the purse in my lap, just in case Chad changed his mind.

Trina shrugged. "Sorry. It's getting close to their nap time."

"Then I'll try to make this brief. Basically I want to know more about Ryson — if he ever had visitors, how he got along with the neighbors, how he harassed you . . ."

Trina held up an index finger, signaling me to wait; then she took the sniffler into another room and came back empty-handed. She poured herself a cup of coffee and sat down again. "Ryson was a weirdo. A number one creep who couldn't get it through his thick skull that I didn't want anything to do with him."

She paused for a sip of coffee. "He kept asking me to go out with him. After I'd said no about, oh, fourteen times, he tried to win me over by bringing flowers that he'd obviously swiped from someone's garden. I made the stupid mistake of taking them the first time, but after that I wouldn't even answer the door. Then I'd find the flowers ripped to shreds on my back porch the next morning."

"That's creepy."

"It got worse. Once he brought over a shopping bag with a leather bra and thong inside and said he'd bought them because he knew I'd look hot in them, and they would be a change from the pink satin set I wore to bed."

"He peeked in your bedroom window?" *She wore pink satin underwear to bed?*

"I told him to get lost and slammed the door in his face; then he started leaving nasty messages on my answering machine and peering in windows, scaring the kids. I had one mother pull her child out of day care because of something Ryson said to her. I called the police several times and they finally had me file a restraining order, but that only made him sneaky about what he did."

When she paused for another sip of coffee, I moved her on to the next topic. I'd heard enough creepiness to get the picture. "How did he treat his other neighbors?"

"Everyone around here hated him, especially Ed Mazella. Ed and Eudora live on the left side as you face Ryson's house. Every night Ryson would play heavy metal rock music from a boom box in his garage while he tinkered with old motorcycles, revving their engines for hours. It drove Ed crazy. Ryson's driveway runs on the side of the house near Ed's bedroom. They've gotten into some wicked shouting matches over it."

I was scribbling fast, and when she paused again, I grabbed a quick gulp of coffee. "Other than you and the Mazellas, has anyone else on the block had a beef with Ryson?"

Trina thought for a moment. "An elderly lady lives on Ryson's other side, and she's very hard of hearing, so the noise probably didn't bother her. My next-door neighbors have griped about him, but I think that's as far as it went."

"Did you ever see anyone stop by his house?"

"There was a girl who used to drop by, but she stopped coming around."

"Can you describe her?"

"I didn't really pay attention."

"Do you remember what kind of car she drove?"

"I think it was white, kind of rusty . . . I'm not really into cars."

"How long have you lived here?"

"About a year and a half. It was a wonderful neighborhood until two months ago. That was when Ryson moved in."

"What did you ask Marco to do about Ryson, specifically?"

"Tell him to stay the hell away from me. Lean on him, if necessary. Marco is good at that kind of thing."

How did she know what Marco was good at? And why did her face glow when she spoke his name? "So you know Marco through his sister?"

"Gina Salvare and I were best friends growing up. My family lived a few doors down from the Salvares." Trina sighed dreamily. "I had a major crush on Marco. All the girls on the block had a crush on him, but he never seemed to notice."

That explained the glow. This woman *still* had a crush on Marco, and I was back to checking her head for split ends. "Did you know the police have focused on Marco as a suspect in Ryson's murder?"

Her eyes welled with tears as she nodded.

"He called me this morning to tell me."

This morning? Hmm. Before or after he'd called me?

"I feel terrible," she said, her chin starting to tremble. "I wouldn't have asked him if I'd thought this would happen — not that I'm sorry to see that creep gone." She carefully wiped beneath her eyes with her fingertips. "I know Marco wouldn't have intentionally killed him."

"Intentionally? Do you mean you think he could have killed him accidentally?"

She put down her coffee mug and raised her chin defiantly. "If Marco says he didn't, that's all that matters to me."

That was a quick sidestep. I decided to let it ride for the present, but I jotted down *intent or accident?* on my pad, to remind me to come back to it. "Were you still at home yesterday evening when Marco went across the street to talk to Ryson?"

"No. Marco told me to take little Mark to my mother's house and stay there overnight, and that's exactly what I did."

"Little Mark is your son?"

"Yes." She smiled, her eyes shining with a maternal love that made me envious — for about a second. Then the sniffler came wobbling in, his nose streaming with yellow goo, his light brown curls stiff along the temples from something that looked like dried pudding. He held up his arms, whining to be picked up. Envy gone.

Marco. Little Mark. Coincidence? Did I even want to go there? Was there any way I could stop myself? "Is this little Mark?" I nodded toward the child now sitting on her lap, the one who looked absolutely nothing like Marco.

"This is Timmy. *That's* Mark." She used her free hand to point through an arched doorway into the living room, where an olive-skinned boy about three years old, with curly dark hair, was stacking wooden blocks and knocking them down. Hearing his name, he paused to glance around at us. Trina wiggled her fingers at him and he gave her a mischievous grin, his mouth curving up at one corner — just like Marco's did.

Damn, I hoped it was a coincidence. "So you weren't here when Marco was inside Ryson's house. What time did you leave for your mother's?"

"Around seven thirty."

"And when did you come back?"

"Why is that important?"

She was getting snippy. I had to choose my response carefully because I didn't want her to realize that she was on my suspect list, not out of petty jealousy, but because she had one major qualification — a motive. What I didn't know was whether she had the opportunity. "I never know what will be important until the investigation is over."

The sniffler squirmed off her lap and headed toward the living room. Trina watched him go, then turned back to gaze at me with unblinking eyes. "I came back early Monday morning, after Marco phoned to tell me what had happened."

I wrote it down and put a question mark after it. I'd have to pay a visit to her mother to check out her story. "Where does your mother live?"

"Why don't you ask Marco?"

It was my turn to narrow my eyes at her — and when I did I noticed that she really did have split ends. I jotted on my notepad: *Split ends, yes!* "I'm sorry if you think I'm being intrusive, Trina. These are just routine questions. I'm somewhat new at this, and if I skip any of them it throws me off."

She toyed with a long silky lock of hair, pulling it from the back to drape across her shoulder. "She lives in New Buffalo, Michigan. Marco knows the address."

By the coy gleam in her eye I could see she'd enjoyed adding that last part.

"Let's go back to yesterday afternoon. Did

Ryson have any visitors that you saw — or maybe you heard a car or motorcycle engine rev, or a door slam?"

She used her small, perfect teeth to tug on her lower lip as she thought it over. "I didn't hear anything and I didn't see any cars or cycles parked out front, either. You can ask Ed Mazella. Maybe he or his wife noticed something. Eudora sees just about everything that goes on in this neighborhood." Trina checked the clock on the wall behind her. "I wouldn't bother going there now. Ed works for a towing service and doesn't get home until after five o'clock. Eudora is home, but I doubt she'll talk to you."

"Why is that?"

"She's weird, kind of a hermit. She keeps the curtains drawn all the time and won't answer the phone. I think I've seen her outside maybe once in the last month, late in the evening, after dark. She had some kind of hood thingy covering her head."

"She must be agoraphobic."

"Agora-what?"

"Phobic. Afraid to leave her house."

Trina shrugged, then twisted to check the gaggle of toddlers in the living room. "I guess so. Are we done? The kids are getting antsy."

I took that to mean we were. There was a stack of orders waiting for me back at the shop anyway, so I hurriedly glanced over my notes and saw the little reminder I'd written earlier. "There's one point I'd like you to clarify. Is there any question in your mind about Marco's innocence?"

"No question at all. I absolutely believe he's not guilty."

Interesting choice of words. From what minuscule information my brain cells had been able to retain from my law classes, I did remember that there was a heck of a lot of difference between being not guilty and being innocent. Did Trina know that? Was she being coy again? "So you believe he's innocent."

"You have to ask me that? Look, Marco is the most decent guy I've ever met. If he says he didn't kill Ryson, that's all that matters to me. And just between us girls, I don't care who killed Ryson. All I care is that the creep is gone."

She wasn't being coy; she was being difficult. "Okay, that's all I have for now. Thanks for the information and the coffee."

I finished my last swallow of coffee, put away my pad and pen, and followed her out of the kitchen, betting that she had no problem finding jeans that fit.

At the front door we were swarmed by small, whimpering bodies with oozing orifices and sticky fingers, making my ovaries shrink up in fear. I raised my purse above my head and plunged through the grasping hands out onto the stoop and into the refreshingly cool September air, where I took a steadying breath and tamped down the urge to make a headlong dash to the car. At the moment, I was very glad that Marco liked his bachelorhood.

CHAPTER EIGHT

When I got back to Bloomers, Grace was in the parlor waiting on several clerks from the courthouse, and Lottie had gone to Rosie's Diner to meet her husband for lunch. All was quiet for now, but that would soon change. At two o'clock, the members of the Monday Afternoon Ladies' Poetry Society would flock in to take up residence in the parlor, where they would spend the next hour and a half sipping coffee and tea, munching on biscuits and scones, and reciting original poems to one another, while Grace fluttered among them refilling cups and Lottie and I hid in the workroom.

I liked the elderly poetesses, but their rhymes of drooping jowls and sagging breasts and stiff hairs sprouting from their chins didn't do much for me other than to give me nightmares about growing old. And poor Lottie had recently begun to check her hand mirror twice a day, tweezers at the ready, in case one of those stiff little suckers should try to sprout from *her* chin.

I put my purse on my desk and pulled a ticket from the spindle for a birthday basket a group of secretaries had ordered for a coworker. They wanted something cute and playful with a fall theme. Super. I was all about cute and playful.

I started with a ceramic vase shaped to look like a green and yellow gourd, then placed in it bright orange epidendrum orchids, vivid yellow sandersonia, sweet little white button mums, and grass green foxtail fern. Then I dug through a box of tiny plastic toys that Lottie had collected over the years, found one in the shape of a typewriter, along with a pair of miniature granny glasses, glued them on tall, wooden picks, and stuck them among the flowers. I tied a bright yellow bow around the gourd, stuck a neon pink pencil through the bow, and wrapped it all in cellophane.

Grace breezed through the curtain with a cup and saucer in hand. "I took advantage of the lull to bring you some mint tea." She placed it on the work table, folded her hands in front of her waist, and smiled. She was waiting for something. Usually that meant I owed her an apology, but I couldn't think of anything I'd done.

"Okay, Grace. What am I supposed to be telling you?"

"You shouldn't suppose anything, dear. It causes all sorts of misunderstandings. But perhaps you'd like to share what it was that Marco needed from you?"

Aha! It was an apology in disguise. She wanted to gloat because her prediction had been right. But why make it easy for her? "Marco asked me to investigate Dennis Ryson's death."

"That's certainly a serious matter. And?"

"And . . . I agreed to help."

She lifted her eyebrows, waiting for the rest.

"You and Lottie were right after all."

"Thank you, dear. When Lottie returns perhaps you'll share the whole story with us."

As she breezed out of the workroom I couldn't help but laugh. Because of her regal bearing and London accent, no one ever suspected that Grace could be devious, but that was one of the reasons I liked her so much.

I took a sip of mint tea, then started on the second order, the ever-popular dozen long-stemmed red roses — we received at least one of these requests a day — which I was able to knock out in fifteen minutes.

Before I could pull the third order, the bell over the door chimed and I heard, "Yoo-hoo. Anyone here?"

Oh, no! My mother had arrived — probably accompanied by whatever feathered sombreros hadn't sold at the festival. I tiptoed to the curtain and peeked through. Yikes! It was even worse than I had imagined. Mom had wheeled in a dolly on which were stacked four cardboard boxes. Obviously, not much had sold at the festival.

I was contemplating slipping out the back door when I heard Grace say, "Maureen, how nice to see you. Aren't you teaching today?"

Rats. I couldn't leave Grace to face the feathers alone.

"Half day," Mom replied. "So here I am. Did Abigail tell you about my new art project?"

I hadn't! She'd be wounded. "Mom," I called cheerfully, entering through the curtain, "you brought your hats. Isn't that wonderful, Grace? Now you'll get to see them close-up."

"Marvelous. I can't wait." No matter what Grace said, she always sounded dignified, so there was no way to tell whether she was being sarcastic or not.

Mom began to unpack the boxes, pulling

110

out big-brimmed downy numbers in a rainbow of hues. "These will be a big draw. You know how women love hats."

Obviously not enough to buy them at the craft fair, even when they were standing in the direct rays of the sun. That should have told her something.

The last two boxes contained an assortment of feathered fans that looked as though the poor birds had been tie-dyed before being plucked, and furry picture frames in all sizes and mixes of colors. I tried to imagine a photo of Grace's classically shaped face surrounded by tufts of teal and purple feathers, but somehow it wasn't working for me.

"Striking," Grace said with a straight face, although I saw her nose twitch. However, that could have been due to the feather motes in the air.

Mom glanced around the shop. "Now then, where shall we put the hats?" She eyed the wreaths hanging on one wall and headed straight for them. I glanced at Grace, but she merely put her finger against her lips, signaling me not to say anything, so I watched mutely as five wreaths came down and five hats went up. The rest of her projects went anywhere she could squeeze them in, against ceramic figurines, brass candlesticks, and silk flower arrangements in the armoire and on the display tables and shelves.

When she was done, the shop looked like a chicken coop that had been attacked by a fox wielding Magic Markers. Lottie chose that moment to return from lunch and had to bat her way through the floating down to get to us.

Knowing the first words out of her mouth would be, *What the hell happened here?* I quickly said, "Good news! Mom brought in her new feather art."

Lottie blinked a few times to clear her vision. "Well," she said, planting her hands on her hips as she swiveled to take it all in. "Well, well, well." I knew what she was thinking: *How soon can we get these down to the basement?*

The poetry society ladies began to stream in, one after the other, exclaiming in delight, "Oh, what lovely hats!"

My mother beamed in delight. She'd finally found her market.

Half an hour later, twelve newly bedecked poetesses were seated in the parlor, sipping hot beverages and sharing their odes, happy as, well, larks, although anyone passing by Bloomers who happened to glance through the big bay window into the coffee parlor would have thought more in terms of escapees from a tropical bird sanctuary. Now, if only we could find customers who'd take the frames and fans off our hands.

With feather particles still settling, my mother went home to start a new project, while Lottie stationed herself at the cash register and I stood in the workroom at the big table, a floral knife in one hand and a handful of daisies in the other, formulating my questions for Ed and Eudora Mazella. By four thirty, business had slowed so much that Lottie and Grace were able to join me so I could fill them in on Marco's request for help and my fear that I would fail him.

"That's why that little wrinkle on her forehead is back," Lottie said to Grace.

"Of course you'll be able to help Marco," Grace assured me. "You're quite a clever girl, really, and you have influential friends in town."

"Like that cutie-pie in the prosecutor's office." Lottie wiggled her eyebrows.

Greg Morgan. Ugh. I'd rather have a mole removed. "The problem with Morgan is that he may be working on the murder case, and even if he isn't, there's no way he'd agree to help the defense team."

"What about Sgt. Reilly?" Grace suggested.

"He's on the other side, too. Besides, Marco doesn't want me to bother him."

Lottie made a clucking sound. "Since when did you listen to Marco? Baby, you gotta stop using law school logic and start using what God gave you."

I glanced down at my chest.

"Not your boobs." Lottie tapped her forehead. "Common sense. Figure out what it will take to get those fellas on your team and go after them."

She had a good point, so I took my wrinkled forehead to the parlor for one last cup of coffee and some serious scheming.

At five o'clock we closed the shop and the three of us headed our separate ways, Lottie to her big, loud brood of teenaged boys, Grace to her cozy little house filled with fine English antiques and Elvis memorabilia, and me back to Ryson's neighborhood. The wind had picked up, bringing a damp chill with it, so I slipped on the denim jacket I kept in the trunk.

I parked in front of Ryson's house and walked toward the Mazellas' tidy, white-frame two-story. A black tow truck was parked in the driveway that ran along the side of the house, and inside the open one-car garage in the rear I could see huge tools hanging from giant hooks on the back wall. I walked up the sidewalk to the front porch and rapped on the door.

My knock was answered by a tough-looking, thick-bodied, middle-aged man wearing an undershirt and blue Dockers that fit below his large belly. He stepped out onto the porch and scowled at me. "No so-licitin'," he said in a gravelly voice, stabbing a lit cigar toward a hand-lettered sign tacked onto the door frame.

"No problem there. I'm not a solicitor. Are you Ed Mazella?"

He gave me a wary glance, scratching the back of his thigh. "Yeah, why? Who are you? Are you from the newspaper?"

"My name is Abby Knight and I'm investigating the death of your neighbor Dennis Ryson."

He took his cigar out of his mouth and peered at me with squinting eyes. "Who you workin' for?"

"I work for myself."

"A private eye?"

"Well, um, yes. Now, if you have a few minutes —"

He stuck the cigar back in his mouth. "Get yer butt off my steps."

Well, *that* was definitely the wrong way to start a conversation. As Ed turned to go inside the house I decided to try appealing to his better nature — if he had one. "You know Trina Vasquez across the street?"

He puffed on his stogie, eyeing me suspiciously. "Yeah, I know Trina. What about her?"

"Did you know Mr. Ryson had been harassing her, following her to the grocery store, peering in her windows, frightening the children?"

He seemed to soften a bit at that. "Yeah. She told me. I even seen him over her way a few times, botherin' her and those kids, so I called the cops on him, you know, tryin' to help her out, poor thing."

Ed grabbed his cigar in the V of two fat fingers, turned his head to the side, and spit a big wad of something gross onto his lawn. "I'll tell ya what. It don't bother me that someone clocked him. He was a real sumbitch. Good for whoever had the balls to do it, too, 'cause he deserves a medal for takin' that scumbag out." Ed stuck his cigar back in his mouth, the veins on the sides of his forehead throbbing. "I hope that sumbitch Ryson rots in hell."

I sensed some really bad karma between Ed and Ryson.

There was a sudden movement in the doorway behind him, a flutter of white, almost like a giant dove had flown past. Ed didn't seem aware of it. He shifted his cigar from one side of his mouth to the other. "So, you're a friend of Trina's, then?"

I was going to have to handle this one carefully, because my response would undoubtedly decide whether Ed cooperated any further. What was it Lottie had told me? I glanced down at the front of my jacket. Oh, right. Common sense.

"I'm a friend of every person who's ever been harassed, Mr. Mazella. My goal is to make sure that the cops find the person who killed Mr. Ryson, for Trina's sake, as well as for your sake and the sake of everyone else in town. After all, we wouldn't want a murderer on the loose." I crossed my fingers behind my back and hoped I'd threw in enough *sakes* to satisfy him.

Ed blew out a thin stream of blue smoke and squinted at me as if he wasn't quite buying it. "What makes you think the cops won't find the killer?"

"To be honest, Mr. Mazella, they've been talking to someone already — they're calling him a person of interest — and I believe they're targeting him unfairly. I want to make sure they get the *right* person, not just

117

someone who's convenient. You hear stories on the news all the time. Some guy spends his life in prison for a crime he didn't commit while a murderer walks."

Ed took another puff and blew it out. "What's really in it for you?"

"You mean like money? Trust me, no one is paying me for this. I'm just big on justice. I don't like to see anyone railroaded by the cops. Surely you can understand my feelings on that. Have you ever been ticketed for something you didn't do and then tried to argue it? Did it get you anywhere? Well, there you go. I really, *really* hate that."

He scratched his leg again, clearly moved by my impassioned speech. "So what d'ya want to know?"

Whew. I'd pulled it off. I dug in my purse for my trusty notepad and pen. "Did you notice if Mr. Ryson had any visitors the day he died?"

"Just that Salvare fella from Down the Hatch. Leastwise, he's the only one I seen."

"How did you know it was Mr. Salvare?"

"I see him all the time down at his bar." Ed made an effort to hitch the waistband of his pants over his belly but it slid back down again. "They sure got into it, I'll tell ya that."

"Did you see Mr. Salvare enter or leave the house?"

"I seen him pull up in front of Trina's house in that black and silver number, and later, after Ryson started his swearin' and stuff, I seen him walk across the street and go into Ryson's house."

"So you heard Mr. Ryson cursing and you saw Mr. Salvare enter his house? What time was that?"

He scratched the front of his thigh. "I'd say around seven thirty, mebbe a little later."

"Did you hear them fighting?"

"Heard it and called the cops. I knew somethin' bad was happenin' 'cause of the glass breakin' and furniture hittin' the walls."

"Did you go over for a look?"

There was a nanosecond of hesitation; then he said, "Naw, I kept my distance from that place."

"You didn't go over at all, not even when the cops were there?"

Another tiny pause before answering. "Wasn't none of my business."

Hesitations, even slight ones, made me suspicious. What normal male wouldn't have gone to see what had happened, especially once he knew the cops were on their way? "Did you see Mr. Salvare leave?"

"Yeah, he took off outta there pretty fast. He was all busted up, like that scumbag got in a few good licks of his own."

He'd seen Marco arrive and leave — in bad shape — not good for Marco's side. If only I could get Ed to admit to having a motive of his own. "What time did he leave?"

"Mebbe a little before eight o'clock."

"Did you get along with Mr. Ryson?"

"You don't *get along* with a scumbag. You keep your distance."

"Did you ever get into an argument with him?"

"Like I said, I kept my distance."

"Did he ever threaten you?"

Ed shifted his cigar from one side of his mouth to the other. "Me? Naw. Why would he threaten me?"

"I was told you had some issues with his motorcycle noise."

"Everyone on the street had issues with that. He'd rev those engines for hours, late into the night, that garbage he called music blastin' from those monster speakers in his garage. Who can sleep with that ruckus?"

"So you *never* tried to talk to him about it?"

"All right, one time I went over there, and that sumbitch had the nerve to come at me with a tire iron. So I called the cops. He didn't like that, I'll tell ya."

"Then he *did* threaten you."

"Naw. Like I said, why would he threaten me?"

Hmm. Ed apparently didn't consider being attacked by a tire iron threatening. I made a note to ask Reilly about Ed. He sounded like one of those people who was always calling the cops, so there was bound to be a file on him. That was supposing I could convince Reilly to help — and not let Marco know about it.

"Was that the only time you got into it with Mr. Ryson?"

Ed leaned close, as though to share a confidence — and more cigar smoke. "I ain't normally afraid of nobody, but some nutcase comes at me with a tire iron, I leave him alone. I got a wife to think of. I can't go gettin' myself hurt and leave her defenseless, know what I mean?"

"Right. You wouldn't want to do that. Did Ryson ever threaten your wife?"

A third hesitation. "No, but I'd have wrung his ugly head right off his neck if he had."

I'd have to get his wife's side of it. Maybe Ryson *had* threatened her and Ed had acted on that urge to do some neck wringing. "Have any of the other neighbors tried to talk to Mr. Ryson about the noise?"

He lifted his thick shoulders. "Search me."

"Did Mr. Ryson have a girlfriend?"

"Yeah, his mommy." Ed chuckled, his belly shaking.

I stared at him in surprise. "Ryson's mother lives around here?"

"I guess so. She stops by here every Saturday afternoon like clockwork. She brings him a box of goodies from the bakery, like he was a little sissy. A mama's boy. I ain't got time for none of that crap, I'll tell ya."

I jotted it down. Marco must not have known about Ryson's mother; otherwise, he would have sent me to interview her. "How did you know the woman bringing baked goods was Ryson's mother?"

"She introduced herself to me once. I think her name was Taylor. Yeah, that's it. Eve Taylor. Mebbe she divorced her first husband or somethin'. I was trimming the shrub out front when she came by. She works at that place on the square — Cake and Icing, or somethin' like that."

"The Icing on the Cake?"

"Yeah, that's the one. Seems like a nice enough lady. How she ever gave birth to that piece of trash Ryson I'll never know." Ed took a puff of his cigar. "Now, I did see a young lady come around here a few times just after he moved in, but I ain't seen her in a while."

"What did she look like?"

"Couldn't tell ya about that. I didn't pay much attention to her looks, but her car sure had seen better days. It was a white Mustang, a 'ninety-one, I think. Local plates. All rusted out along the bottom. What a shame. They don't make Fords like they used to. Chevys, neither. By the way, that's a good-lookin' Corvette you got there. A 1960, ain't it? What's it got, like, a four twenty-seven engine? Now *that's* when they knew how to make a car. Am I right?"

Another flutter of white drew my attention to the doorway, where I caught a glimpse of a face — a strange, almost tribal-looking wooden face — that popped up, then disappeared. I pointed to the doorway. "What was that?"

He turned for a look. "What?"

"I'm not sure. It kind of looked like an African tribesman."

"That's just my wife."

"Your wife is a tribesman?"

"Naw. She collects masks." He didn't explain further, so I dropped it for the time being.

"Got any more questions?" he asked, shifting the area of his scratching.

Afraid of where that itch might travel next, I packed up my pad and pen. "That's all I have for now. Thanks for talking to me."

Ed reached for his wallet in his back pocket. "If you want to know anything else, come see me here." He handed me a plain white business card, bent at the corners, with WALT'S TOWING SERVICE in bold black letters on it. An address and phone number were underneath.

"Thanks." I tucked it in my purse, and when I looked up, Ed was already inside the house, slamming the door behind him.

Not a bad interview considering he hadn't been very cooperative at first, but also not a good one, either. Although Ed hadn't been a fan of Ryson's, he seemed more the type to do a lot of barking but no biting. In fact, his motive, such as it was, wasn't anywhere near as strong as Trina's, and she allegedly wasn't even in town at the time of the murder. And neither of their motives was as strong as Marco's. As for the mysterious former girlfriend, neither Ed nor Trina could give me a description. But it didn't seem to matter since she hadn't been seen near Ryson's house in a long time anyway.

I spent the next hour talking to neighbors in the houses closest to Ryson's, but didn't turn up any new information. Apparently,

Marco was the only one who'd been seen there the evening of the murder. And now I had to meet him for supper and give him the news. Some investigator I was. Miss Marple would hang her head in shame.

CHAPTER NINE

On a dark autumn evening, what could be better than sitting in a cozy back booth at Down the Hatch, having a bowl of steaming ham and split pea soup and a thick, gooey grilled-cheese-and-tomato sandwich on crisp rye bread, accompanied by a cold Bud Light, with a Paul McCartney song playing in the background? Just one thing — sitting there with Marco.

There were two things wrong with that setting tonight, however — Marco's bruised face and somber mood. I couldn't complain. My mood was just a notch above his.

He had ordered only a lager for himself, ostensibly because of a late lunch, but I had a feeling his appetite was as low as his spirits. He made notes in pencil on a legal pad as I nibbled my food in between filling him in on my conversation with Trina and my rounds of the neighborhood.

"So we have a gruff next-door neighbor

who Ryson threatened with a tire iron and an unknown female who used to visit him." Marco rubbed his forehead. "It's thin."

Thin was an understatement. Pitiful was more like it. I felt terrible that I hadn't come up with more. "There's one more person we need to consider as a suspect, Marco. Trina."

His gaze darted to my face as though he couldn't believe I was serious. "Trina was out of town."

"We need to verify that."

"I *sent* her out of town." He said it as though my brain was operating on low batteries — an attitude that wasn't like him, and that ticked me off. Marco wasn't the only one who'd had a bad day. I'd had to deal with Miss Split Ends and her host of runny-nosed kids, a burly, cigar-chomping tow-truck driver, and all those *feathers.*

"I know you sent her, but are you sure she went? She may be your sister's best friend, Marco, but you're the one who's always saying we can't cross anyone off the list until we check them out."

He frowned, bending his head over his notes once again. "Point taken."

"Trina said you'd have her mother's address in New Buffalo, Michigan. If you'd like to share that with me, I'll go see her in the morning before work."

He wrote a name and address at the bottom of a sheet of paper, tore it off, and pushed it across the table. He had it memorized. Why did he have it memorized? How close *was* he to Trina?

Gert, a skinny waitress with a bad cough and tobacco-stained teeth who'd worked at the bar since before the blue anchor and fake carp made their appearances back in the 1950s, halted in front of our booth. "You two need anything?"

Marco shook his head, so Gert glanced at me. "I'm fine, thanks."

"Good." Then she left. Gert didn't waste words on anyone. She didn't have the lung capacity for it.

I nibbled a corner of my sandwich. "Ed Mazella was probably the neighbor who identified you to the police. He mentioned several calls he'd made about Ryson. It seems to have been a habit of his. I can check that out with Reilly."

"Didn't we decide to leave Reilly out of this?"

"But I'm sure he'd want to help."

"I don't want to cause any trouble for him, so let's leave him out. Okay?"

He pinned me with those dark eyes, so I gave him a nod. I knew Marco well enough to stop pushing him on the issue. When he dug in his heels, arguments didn't sway him. What he failed to take into account were my heels, and I didn't mean the spiked kind. They dug even deeper than his, especially when his life was at stake.

"Did Mazella say how he knew me?" Marco asked.

"He mentioned seeing you at the bar, so he must come here."

"What was your impression of him?"

I swallowed a mouthful of bread and cheese, wiped my buttery fingers on a napkin, and readied my soup spoon for a dip in the bowl. "He's a thickset guy with a south-side-of-Chicago accent who seems to have little patience for things that irritate him, like noisy motorcycle engines. But he didn't strike me as a killer, just a tough talker. I'm guessing he's the all-talk no-action type, although he got very riled when I asked if Ryson had ever threatened his wife. He also seemed to have a soft spot for Trina."

"Understandable. Go on."

The spoon was almost to my lips, but at his remark I put it back in the bowl. "Why is that understandable?"

I was smiling — okay, perhaps glowering was a better word — which might have been why Marco started to stammer. "What I meant by that — what he probably — never mind. It's not pertinent. What was your impression of Mazella's wife — what was her name, Eudora?"

Well, of course it wasn't pertinent, but *never mind?* Was he saying Ed's reaction was understandable because of Trina's looks?

I suddenly realized Marco was waiting for an answer. What had he asked again? Oh, right. Eudora. Why was I worrying about some innocuous comment at a time like this? "I couldn't form an impression of her because she only flitted by, and I mean flitted, like a bird. All I know for sure is that she collects masks and Ed is protective of her."

"Halloween masks?"

"He didn't elaborate, but I think not. I caught a glimpse of her wearing what looked like an African tribal mask. Then he told me to contact him at work if I have more questions, which makes me suspect he doesn't want me speaking to her. Maybe she has a mental problem."

"Or maybe she's just shy."

"So she hides behind a big, ugly wooden mask? Wouldn't that be counterproductive?"

"In the world of a private investigator, anything is possible." He studied his notes, then looked up at me. "Let's leave Eudora alone for now and try to locate Ryson's former girlfriend instead. I'll give my contact at the DMV a call and ask her to search the database for a 'ninety-one white Mustang with local plates."

"Shouldn't I do that?"

For a moment Marco seemed nonplussed. Then, with a heavy sigh, he scribbled out the note he had made. I could see by the frustration on his face how difficult it was for him to step back and let someone else take the reins. "Yes, you should do that. Her first name is Eileen. I don't know her last name, but she's the only Eileen at the license bureau. Just make sure you call her between noon and one o'clock."

"Got it. Okay, here's a thought. Maybe Ryson's mother knows who the girl is."

Marco's head came up. "His mother?"

"Yes, apparently she lives in town. Ed Mazella said she works at the bakery on the square. Her name is Eve Taylor."

Marco tapped the pencil against the paper, working his lower lip with his teeth as though deep in thought. "Taylor," he muttered.

"Different last name, so she must have remarried. I'll drop by the bakery first thing in the morning and see what she can tell me about her son's friends."

"Leave her out of it. Just stick with Eileen at the DMV."

I stared at him, puzzled. "Leave her out. Leave Reilly out. Leave Eudora out. You're tying my hands, Marco. I don't get it. Eve Taylor is Ryson's mother. She's bound to know things about his friends. Why shouldn't I talk to her?"

For the first time ever, Marco glared at me — I mean really glared. "Because her son is dead and she hasn't even buried him. She doesn't need to be pestered with questions."

I was on the verge of putting a little pomade in his hair with my grilled cheese sandwich, but instead I took a breath, considered his situation, and tried to put my annoyance on the back burner. "Okay. I don't have to go *tomorrow,* but that doesn't mean I can't go at all, and I certainly won't *pester* her with questions. Give me a little credit."

"You know what I mean."

I drummed my fingers on the table, stewing about his pestering remark, which also brought to mind his comment about Trina's looks. One comment I could handle, but I drew the line at two. "Sure, I know what you mean. Be tactful, because apparently

I'm *not.*"

His left eyebrow rose. "*Someone* got up on the wrong side of the bed today."

That did it. "*I* got up on the wrong side? What does that mean, anyway? How do you even know which side of the bed is the wrong side? What if there's only one side?"

In typical male fashion Marco ignored *my* testy remarks — if you didn't notice them, they didn't exist, right? — and instead reached for his beer, which only vexed me more. Why was I letting his comments annoy me so? The man was under enormous stress. Shouldn't I be more sympathetic?

Okay, fine. I would own up to the fact that my irritation had started at the parade, when I saw the longing look on Trina's face after she and Marco had talked. It had heightened with his remark about how it was understandable that Ed would have a soft spot for Trina. Was he simply being a "big brother" to Trina, or was there a mutual attraction that he hadn't yet owned up to? If there was, fine. All I wanted was his honesty.

I opened my mouth to ask him, then shut it again. Sometimes, the point-blank method wasn't the best route to take.

Fortunately, I knew another way to get an answer, a method known only by magicians and every single woman on the planet over the age of thirteen. I had stumbled onto it as a preteen, when my brothers decided they wanted to be illusionists and my dad took us to a class sponsored by the YMCA, where a local prestidigitator gave a demonstration that stuck with me to this day.

It was a simple matter of using diversions: Keep the audience's attention focused on one thing so they won't realize what you're doing somewhere else. Being of the feminine persuasion, it had quickly occurred to me that this sleight of hand would work in other situations, too, such as getting someone to answer a question.

With that in mind, I stood my remaining sandwich half on one short end to see whether I could get it to stay there. Then I let it go, watching as it toppled over. I tried it again, balancing it carefully, watching as it wobbled a bit but held its ground. Marco, I was pleased to see, was watching, too.

"Look, Marco. I'm sorry I went off like that. I promise I won't pester Eve Taylor. Okay?"

He raised those beautiful brown eyes to mine, looking so utterly miserable I felt terrible for snapping at him. "I'm sorry, too, Sunshine. This is really getting to me. I hate not having control over my own life."

"I understand completely."

And now to pull the rabbit out of my unfeath-ered hat.

"So, just out of curiosity —" The sandwich began to lean to the left. I cupped my hands on either side, ready to catch it. Marco seemed to be holding his breath, waiting to see whether it would fall. "Why do you think it's understandable that Ed would have a soft spot for Trina?"

Abracadabra . . .

"Hey, Marco," Bob, one of the bartenders, said, coming toward our booth. "Phone call. You should take it in the back, man." He lifted his eyebrows as if to signal that it was too personal for me to hear. Bob was high on my list of guys who thought they were hot but in reality had all the spice of white bread. Too bad no one had ever clued him in on it.

Marco slid out of the booth and rose in one smooth, pantherlike move. "I'll be right back."

Presto! The man disappears.

"Want another beer?" Bob asked me.

I let the sandwich fall, then propped my chin on my hand and sighed morosely. "No, thanks. I'm fine. Hey, Bob, who's on the phone with Marco?"

He grinned smarmily. "Wouldn't you like

to know?"

"That was the whole point of my question, *Bob*."

He winked and walked away. Boy, did I wish I was a real magician, because Bob would make a great toad.

I was considering a trip to the bar with my sandwich to distract information out of Bob when Marco returned. "I have to run home for awhile. Stay and finish your food. I'll talk to you tomorrow."

"Is there an emergency?" I asked, trying to appear innocently concerned.

"Family matter. Nothing to worry about."

I hated it when he said that.

As I left the bar I heard the lively strains of "The Beer Barrel Polka" coming from the green and white striped tent behind the courthouse and remembered that tonight was the Pickle Polka dinner dance. Since my Vette was parked in a lot in that direction, I decided to stop by for a peek inside. If nothing else, seeing a tent full of drunk people careening around like wounded llamas might improve my mood.

I entered through the wide doorway, the tent's flaps held back with giant hooks, and was nearly bowled over by the pungent aromas of sauerkraut and Polish sausage.

Picnic tables and benches were set up on either side, while at the far end a long banquet table held large platters of food, which, along with the sausage and kraut, included Wiener schnitzel, German potato salad, green beans with bacon, hard rolls, and tall torte cakes, some stuffed with strawberries and whipped cream, and others layered with creamy chocolate.

To my right, a four-man band played the usual selection of polkas, while at least two dozen couples galloped around the dance floor to the delight of the diners who clapped to the beat and shouted their encouragement. I wasn't surprised to see the mayor and his wife and members of the town council among the rollicking group. The only person that was a surprise was Reilly. Who knew he could polka?

Reilly was a good-looking man, about forty years old, who displayed an air of confidence without the normal policeman posturing. He had intelligent hazel eyes, good bone structure, medium brown hair that was beginning to show a teensy bit of gray at the temples, and, more importantly, no gut hanging over his belt. He was dancing with an attractive blonde who was almost as tall as he was, which would have made her nearly six feet tall. Was she his steady? I'd never seen him out with anyone, so I was curious about her.

As they swung past, Reilly's gaze landed on me, and I held up a hand in greeting. He instantly turned red, as though he was embarrassed to be caught being human. When the song ended, he came over, leading his partner by the hand.

"Hey, Sarge," I said, sizing up the woman and deciding she was okay. "I didn't know you polkaed." I stuck out my hand to the woman. "Hi, I'm Abby Knight."

Reilly took over as I shook her hand. "Abby, this is Karen Jenkins. Karen, Abby owns Bloomers Flower Shop. Her father is former police sergeant Jeffrey Knight."

"Of course." She gave me a warm smile, her eyes crinkling at the corners. "Hi, Abby. I love your little shop, and Sean has told me wonderful stories about your father."

Yes, indeed. This woman was a winner.

"You should have brought Marco over," Reilly said.

"Considering what's going on, he wasn't exactly in a dancing mood. . . . But since you brought it up —"

Are you sure you want to do this? Don't you remember what Marco said about putting Reilly's job at risk?

Pffft. A few harmless questions wouldn't

make him lose his job.

"I really need to talk to you about Marco — when you have time, of course."

"Abby," he said, using the same tone my mother always used when I was on the verge of doing something I shouldn't — as if a tone of voice would have stopped me.

I moved closer to him. "He's your friend, Reilly. I'm sure he's done plenty of favors for you. Come on. I just want to talk."

Reilly glowered down at me and I glowered back.

Karen glanced from me to him, then patted his arm. "Why don't you talk to Abby and I'll go get us some of that luscious strawberry torte cake. I hear it came from the Icing on the Cake. Would you care for some, Abby?"

"No, thanks."

Reilly jerked his head toward the doorway, so I followed him outside to a recessed area along one side of the courthouse. He folded his arms and looked down at me. "How many times do I have to tell you I can't give out any information?"

"So, you don't care if Marco goes to prison?"

"That's not fair."

"Then what's the problem? Marco needs your help, Reilly. Pretty please? I promise

Kellerman won't find out." I gave him my most winning smile, the one that had always worked on my dad after my mom had said no.

Reilly gave me a skeptical glance. "How do you know about Kellerman?"

"Everyone knows about him."

Reilly studied me a moment, not quite believing me. "What do you need?"

I pulled the notepad from my purse and wrote Ed Mazella's name and address on it. "For starters, this is Dennis Ryson's next-door neighbor. Will you find out if he was checked out as a potential suspect?" I tried to give him the paper but he wouldn't take it.

"I'm familiar with Mr. Mazella and I can't tell you that."

"Sure you can. We can use hand signals, like thumbs up or thumbs down, or the wink system, one for yes, two for no. Work with me a little, Reilly. I've got to find out who killed Ryson before the grand jury meets next week."

He glanced around to be sure we were alone. "Look, Abby, I'm just as concerned about Marco as you are, but I'm a divorced dad. I've got two kids to support. I can't risk losing my job."

"You have kids? I didn't even know you

were married."

"It was a long time ago. You were probably in high school then — and do you really want to get into that now?"

He was right. I'd save that for the future, since Reilly was almost as much of a mystery as Marco was. "Come on, Reilly. You can't even look in a file for me?"

"If there *is* a file on Mazella it's bound to be in with the rest of the investigation. I don't want to be caught digging through it."

"So I'm on my own, then?"

"You're on your own."

I threw my hands up in frustration. "Okay, if that's the way it is, then I'll have to handle it — somehow."

"We're good, then?"

"Good? You know the prosecutor will railroad Marco if no one stops him. It's a sorry situation when a guy's best buddy is so intimidated by his bully of a captain that he'd let him go to prison for something he didn't do."

"Look, Abby, before you start passing out the insults, are you sure about —" He paused to scratch behind his ear, clearly uncomfortable with what he was about to say.

"Sure about what?"

"Marco?"

I stared up at him, stunned. "You're joking, right? You don't honestly think he would kill someone."

"Maybe not on purpose, but think about it, Abby. He was an Army Ranger, special operations, trained to kill a hundred different ways. And don't forget, I've seen him in action. He's got a long fuse, but he'll only allow himself to be pushed so far and then he reacts — swiftly. Efficiently."

Oh, my God. Reilly *did* think Marco could have killed Ryson. I felt a knot of anxiety in my stomach. If Marco's buddy didn't believe in him, what chance would Marco have convincing twelve jurors of his innocence?

I stuffed the piece of paper with Ed's information into my purse. "Well, thanks, Reilly. At least I know where you stand. And it's not beside Marco."

I started to walk away, but Reilly said, "Hold it, Abby. I don't want you to get the wrong idea. I'm not saying Marco is guilty, just that you shouldn't, well, assume anything."

"I'm not assuming, Reilly. I know Marco didn't kill Ryson."

He studied me for a moment, then rubbed his forehead as though agitated. "Okay, look. Let me do some thinking on it tonight and maybe I'll drop by Bloomers for a cup of coffee one of these days."

"Thanks, Reilly."

"Don't give me that *I want to hug you* look. I haven't agreed to help."

"I know you haven't. Besides, I wouldn't want to start rumors about us. Karen might get jealous."

"Yeah, right."

He was scowling, but I could tell that inside he was smiling. And by that I knew Reilly would join my team . . . if I had a team.

As we started back for the tent, I asked, "So how did you meet Karen, by the way? What does she do for a living? Does she have family in the area? Has she been married before?"

Reilly just rolled his eyes and kept walking.

CHAPTER TEN

Instead of my usual gulp of morning coffee to jolt me awake, I took a careful sip, rolling the brew over my tongue as if it were a fine wine. *Ahhh.* This time I'd gotten it right. Not too bitter, not too weak. I downed half the cup; then, as the caffeine molecules hit my stomach lining and began to paddle upstream into my sleepy brain, I slathered chunky-style peanut butter on a slice of toasted multigrain bread and drizzled honey on top. It was my new power breakfast, guaranteed to keep me going until noon.

"Tell me the truth," I said to my breakfast companion as I hopped onto a stool at our kitchen counter. (Being short necessitated a lot of stool hopping.) "Am I off base to think there might be something between Trina and Marco?"

I got a bored stare as a reply.

"Don't be so quick to judge. Look at the facts. First of all, I did see them gazing into each other's eyes right there in front of the whole town. Then there's her son, a little boy who — I am not joking — looks so much like Marco that it's frightening. Same skin tone, same color eyes, same wavy hair, and his name is — are you ready for this? — Mark. And then there's the fact that Marco knew Trina's mother's address in New Buffalo. What is *that* about?"

The bored stare was followed by a yawn.

"You think I'm being superficial, don't you? For your information, hotshot, I'm fully aware of the serious nature of Marco's predicament, but that doesn't prevent me from having a few minor, shall we say, *questions* on the subject? Okay, fine, maybe I'm overthinking it, but I can't help feeling you're not giving the topic your full attention." I tore off a corner of my toast and held it out. "Here. This is all you're getting. Now what do you have to say?"

Simon, Nikki's white cat, rose on his hind legs, sniffed at my paltry offering, and went to find a sunny corner to wash his face. He liked his peanut butter smooth.

Nikki came around the corner, sleepy eyed and with her hair sticking up at angles that even the best gel couldn't duplicate. "He's a cat, Abby. Did you really expect him to give you advice?"

"Hey, don't knock him," I said as she pulled out the carton of orange juice. "Simon is a good sounding board. So what are you up to? Another day shift?"

"Early dentist appointment. I have a tiny cavity" — she paused to stick a finger deep into her mouth — " 'ack 'ere."

"Ew. Sorry."

She set the juice on the counter and hunted in the cabinet for a glass. Since most of them were in the sink waiting to be washed, it was a long hunt — more like a safari. "If you were *really* sorry, you'd go in my place."

"They might suspect something when the X-rays didn't match. Besides, I had my teeth cleaned two weeks ago."

"I'm just saying." She splashed juice in a shot glass and drank it down, then poured herself another. "What did I hear you telling Simon about Trina's little boy — that you think he could be Marco's son? Why didn't you tell me this last night? You told me everything else — the weird neighbors, your conversation with Reilly, Reilly's new girlfriend, Marco's secret phone call and family emergency — so why not that?"

"It was a *personal* phone call, not a secret one, and a family *matter,* not an emergency — not that splitting hairs makes me feel better. I didn't tell you the rest because it seems so, I don't know — petty — worrying about whose son little Mark is when Marco's life is at stake."

"Totally petty, so knock it off."

"Got it. Thanks for setting me straight. The thing is, Nik, little Mark looks a lot like Marco."

Nikki took a seat on the stool next to mine. "A lot of people have an olive complexion and dark hair and eyes, Abby."

"You're right. I should totally drop it. But then there's the name similarity and the fact that Marco knows Trina's mother's address."

"Think of it this way. If Trina really wanted to establish her son's identity as Marco's child, she would have named him Marco Junior and had a paternity test. As for the address issue, you said Trina's family and Marco's family lived in the same neighborhood, right? And Trina is friends with his sister? So maybe the two families are still close and send each other Christmas cards or something. Okay, that sounds lame, but there could be a good reason why he knows Trina's mother's address. Stop nitpicking."

I thought it over as I sipped my coffee, holding the warm mug between my hands.

"I've always assumed Marco didn't have any kids because he never mentioned it. But you know what *assuming* does."

"Please don't finish that. I've heard it, like, a thousand times."

"Maybe I should adopt a policy that whenever I meet a guy I automatically ask if he has any children."

Nikki gave me a knuckle rap on the top of my head. "Hello-o-o. Why would you do that? It's not like it comes up in conversation. 'Hi, I'm Abby. Great to meet you. Do you have any kids scattered around the country?' " She paused, her brow furrowing. "On second thought, that might be a good idea."

Nikki had been hurt several times by guys who'd hid their wedding rings — and, in one case, two wives — from her. She swiveled to look at me. "Okay, here's a question for you. What if Mark *is* his son?"

I took a bite of toast and pondered her question. The peanut butter stuck to the roof of my mouth, so I had to swallow more coffee before I could reply. "I guess it wouldn't matter, as long as he was honest about it. It's not like we're married, or are even considering marriage." I sighed longingly. "Wouldn't it be nice to be engaged? I've always wanted to hold my left hand up to the light to display the sparkle of a cute little diamond so everyone could ooh and aah over it."

"You're scaring me now. You're sounding way too much like Jillian. And don't bug your eyes at me, Abby. Just think about your last comment."

Well, whose eyes wouldn't bug out at being compared to Jillian? My cousin was a childlike, self-absorbed drama queen. She had recently wed Claymore Osborne, the younger brother of my former fiancé, Pryce, the chump who'd dumped me because I'd flunked out of law school. Jillian's wedding ceremony had been a lavish Fourth of July garden spectacle timed to precede a splashy fireworks display, so the sky would explode as if the heavens were giving her a standing ovation. (She hadn't counted on someone being murdered during the fireworks show, but that was another story.)

It hadn't mattered to Jillian that her new hubby was a nervous nerd or that his family were snobs. What had mattered was that Claymore would one day inherit half the Osborne fortune. Thank goodness I had no such ambitions. I just wanted a hardworking, honest guy who loved me for my good qualities, accepted my limitations, and didn't care that I was short, freckled, busty, and a bit feisty at times. And if that special guy gave me a ring, any ring, I'd love it no matter what its size.

"Wait, Nikki. I see a way out of this. Didn't I say cute *little* ring? There you go. If I were making Jillian statements, I'd be talking carat size."

"That's true."

Whew. I blinked a few times to make sure my eyeballs were back in place.

"But going back to my original point, Abby, if Mark is Marco's son, and Ryson had been frightening Mark and stalking his mother, wouldn't that give Marco an even stronger motive to get rid of Ryson permanently?"

"Don't even think such a thing." I shoved the last bite of toast in my mouth and chewed furiously so *I* wouldn't think about it.

Nikki slid off the stool, rinsed out her shot glass, added it to the herd in the sink, then put a hand on my shoulder. "You need to have a talk with Marco."

I knew she was right, but my mouth was stuck together again, so all I could do was nod.

"What's this?" She reached for a square of paper that had been on the counter. "Juanita Lopez. New Buffalo, Michigan. Is that

Trina's mother?"

I rinsed the toast down with a gulp of coffee. "I'm going there this morning to check out Trina's story. I want to hear it from the woman's own lips that her daughter was there when she said she was."

"You don't trust Trina?"

"It's not about trust. It's about checking alibis and eliminating suspects."

She studied me. "Are you sure there's not more to it than that?"

"All I want to do is prove Marco's innocence and let the blame fall where it may."

"Hey, maybe Mrs. Lopez will tell you who little Mark's father is."

"I'm way ahead of you on that one, Nikki."

Wearing a long-sleeved, fitted white blouse, khaki pants, and a pair of tan ballet flats I'd found on a deeply discounted shoe rack at Target, with my hair pulled back in a brown plastic barrette, I took off for New Buffalo, Michigan, stopping at Bloomers first to pick up a bouquet of flowers. Whenever I had to question a woman I'd never met before, I'd found it advantageous to dress conservatively and carry flowers. After all, was there any better way to disarm a female than to present her with a handful of lovely, fragrant blossoms? I called it my Investigator's Tactic Number One.

After leaving a note for Lottie and Grace, I headed north on I-49 as far as I could go, then east around the lower end of Lake Michigan. The trip to the tiny tourist town of New Buffalo normally took an hour and ten minutes, but in my Vette, I was there in fifty-five minutes flat. It was a scenic drive that I'd made many times, but when it came to finding the address on the slip of paper, I turned to the Yahoo driving instructions I'd printed out.

Juanita Lopez lived a mile from the lake, in a narrow, two-story duplex in a new neighborhood of identical aluminum-sided patio homes, with garages in the middle and little pockets of lawn in the front and back. I rang the doorbell and a woman in a baby blue terry cloth jogging suit answered it. She was an older, heavier version of Trina, her dark hair threaded with white.

"Mrs. Lopez?"

She took a look at me, then at the flowers in my hand, and her eyebrows drew together. *"Sí?"*

Spanish. Yikes. I hoped she spoke English, too, because my Spanish was limited to a few cuss words, a body part or two, and a working knowledge of Cuban and Mexican food. "I have a gift for you." I held out the bouquet with a smile.

Her eyebrows relaxed and her mouth curved upward. "Really?"

That sounded English enough. She opened the screen door and took them from me, then proceeded to search for a gift tag.

"There's no tag. The flowers are from me. I'm Abby Knight from New Chapel and I own Bloomers Flower Shop on the square. Did Trina mention that I might be coming up here to talk to you?"

The eyebrows resumed their knitted position. "No."

Perfect. I liked the element of surprise. "I'm sure you've heard about the death of her neighbor, Dennis Ryson."

"*Sí.*"

"And I'm sure you remember Marco Salvare. Did you know the police are investigating him as a suspect?"

A pause, and then another hesitant, "*Sí.*"

"Mrs. Lopez, I don't believe for a minute that Marco killed Mr. Ryson, and I don't want him to be blamed for something he didn't do, so I'm trying to gather as much information as I can to prove his innocence. Would you like to help?"

"How do you know Trina?"

She was still skeptical, so I commenced

153

Investigator's Tactic Number Two: flattery. "I was fortunate enough to meet your lovely daughter through Marco. Trina is also very concerned about Marco, which I'm sure she told you. And I must say, your grandson, little Mark, is a real cutie. He certainly takes after his mother in looks."

Her grandmotherly pride finally overcame her wariness. "He's a handsome child, and very smart, too."

"Yes, I saw that right away." I paused a moment. "I understand you knew Marco when he was a boy."

"I have known Marco since he was five years old."

"So you know what a good person he is."

"*Sí*. He's a good man, just like his papa was."

"Can I count on your help, then, to prove Marco's innocence?"

Her mouth shifted to one side, as though she were thinking about it. Maybe Investigator's Tactic Number Three would help her decide: guilt.

"If Marco were to be convicted, he'd get life in prison, Mrs. Lopez. I'm sure you can imagine the pain his mother would feel if her son went to prison. Imagine your grandson in that situation. Wouldn't you hope someone would step forward to help him?"

Mrs. Lopez made a quick sign of the cross. "*Madre de Dios,* it is too horrible to think about. But I don't know what I can tell you."

"How about if I ask you a few questions, and we'll see. You might have some answers that will clear up the situation right away."

She studied me for a moment, then opened the screen door and let me in, showing me in to a tiny living room decorated in shades of blue, with a fishbowl full of seashells on the coffee table, and an ornately framed print of the Last Supper over the blue crushed velvet sofa. I took a seat at one end of the sofa while she settled at the other end. She motioned for me to start.

This was the tricky part — winning her cooperation without letting on that her information might make her daughter a suspect. "I'm trying to get an idea of what Dennis Ryson was like. Had you ever met him?"

She shook her head. "I don't get down to New Chapel much anymore, but Trina told me about him plenty of times, how he was always hitting on her and scaring little Mark and the children in her day-care class. The police, they weren't much help. They had her fill out a paper. What good is a paper?

So she asked Marco to make him leave her alone."

"Do you know how Marco tried to do that?"

She pushed the tip of her index finger against her lip. "I think it was last Friday that Trina called him. She said he agreed to help her; then I didn't hear from her until Sunday evening when she called to tell me she was coming up here with little Mark."

"Did she tell you why was she coming?"

"*Sí.* Marco wanted her and little Mark away from there in case there was trouble. I was very frightened when she told me that, but she said Marco knew what he was doing."

"Do you remember what time she got here?"

"Let me think . . . it was late. My program had already started, so probably ten minutes after ten o'clock."

I did some quick calculations. Allowing seventy minutes driving time, that meant Trina wouldn't have left New Chapel until around nine o'clock. Yet Marco had gone to see Ryson at approximately seven thirty. If she was supposed to get out of town for safety reasons, why had she waited so long to leave? Did Marco know she was still in her house when he went to see Ryson?

Could Trina have stayed behind so she could slip into Ryson's house to finish him off after Marco left?

I instantly saw two problems with that. First, the only way she would have braved entering Ryson's home was if she knew she wouldn't be in danger. But how would she know that unless she had watched the fight through Ryson's window and saw that he had been hurt? Or could she have had someone watching for her? A neighbor, perhaps?

Second, she would have had to deliver a fatal blow to Ryson's head, which meant she'd either grabbed something heavy in his house or brought a weapon with her. I needed to know what had been used to kill Ryson and whether Trina had access to such a thing. Maybe I could get Reilly to tell me.

"Was Trina upset when she arrived here Sunday night?"

"Very upset. That man — Ryson — she knew he could be dangerous, and Trina didn't want anything bad to happen to Marco."

"Has Trina said anything about who she thinks might have killed Mr. Ryson?"

"No, she doesn't like to talk about it."

"Has she ever mentioned a neighbor by the name of Ed Mazella?"

"Oh, *sí.* Señor Mazella has been so kind to her. He even takes little Mark to play at the park. Little Mark calls him *Abuelito* — Grandpa."

That was so not the picture I had of Ed. "What about Mrs. Mazella?"

Mrs. Lopez tapped the side of her head. "Trina said she's *loca.*"

Crazy. That was one Spanish word I knew. "Is your daughter divorced or widowed, Mrs. Lopez?"

"She is a widow. Why?"

"I was just wondering if there was an ex-husband in the picture — someone who might have been angry about the way Mr. Ryson was treating her."

She made the sign of the cross again. "Luis was killed in a car crash over a year ago. She didn't tell you?"

No one had told me. "I'm so sorry. I hadn't heard. How awful for Trina. And Luis was little Mark's father, right?"

"*Sí.*"

Whew. That was one question that I was very glad to have out of the way. "How long were Trina and Luis married?"

She had to think about it, counting back on her fingers. "It was four years ago that they got married. Such a beautiful ceremony, too."

158

If I wasn't mistaken, little Mark looked about three years old. Hmm. Had Marco been around then, or were those his Army Ranger years?

I glanced around, spotted a group of framed photos on an end table, and got up to look at them. Two were snapshots of Trina and her son, one was of Mrs. Lopez with Trina and Mark, and one was a posed photo of Trina, Mark, and a man who had an olive complexion, curly dark hair, and dark eyes — a grown-up version of little Mark. I picked it up. "Is this Luis?"

"*Sí.*" She sighed longingly. "He was such a good man, and a handsome man, too. Luis, he was good to my Trina. He did everything for her. Now she must do it all herself. I hope someday she will find another man like him."

I wondered whether either she or Trina was picturing Marco in that role. I set the frame on the table beside the others, satisfied that the names Mark and Marco were merely coincidence — plus I couldn't think of any way to question her about it that tied into the murder investigation. "You have a beautiful grandson, Mrs. Lopez. He'll grow up to be a fine man someday."

As I drove back to New Chapel, I made a mental list of what I had learned from Juanita Lopez that would need further investigating and came up with a whopping two items. One: Trina hadn't reached her mother's house until after ten o'clock. Two: Trina was upset when she arrived. I wasn't sure whether item two was even a legitimate concern. I would have been upset, too, if a friend of mine was putting himself into danger for me.

Item one was the clincher. Why had Trina waited so long to leave home?

CHAPTER ELEVEN

There were a handful of customers shopping at Bloomers when I got back, some browsing the silk floral arrangements scattered throughout the store, one paying for a purchase, and one brave woman trying to convince the gentleman with her that she really needed a feathered fan. There was also a coating of neon-colored down on the floor, making the waxed wood as slick as an ice-skating rink, which I discovered when I slid from the door to the cash register. As my arms windmilled to keep my body upright, one thought screamed through my head — *lawsuits!* I had to get that floor cleaned before a customer took a nosedive.

Lottie didn't even blink when I collided with the counter. She was busy ringing up a twig garland entwined with moss, cones, fungi, catkins, and bright pink heather for a young woman holding a four-year-old girl by the hand. The little girl had several bright green feathers clutched in a chubby fist and was using them as tiny whisk brooms to sweep out the contents of her nostrils. She and her mother seemed startled by my dramatic entrance.

In the parlor, Grace was pouring coffee for a group of women seated at a table in front of the big bay window, her nose screwed up as though she smelled something distasteful. Had something died behind the coffee counter overnight? It was an old building, but I thought my pest control was up-to-date.

I was about to glide across the room to investigate when I saw her put the pot back on the warmer, then scurry past me, through the shop, and into the workroom. I followed her, curious as to what she had smelled, only to find her blowing her nose. She threw the tissue in the trash can and turned toward me with a sigh. Her eyes were red, her nose was red, and she looked miserable.

"My sinuses are acting up today. There must be rain coming in."

I was afraid what she really had was a case of featheritis, but I didn't want to put any ideas in her head. "I'm sorry."

Grace took her purse out of a cabinet over the work counter, pulled out a bottle of antihistamine, and proceeded to dispense two tiny red pills from it. "Perhaps this will solve the problem. I should have taken them earlier."

She blew her nose again, then went to the kitchen to wash her hands, while I got a damp mop to clean the floor in the shop. I was going to have to do something to end Grace's torture and eliminate any risk of customer injuries, but what was I going to do with all those fans and frames?

Once the floor was feather-free, I tackled the stack of orders on the spindle. Four were for Dennis Ryson's funeral service that evening at the Happy Dreams Funeral Home. Wait. That evening? Could that be right?

I found the newspaper and checked the obits. The viewing was scheduled for seven o'clock with the service to start at eight. Wow. Someone was in a hurry to get Ryson buried. His mother? I'd have to check with the funeral director. Also, since the body had been released for burial, that meant the autopsy had been done, so hopefully Dave would have the results soon.

In the meantime, I had to get busy so I could get the arrangements delivered before Ryson's friends and family arrived at seven. Hmm. Friends and family. A potential source of information. In fact, maybe that group would include former girlfriends. I'd have to drop by during the visitation to pay my respects — and see whether any young females driving a 1991 white Mustang with local plates had the same idea.

I checked the names on the four orders. The casket blanket had been ordered by Eve Taylor. The other arrangements were from "the gang at the motorcycle shop," the Icing on the Cake Bakery, and someone who wanted the card signed, "Clowns-on-Call."

By noon we had the arrangements ready to deliver. While Lottie loaded our rental van, I placed a phone call to the license bureau to talk to Eileen. After working my way through a confusing automated menu (I didn't know anyone's extension number; I didn't want to hear anything in Spanish — unless they were teaching new cuss words; I didn't want to report a lost license; and I certainly didn't want to schedule a driving test), I finally reached a live person.

Fearing I'd be transferred back to the menu or put on hold, I said quickly, "Hi, I need to speak to Eileen. I'm a friend of hers and this is really important."

"Eileen who?" a bored female asked.

"I don't know her last name. How many Eileens work there?"

She stopped doing whatever was making a

rasping noise, possibly filing her nails. "One."

"That should make it easy, then, shouldn't it?"

She didn't seem to find that amusing. "Hold plea—" She punched a button before she'd even finished her sentence.

I stood up at my desk and reached for the cup of coffee on the worktable about two feet away from my fingertips. I stretched the cord as far as it would go, sliding the phone precariously close to the edge of the desk, and still no luck. I had just put down the handset when I heard, "This is Eileen. How may I help you? Hello?"

"Don't hang up," I yelled, grabbing the handset. "I'm here. Hi, Eileen. My name is Abby Knight, a friend of Marco Salvare's. I own Bloomers —"

"On the square. Sure, I remember you. I worked here when your Corvette was in a hit-and-run accident last June." She cupped a hand around the mouthpiece and whispered, "I got the information for Marco on the SUV that hit you."

Good memory. And she'd heard of Bloomers, too. I liked this friend of Marco's. "That was really super of you to help us out, Eileen. We were able to solve that case thanks to your information. And now I'm hoping you'll help again."

She whispered, "Is this for Marco?"

"Um . . . Well . . . I can't really say. So let me just ask if you read about the Ryson murder in the newspaper?"

"Yes, and I saw Marco's name in it. I think it's terrible that the cops questioned him. He's such a sweet guy."

"So do you think you could give me a little help, like by looking up a car registration?"

"Hold on."

I heard someone speaking to her, and her reply of "Okay, in a minute," then she whispered again, "What do you need?"

"The names of everyone in the county owning a nineteen-ninety through ninety-two white Mustang."

"It might take a few days. Is that okay?"

"The sooner the better, but whenever you can get to it is fine."

"I'll see what I can dig up. Give me your number, Abby."

I rattled it off and listened as she repeated it. "That's it. Thanks, Eileen. This could help me make a breakthrough on the case."

"Tell Marco a lot of us are pulling for him."

Wonderful. Marco had a fan club. As I hung up, Grace poked her head through the curtain. "Line two, dear. It's Marco."

Speak of the devil. If only I had some good news for him. I punched the button and forced a cheerful tone. "Hey. How's it going?"

He grunted. That wasn't a good sign. Neither were his brusque words. "Anything new to report?"

"I just talked to Eileen at the DMV and she's going to do a database search on the Mustang. She said to tell you she and many others are pulling for you."

"Did you get up to New Buffalo?"

"I did."

"And?"

"Mrs. Lopez is a very nice woman, and I got to see photos of Trina's husband, Luis, who I was not aware died last year."

"What about Trina?"

Marco had always been a cut-to-the-chase guy, but never more so than now. "One interesting item turned up. She didn't arrive there until after ten o'clock Sunday night. So if she left her house around seven-thirty, why did it take her until ten o'clock to make an hour-and-fifteen-minute trip?"

"You'll have to ask Trina. I'm sure there's a logical explanation."

"It's on my to-do list. I'm also going to pop into the Ryson funeral service this evening to see who turns up."

"Good."

"I'll report back afterward."

"Sure."

The conversation was stilted and Marco seemed distant. It felt as though someone were sliding a wedge between us, and I didn't like that at all. "Marco?"

"Hmm."

"I need a little sunshine."

"What?"

"You know . . . Sunshine?"

"I'm not getting it, Abby. What are you saying?"

Men. They can be so dense at times. "I'm sending you a metaphorical message. You haven't called me Sunshine lately."

There was a long pause; then he said in a discouraged voice, "I met with Dave today, and things aren't looking good. The prosecutor isn't even trying to find another suspect. It's like the entire force of the government is focused on one guy — me. I honestly don't think I have a fighting chance, Abby."

I'd never heard him sound so down before. Marco had always been solid, confident — my rock. It tore at my heart. "Marco, you *do* have a fighting chance. You have me. I know you didn't do this and I'm going to find the person who did. Just keep your hopes up."

"I know how the system works, Abby. We have only a few days until the grand jury meets and not one good suspect has turned up."

As if I needed a reminder. "I'll come through for you. Just try to relax, okay? Remember this song." I cupped my hand around the phone and crooned softly, *I've got sunshine — on a cloudy day . . ."*

"It's hard to find the sunshine when the clouds are so thick."

Proving that he could make metaphors, too. "I'm right here, Marco."

"Hang in there with me, okay? This isn't easy."

"Of course I'll hang in there. You've been there for me, haven't you? I believe in you, Marco. Don't ever forget that."

"I hope *you* never forget it."

It was my turn to pause. "What?"

"I'll call you." He hung up, leaving me to puzzle over his words.

"Oh, for goodness' sake," Lottie said, coming through the curtain. "Why is that wrinkle in your forehead back?"

"Because I'll never understand men."

"Sweetie, join the club."

We both had a laugh at that, only mine was forced because inside I wasn't laughing at all. What had Marco meant? Was there a reason I might stop believing in him?

CHAPTER TWELVE

As soon as I'd eaten a quick supper of leftover chicken salad and stale tortilla chips (clearly I needed to make a trip to the grocery store), I put a short black jacket over my shirt and changed from khakis to black slacks, then sped to Bloomers to pick up one last funeral arrangement (which I'd purposely waited to deliver). Then I zipped around the corner to the Happy Dreams Funeral Home, owned by Maxwell and Delilah Dove.

The huge, cream-colored Victorian house had dark green and light green trim and accents of mauve, in a style commonly known as a painted lady. It had a reception area in front and two parlors, A and B, one on each side, that ran from the front to the back, with an entry on both ends that led to a hallway between the two. When I arrived at ten minutes before seven o'clock, I was relieved to see that parlor A was empty and dark, which meant that any guests arriving tonight would be there for Ryson's service in parlor B.

I checked in with Max, a genial man with a calm, pleasant demeanor, to let him know I was bringing another arrangement; then I casually mentioned my surprise at how soon the Ryson funeral was being held.

"What can I say, Abby? Those were his mother's wishes. I always follow the family's wishes."

"I'm just saying it seems so rushed. Was it just Mr. Ryson's mother who met with you? No other family members, or girlfriends, by any chance?"

"No one else." Max opened a file on his desk and scanned the information. "Apparently there are no other siblings or close relatives, and she didn't want anything elaborate or drawn out."

"How did she seem to you?"

Max shrugged. "She was doing all right. I've seen a lot worse."

"Is she here yet?"

"I haven't seen her."

"Okay, thanks, Max. I'll drop off these flowers; then I might hang out for awhile to pay my respects."

"You're always welcome, Abby. The service is scheduled for eight o'clock."

I left his office and slipped quietly into room B, surprised to find myself the only one there. At the back of the room was the closed casket, covered by my floral blanket of cream- and peach-colored roses. Another surprise was that there were so few flowers in the room. Normally, the floor on either side of the casket and the console tables along the side walls were filled with arrangements of all kinds, but tonight there were a mere seven, and most of those were mine. Obviously Dennis Ryson was not a popular person.

I waited more than fifteen minutes for someone to show up — where was his mother, for heaven's sake? — and was on the verge of leaving when suddenly I heard loud male voices outside the parlor. I hurried to the front doorway and peered into the reception area, where I saw a group of men wearing various black leather items and sporting lots of tattoos headed my way. I was betting they were Ryson's coworkers at the motorcycle shop, but I hated to typecast. I quickly took a seat at the end of the fourth row of chairs and dug for a tissue in my purse, trying to look properly mournful.

Their loud voices ceased the moment they entered the parlor. With heads bent and meaty hands hanging limply at their sides, they shuffled up one side, past the closed coffin, then down the other side, where they stood in a huddle, talking in low murmurs. Although I wasn't keen on interrupting a pack of alpha males, I also wasn't one to let an opportunity pass. I gave them another five minutes, then scooted out of the row and walked up behind them.

"Excuse me. Sorry to interrupt, guys, but would you mind if I asked some questions?"

Heads swiveled to give me a slow once-over, making me feel like an ice cream sundae on display in a Baskin-Robbins window. Then they turned away to resume their conversation.

As if a snub would discourage a redhead. "Excuse me again. I know this isn't the best time, but I have some questions about your friend —"

"Dude, do you hear something?" That was from a big guy in a studded black leather vest and white T-shirt, a pack of cigarettes wedged under one rolled sleeve. (Now *there's* a funeral outfit.)

A guy with gold rings stacked on his thick fingers cupped a hand around one ear. "I don't hear nothin'."

"Me, either," grunted another fine product of our educational system.

"Sounds like a gnat buzzing around to

me," Leather Vest said.

"You know how we get rid of gnats?" To answer his own question, Gold Finger smacked his palms together, making the other guys snicker.

Very cute. They were playing *Let's be cool macho studs and ignore the nosy chick.* Well, I could play games, too, and all I had to do to outsmart them was dumb down to their level.

Within ten seconds I had the clip out of my hair, two shirt buttons opened to reveal cleavage, and a coat of gloss on my lips. I tossed my hair back and said in a husky voice, "I prefer to think of myself as more the ladybug type. You know . . . all red-hot and hungry."

Five heads turned and five pairs of eyes devoured me from the scalp down. Time to turn on the bimbo act. Shameful, perhaps, but, hey, what wouldn't I do for Marco?

I tilted my head, batted my eyelashes, and pushed my lips into a pout. "I saw you big, tough guys standing here and was really hoping you could help me out. See, I'm a very curious girl. In fact, some people say my curiosity is, well . . ." I twirled a lock of hair around my finger and let them fill in the blank any way they wanted. "So, any of you hunks feel up to answering some questions?"

I could see drool forming in the corners of their mouths.

"What do you want to know?" Leather Vest said, his voice thick with saliva.

"For starters," I purred, "tell me what a bunch of macho guys like you do for a living."

Gold Finger undressed me with his eyes, causing an unpleasant shiver to crawl up my spine. "We're mechanics at Wheel and Deal Motorcycles." He cracked his knuckles, as if to prove how manly he was. "We know bikes inside and out. You got a problem, we can fix it."

"*Very* impressive. So you and Dennis must have worked together."

That was clearly the wrong comment to make, because immediately a surly, thick-necked man stepped forward as the rest closed ranks around me. "How do you know Denny?"

He had a shaved head, wore a black T-shirt with a HOGS' BREATH SALOON logo on it (motto: "Hog's breath is better than no breath at all," something I would not dispute) and black leather pants, and sported a tattoo of a wicked-looking cobra down his arm.

Obviously I shouldn't have jumped into the serious questioning so soon. Now I'd have to backpedal into bimbo mode to put them at ease.

I glanced at each one of them, my hand at my heart in a gesture of complete surprise (drawing their gaze straight to my cleavage), and in a breathless voice exclaimed, "Oh, I didn't know him at all. I just came to deliver flowers. But I read about the murder in the newspaper this morning, and then when I saw your friend up there I couldn't help but wonder what brought him to such a terrible end."

That seemed to satisfy them.

"Yeah, poor bastard," Gold Finger said, making no attempt to raise his eyeballs away from my breasts. "I'll bet he didn't see *that* one coming."

"And you've probably been friends with him, like, forever, right?" Boy, was it difficult to do any intelligent questioning while pretending to be a twit.

"Only a couple of months," Cobra Man replied, "when he started working at the shop."

"I see." I paused to glance around the nearly empty room. "I can't believe you're the only ones here."

"Doesn't surprise me none." Cobra Man

flexed the biceps on one arm. "Denny wasn't what you'd call easy to get along with."

"But you'd think he'd at least have a girlfriend, right?" I smiled prettily. I didn't dare come right out and ask about the girl in the 1991 Mustang.

"No girlfriends. Only the chicks he paid for." Gold Finger snickered.

Okay, I didn't want to go there. Forget that line of questioning. "So you guys hung out together?"

"Nah. We didn't see him too much outside work," Leather Vest said. "He did his clown gigs on weekends. Sometimes he'd drop by the bar, but he was always alone."

I tilted my head and gave him a coy smile. "So where do you guys hang out? I'm always looking for a new place."

Leather Vest snapped his fingers. "What's the name of it? You know, that mick place out by Dunes State Park."

Mick place? Lovely. "Do you mean Luck O' the Irish?"

"That's the one." Leather Vest winked. "You should drop by some Friday night."

"I might do that." *Like never.* I had to suppress a shudder, remembering the one and only time I'd been there, tracking clues to find a missing groomsman in Jillian's wedding party. I was still having nightmares about guys with greasy beards and nose hair long enough to braid. Who would have guessed facial hair could hold so much food?

I turned to glance at the coffin. "So what do you think happened? A robbery gone bad or maybe someone with an ax to grind?"

Clearly puzzled, Gold Finger glanced at Cobra Man. "Denny was offed with an ax?"

"Hey, numb nuts," Cobra Man snickered. "Don't you know what *ax to grind* means?"

"It means that someone had a beef with him," I explained, making a note to myself not to use big words with them — like *ax* and *grind.*

Leather Vest said, "I'd bet you any money it was someone who had a beef. Denny had a way of pissing off people."

"Even you guys?"

"Whoa there, girly," Cobra Man said, stepping closer. "We didn't have any beefs with Denny."

Yikes. Bad move, Abby. "I didn't mean to imply —"

"When we have a beef with someone, we settle it like men." He balled one hand and smacked it against his open palm.

"Only a pansy attacks with a weapon," Gold Finger added.

And here I had mistakenly believed real

men settled their differences by talking things out. Silly me. At any rate, I was fairly confident that none of them had killed Ryson. They weren't bright enough to sneak into Ryson's house without attracting attention.

I tossed my hair back and gave them a pouty smile. "You are so right. Aren't the cops questioning someone for the murder anyway?"

I waited for an answer, but all they did was glance at one another. I couldn't tell whether they hadn't read the article or were just playing dumb, so I pressed a little harder. "I read his name in the paper just this morning. Salvare, wasn't it? Do you guys know anything about him?"

Leather Vest started to answer, but Cobra Man put out a hand to stop him. "Wait just a damn minute, here. You think we're stupid?"

No way I was going to answer that. I tilted my head and pushed my lips into another pout. "What do you mean?"

Gold Finger said to him in a hushed voice, "Take it easy, dude."

"I'm not going to take it easy until she tells us what's up with all the nosy questions. Now she's asking us about the guy who offed Denny. What gives?" He glared down at me. "You're no delivery girl. Who are you?"

"Okay, let's all take a deep breath and calm down," I said, deciding a little bit of the truth wouldn't hurt. "You're partially right. I'm not just a delivery girl. I'm a florist. I own a flower shop." I pulled a business card out of my purse and handed it to him. "See? Bloomers Flower Shop. It's right around the corner, facing the courthouse."

He read it, then passed it to Gold Finger. "Big freakin' deal. Anyone can have a card printed up."

I was on the verge of simply walking away, but I figured I had more to gain by giving them some kind of explanation and winning their confidence. "Can you guys keep a secret?"

They exchanged glances; then Cobra Man said, "Let's hear it first."

Make it good, Abby. "Okay. Here it is." I took a deep breath, giving me a precious moment to gather my wits. "First of all, I really am a florist. See all those arrangements up front? They're mine. I did them. I'm also a private investigator, kind of as a sideline business. You know, florist by day, PI by night? Here, I'll show you."

I flipped open my wallet and pulled out the yellowed clipping from the *News*. "This

181

is an article about how I solved a hit-and-run accident and caught a murderer. It was my first case." I held it out, waiting for a taker. "Go on. Read it. My name is in there."

Cobra Man took it, looked it over, and passed it along. "So how come you're working on Denny's case? I thought the cops had their guy."

"Again, this is strictly between us, okay? I'm working on it because I think the man the cops have targeted is innocent." I glanced around to be sure no one was near. "Do you guys know Marco Salvare? He owns Down the Hatch Bar and Grill."

"Yeah. I know him. He used to be a cop," Leather Vest said.

"And before that," I told them, "he was an Army Ranger."

Cobra Man rubbed his whiskered chin. "Tough dude. He busted my chops a few times."

"Salvare was okay," Gold Finger said to him. "He was on the up-and-up."

"That's exactly why I'm investigating. Why would someone like Salvare commit a cowardly act of murder?" I let them digest that a moment. "It sounds to me like he's being railroaded. You guys know how the system works. The DA finds a guy to pin it on; then he doesn't have to look any further."

"Yeah, but the newspaper said Salvare was at Denny's house right before the cops got there," Cobra Man pointed out.

"It's circumstantial, guys. That doesn't mean he killed Denny." I did a quick check of the time — yikes, it was almost eight o'clock — and forged ahead, talking fast. "You know, if Denny were my friend I'd want to see justice done. I mean, think about it. If the prosecutor indicts Salvare and they put him away because of some flimsy, circumstantial evidence, someone out there is going to get away with murder. So, come on, help me out. Is there anybody you can think of who might have had a beef with him, like a former girlfriend, or an angry customer . . ."

"Well . . . there was this chick who came to see Denny at work last week," Gold Finger said. "She was really pissed off at him."

Hmm. The mystery girlfriend, perhaps? "What day was that?" I asked him.

"Last Tuesday. Denny and I stayed late to work on a 'ninety-five Harley. So this chick comes tearing into the garage in these boots with, like, five-inch heels — man, one kick with those suckers and you'd be singing soprano. She cussed Denny up one side and down the other. Said if he ever came near her again, she'd kill him."

"Did you get her name?"

He scratched a thick sideburn. "I think Denny called her Trina. Yeah, that was the name."

Trina had confronted Dennis Ryson, the man she feared? Why hadn't she told me?

Out of the corner of my eye I caught sight of Max at the front of the room getting ready to start the service. I pulled more business cards out of my purse and passed them around.

"You guys have been great. If you think of anything else that might help me crack open this case, or anyone who might have had a grudge against Dennis, will you let me know?"

Cobra Man tucked the card in his pants pocket. "Yeah, we can do that. And next time you need a tune-up, you come see me." He gave me a lecherous wink, then followed his buddies into the back row of folding chairs.

Right. Like I'd let him touch *my* spark plugs.

As I headed toward one doorway, four women entered the parlor from the other and lined up in front of the casket. They all wore dark dresses, two had on black hats, and one had covered her head with an old-fashioned scarf — what Nikki's grandmother always called a babushka. I was guessing one of the ladies was Ryson's mother, but none of them stood out as the obvious choice. No one began to sob or did anything else that might be expected from a mother who'd just lost her son. Instead, they turned and took seats in the front row.

Max cleared his throat, darting a glance my way, as if to say, *"If you're going to stay, please take a seat."*

As much as I would have liked to stick around to question Ryson's mother after the service, I couldn't bring myself to put her through such an ordeal. I walked up the hallway and into the reception area just as the front door opened and two men in their late twenties or early thirties hurried in. They nodded to me as they passed, then slipped into parlor B.

I headed for the small front foyer and pushed on the old wooden door to go outside, but it wouldn't budge. That was odd. It had worked fine for the two who'd just entered. I grabbed the handle with both hands and tried again, but it still wouldn't give, so I stepped back, hit it with my shoulder, and — *bang!* The door flew open and I stumbled outside, nearly falling over a young woman who sat on the sidewalk gaping up at me, legs sprawled, as if she'd fallen backward.

"I'm so sorry," I cried, helping her to her feet, which was more of a task than I'd imagined. She was very solidly built. "I thought the door was stuck."

She laughed, then in a soft southern drawl said, "Ah did, too."

She had a wide, square face, upturned nose, and big, expressive brown eyes. Hmm. Young woman . . . Ryson's funeral . . . his ex-girlfriend? She straightened her navy jacket and brushed off the back of her navy skirt.

Her face seemed familiar, but I couldn't place it. "Do I know you?"

She gave me an skeptical look. "Ah don't remember ever meetin' y'all."

"I'm Abby Knight. I own Bloomers Flower Shop on the square."

I was hoping she'd reciprocate with her name, but all she said was, "Ah've been there a few times. Pretty little shop."

"Thanks." I stood directly in front of her, blocking the path to the door, hoping I could get more information before she went inside. "Are you here for the Ryson funeral?"

She grimaced as though the subject was distasteful. "Ah sure wish Ah could say no to that."

"Were you a friend of Dennis's?"

"Now, there's a *no* Ah'm delighted to say."

She wasn't a friend, and was quite glad of it, yet she'd come to his funeral service. Sounded like an ex-girlfriend to me. The test would be the car in the parking lot, but, as I discovered when I glanced to my right, I couldn't see the lot from where I stood.

She checked her watch as though she was in a hurry, so I said, "I'd better let you go inside. The service is about ready to start."

"Oh, no. That's all right. Ah'm waitin' for someone. Ah hope he gets here soon. Ah hate funerals enough as it is."

"So, how did you know Dennis?"

"Ah worked with him," she said vaguely, glancing toward the parking lot.

"At the motorcycle shop?"

"No, as a performer."

A performer? Aha! I had it. She was in the clown troupe. And since there'd been only one female clown, I knew exactly who she was. "I saw you last Saturday in the parade. You had a purple lily on your hat."

"Ah surely did. How quaint that you remembered my hat."

"I never forget a flower."

She laughed, a deep throaty laugh, her cheeks turning a pretty pink. Over her shoulder I saw a tall man come striding around the corner from Franklin Street. "Lily!" he called.

Her name was Lily? Well, that explained the flower.

The young woman turned toward him, hands on her hips. "There you are, Trent! Ah'd just about given up on you."

"Sorry I'm late. Are Gil and Brad here?"

"Their cars are here," she replied. "They must be inside."

I was guessing she meant the two guys who'd arrived earlier. Maybe they were also in the troupe.

"Pleasure to meet you, Abby," she called over her shoulder, hurrying away.

"Same here, Lily."

I immediately headed for the parking lot, where I found five gleaming Harley-Davidsons and a few nondescript older cars — but not a rusty white Mustang in sight. Damn.

Sitting in my Vette, I checked my cell phone for messages and was disappointed to see that neither Dave Hammond nor Marco had called. I'd been hoping Dave would have phoned with the autopsy results, and of course I always wanted to hear from

Marco. I hit Marco's speed dial button but got his voice mail, so I headed for Down the Hatch to try to catch him there.

"He went home," Chris told me when I dashed in. "Said he had to handle a family matter."

Another family matter? What was going on?

Hmm. There was one sure way to find out.

CHAPTER THIRTEEN

Marco lived in an apartment above a white aluminum-sided home on Napoleon, a quiet, tree-lined, residential street near the town square. The house had a big screened-in porch across the front and a garage in back for the landlord's use only, so I could tell immediately that Marco was home because his black and silver Toyota Prius was there. As I got out of the Vette, I noticed a 2001 Buick LeSabre parked almost nose to nose with the Prius. Did he have company?

Inside the long porch, I checked the name above the buzzer beside the first door — it wasn't Marco's — then went to the second door, saw SALVARE, and pushed the button. I had never seen the inside of Marco's apartment for the simple reason that he had never invited me there, and I wasn't one to drop by someone's place unannounced. Blame it on my upbringing.

I wasn't sure *why* Marco had never invited me to his place, unless he was one of those clothes-all-over-the-floor, dirty-dishes-in-the-sink types. Somehow I couldn't see him being that way, but who knew?

After a moment I heard footsteps pounding down the stairs; then the door opened and Marco stood there in all his hunkiness — snug-fitting, ribbed navy tank top that showed off those rippled abs, tan cargo pants that rode low on his hips, and bare feet.

I lifted a hand in greeting. "Hi, there."

He gazed at me as if I'd just flopped out of a fish tank dripping green algae. Obviously he wasn't as pleased to see me as I was to see him. He stepped out onto the porch, pulling the door shut behind him. "What are you doing here?"

"Nice to see you, too."

He rubbed his eyes, looking tired. "Sorry. I didn't mean that the way it sounded. It's been a long day."

"No problem. I just came from the funeral home and thought I'd report in."

He hesitated. "Sure. Okay. I'll get my shoes and be right down. We can go get coffee or something."

"Or we can just stay here and talk."

He started to say something, then signaled

for me to wait a minute, slipped back inside the door, and shut it behind him, as though afraid I would try to follow. Feeling a little hurt, I left the porch and went to wait by my car. As I cut across the lawn I spotted that LeSabre again and detoured around it to check out the license plate. Ohio. Hmm. Hadn't Marco told me his mother had moved to Ohio? But if she was staying with him, why wouldn't he want me to know?

I had just slid into the Vette when Marco came jogging out, a denim shirt thrown over his navy tank and a pair of black flip-flops on his feet. He climbed into the passenger side, fastened his seat belt, and glanced at me. "All set?"

"All set." I started the engine. "Do you have company?"

"Why?"

I hitched a thumb over my shoulder. "That Buick with Ohio plates."

"Oh, yeah. It's my mother's car."

"Your mother is visiting? Why didn't you tell me?"

"Because you'd want to meet her, and now isn't the best time. My sister Gina is there, too, and things are a little tense between them. Gina hasn't been feeling well, and Mama thinks she should step in — confer with the doctor, order tests — you know how heated those mother-daughter conflicts can be."

"Gee, no. Tell me about it." I pulled away from the curb and headed for the Daily Grind coffee shop about five blocks away. "Is that the family matter you left work to handle?"

"That's one of them."

"The other one is your situation?"

"You got it. Mom says they'll arrest me only over her dead body. Try to imagine what your mother would be like, then add a dose of Italian passion."

I couldn't help but shudder. Marco had my sympathies.

On the short trip to the coffee shop I gave him a rundown of my conversation with the five grease monkeys, ending it with the startling revelation of Trina's visit to Ryson at the motorcycle shop. I pulled into a parking space along Lincoln and turned off the motor, then sat there waiting for Marco's reaction, but he merely opened the door and got out. That was odd. Surely he had to be somewhat astonished.

Inside the brightly painted coffee shop, with its mismatched wooden tables and chairs, soft lighting, and crowd of students from the university campus, we found a table in the back; then Marco went up to place our order and came back with two steaming cups of coffee. "Did you learn anything else?"

Still no comment about Trina's behavior. As I stirred sugar into my coffee and dumped in two of the tiny thimbles full of half and half, I told him about meeting Lily outside the funeral home.

"Sounds like Lily needs further investigation," Marco said. "It'll be interesting to see if she owns that white Mustang."

"That reminds me. I haven't heard back from Eileen at the DMV."

"She'll call soon. She always comes through for me. Do you know the name of the clown troupe?"

"Clowns-on-Call." I blew steam away from my cup, then took a drink. "So what do you think about Trina's visit to the motorcycle shop?"

He put his hands behind his head and leaned back in his chair. "You're itching to pin this on her, aren't you?"

My cheeks instantly grew hot. "That is totally untrue. I don't care who the suspect is as long as it's someone other than you. And please, you have to admit it's odd that she would seek out Ryson and threaten to kill him when she claimed to be scared to death of him. Add that to the puzzle of why she waited so long to leave her house Sunday night — and tell me I shouldn't be suspicious."

He didn't say a word. I knew he agreed with me, but he wouldn't say so, and that really bugged me. "I'm going to pay Trina another visit tomorrow to see what she has to say about it." I folded my arms and silently dared him to say otherwise.

"I'll tell you right now, she's not the killer."

"And you know this how?"

"The same way you know things. I feel it in my gut."

Wasn't that a comfort.

Driving Marco back to his apartment, I turned on the radio and cranked up the volume, partly because my temper was still simmering, and partly to drown out the silence that stretched between us. I pulled up behind the LeSabre and sat there, engine running, not sure what to say to banish the tension. A curtain lifted in an upstairs window, then dropped again.

"We're being monitored," I told him.

"I don't doubt it." He leaned over to plant a chaste kiss on my cheek. "I'll see you tomorrow."

"If you're lucky."

"Then I'll keep my fingers crossed." Marco gave me that little quirk-of-the-mouth smile that always zapped me through the heart, then got out of the Vette and strode up to the house. I glanced at the upstairs window again and waved good-bye to whomever might be watching, then gunned the engine and took off, squealing my tires and feeling very satisfied about it.

When I got back to my apartment, the message light on the answering machine was blinking and Simon was meowing for food. Being the kind, caring person I was — and also because Simon's howling could drown out the voice on the machine — he got fed first. Then, after kicking off my shoes and grabbing the carton of frozen chocolate yogurt and a spoon, I hit the Play button and plunked down on the sofa to listen. Simon jumped up beside me and stared longingly at the container, having abandoned his food in favor of a sweeter treat. I kept my eye on him as I shoveled a spoonful into my mouth. He was a shameless hustler.

"Abigail, where are you? I haven't heard from you in two days. How are my frames and fans selling? Do I need to bring more? And don't forget about dinner Friday night. Call me."

No need for that. Mom would be phoning

in a few minutes anyway. Another mouthful of yogurt went in as I contemplated our weekly custom, when my entire family gathered together to share a meal and hear from my sisters-in-law just how successful my brothers were. Always a delightful time. My spoon hit the bottom of the carton with a dull thud. I glanced inside. Where had the yogurt gone?

I went to the kitchen for something else chocolate and had just spotted a Ghirardelli bar at the back of a cabinet when the phone rang. I peeled away the gold foil and bit off the end before answering with a cheerful, if somewhat mumbled, "Hi, Mom."

"This is Dave."

I swallowed the bite. "Oh, sorry, Dave. What's up? Please tell me you have good news."

By the long moment of silence that followed, I knew he didn't.

"Here's the story, Abby. I received a preliminary report from the prosecutor's office that says Ryson suffered blunt-force trauma to the left temporal area, causing a subdural hematoma. They're still trying to determine if a weapon was involved, and they don't have toxicology results, but at this point it appears he suffered the trauma falling against something wooden, possibly the corner of his coffee table. They're analyzing wood fibers found in the scalp to see if they match the table. The prosecutor is alleging the fall occurred during the fight with Marco." He paused a beat, then added, "You know what that means. A charge of voluntary manslaughter."

I sank to the floor with my back against a cabinet as a wave of nausea swept over me. "Voluntary manslaughter? Marco acted in self-defense, Dave. And Ryson was alive when he left."

"You and I may believe that, Abby, but will a jury? Because if we go to trial, that's what this whole case will hang on. I'll present Dennis Ryson in the worst possible light, of course, and Marco in the best light, but it still boils down to what the jury believes. And with the amount of circumstantial evidence the prosecutor will present — I have to be honest with you. It's not looking good for our side."

My stomach was knotted so tightly I couldn't stand to look at the chocolate bar in my hand. Voluntary manslaughter?

My gaze darted to the calendar on the wall. Only five days left to make sure that didn't happen.

CHAPTER FOURTEEN

I cupped my hands around my eyes to peer through the plate glass window of the Icing on the Cake and saw more than a dozen customers queued up inside, waiting to choose their donuts from the big display case. Rats. This was going to take longer than I'd expected. Why hadn't I left home earlier? The bakery opened at seven a.m., and I was fully aware of how popular those donuts were.

You know why, my conscience chided. *You're stalling because you feel guilty bothering Ryson's mother so soon after his funeral. How passive-aggressive of you.*

I never should have taken those psychology classes in college. I glanced at my watch. It was eight o'clock, the time I normally showed up at Bloomers. I'd just have to try the bakery again after work.

Right. Like you have a day to spare. And by

the way, you didn't do all that well in psychology.

Damned know-it-all conscience. Fine. I'd stay.

I hugged my denim jacket close as a gust of wind blew my hair into a tangle of red straw, always an attractive look for me. As I stepped inside, I ran my fingers through the blunt-cut ends, wincing as I encountered a knot. But the tangle was instantly forgotten when I got a whiff of the yeasty, sweet aromas of glazed, powdered, and jelly-filled donuts. I was drooling before the door shut behind me.

The Icing on the Cake was primarily a carryout store, although the owner had managed to squeeze in four small tables along the right side of the narrow shop. The bakery had a long, glass-fronted counter along the left side, a faux-brick linoleum floor, peach-colored walls, and a blue ceiling painted with clouds to look like a sky. The store had been open less than a year but had quickly become a town favorite, known largely for its artistically decorated cakes.

I sized up the two female clerks waiting on customers, trying to guess which one was Eve Taylor. Both women appeared to be in their fifties and wore peach-and-white-checked bib aprons and little white caps pinned into curly salt-and-pepper hair. One had a thin face and pasty complexion with a long, hooked nose and deep creases from nose to chin that gave her a permanently exhausted look. The other woman was cheerful and robust, with creamy caramel-colored skin, a generous mouth, a double chin, and gigantic gemstone rings on the fingers of both hands. She looked too happy to have been Ryson's mother, so it fell to the thin-faced woman.

As I waited in line, I couldn't help but sigh over the pastel-frosted cakes on display, some decorated with marzipan figures, some with sugared berries, and — the biggest draw — some with real flowers. My favorite was a small, two-layer chocolate cake, enough for four generous slices, with creamy vanilla frosting topped with pink crystallized roses, deep purple violets, blue orchids, and shiny, mint green leaves, which I decided to buy to take back to the shop for Lottie and Grace. After the cheerful woman rang it up, I asked whether I could speak privately with Mrs. Taylor.

The woman gave me a skeptical glance as she handed me a white box tied with string. "You're not a reporter, are you? We've had our fill of reporters lately."

"Oh, no. I'm not a reporter. I'm Abby Knight. I own Bloomers Flower Shop on the other side of the square."

She folded her arms and gave me a long, appraising look. "Is your brother a bone doctor?"

From her tone of voice, I wasn't sure whether I should admit to it or not. "You might be talking about my brother Jordan."

"That's the one. Dr. Jordan Knight. He set my grandson's ankle and did a terrific job of it. He's got a nice bedside manner, too. You tell him Sharona says hi, okay?" She waggled a finger at me. "Wait a minute. Did you say Abby Knight? Are you the sister who flunked out of law school?"

As if Jordan had more than one sister. I hung my head. In a small berg like New Chapel you couldn't hiccup without everyone knowing. "Yes. That was me."

"That's okay, sugar. Everyone fails at something. Take Evie, for instance. She knows. Uh-huh, she sure does."

"Evie?"

"Eve Taylor." Sharona held a hand to the side of her mouth so no one else would hear her. "I don't like to speak ill of the dead, but that son of hers was nothing but a giant pain in the ass, pardon my French. Poor

202

Evie blamed herself for not raising him better."

From what I remembered of my high school French lessons, *giant pain in the ass* was not a French expression, but in the spirit of cooperation I decided not to mention it. "I take it that Eve is either divorced or widowed?"

"Widowed six months now."

"I'm sorry to hear that. Was Mr. Taylor from New Chapel?"

"Not Taylor, baby. Ryson. Her husband, God rest his soul, was Douglas Ryson. Taylor is Evie's professional name. I think it's her maiden name, too."

I cast a quick glance at the thin-faced woman plucking donuts from the case. "Eve needs a professional name?"

Sharona planted her hands on her hips. "Come on, girl. Everyone knows Evie's our resident ar-*teest*."

"I beg your pardon?"

"Our artist, sugar. Evie Taylor. See all these pretty cakes? They're Evie originals."

"*She* decorated these?" I pointed to Sharona's coworker.

"No, baby. Evie's in the back. She owns this bakery."

"Eve Taylor is the owner?"

"She sure is. She built this business from

the bottom up. Why, if it wasn't for her cake decorations, we'd be just another donut shop."

The news was settling in when Sharona motioned for me to meet her at the far end of the counter, where there was a door marked PRIVATE. She knocked twice on the door, then pointed her index finger at me. "Now, you make it quick, girl, okay? Considering what she's been through, Evie shouldn't even be here today, but she's one stubborn woman. This bakery is her pride and joy, and it gives her great —"

The door opened and Sharona cut short her sentence to say with a smile, "Evie, honey, this is Abby Knight. She owns Bloomers Flower Shop and she wants to meet you."

"How nice. Thank you, Sharona."

"There you go, sugar." Sharona gave my shoulder a friendly pat, then headed up to the cash register, while I merely stood there blinking in surprise. If I could have imagined anyone to be Dennis Ryson's mother, Eve was not her. But if I'd ever wondered what Santa Claus's wife would look like up close — she was a dead ringer.

Eve Taylor was a short, plump, rosy-cheeked woman who smelled like a vanilla milk shake and whose blue eyes behind her

204

silver-framed granny glasses twinkled when she smiled. She had snow-white hair that curled softly below her white chef's toque, with tiny pink rosebud earrings on her earlobes. She was wearing a white bib apron over a navy floral print dress that fell to mid-calf, nearly obscuring her white nurse's shoes.

The only flaw in her otherwise perfect Mrs. Claus look was her gap-toothed smile — a space between her front teeth large enough to whistle through, making her resemble *Mad* magazine's impish mascot, Alfred E. Neuman.

With the white box tucked under my left arm, I held out my right hand, which she took in her two soft, warm ones. "I'm tho pleathed to meet you, Abby."

Um. Make that two flaws. "I'm pleased to meet you, too, Mrs. Taylor. I don't mean to interrupt you — I'm sure you're busy — so would there be a better time to talk?"

"I don't mind if we talk while I work. Come inthide."

I followed her through the door into an immaculate kitchen filled with ovens, stainless steel sinks, a black marble-topped counter, and white wire shelving stacked high with white boxes. The room would have been colorless but for a row of glass jars filled with brightly hued sprinkles, powdered dyes, and candy figures, and a line of cakes in a rainbow of frostings.

Eve introduced me to Maxine Grindley, the actual baker, then led me to her marble-topped island in the back, where she was in the process of creating a garden scene on a lemon frosted cake, with a gazebo on top constructed of brittle strands of what appeared to be spun sugar. On a waxed paper–lined tray beside her were pale pink miniature roses, deep pink dianthus, blue bachelor's buttons, tiny yellow marigolds, and an array of mint leaves, all with a sugary glaze on them that made them sparkle in the flourescent glow of the overhead lights.

Eve pulled a pair of latex gloves from a box on the counter and put them on, then carefully selected one of the roses and placed it under the gazebo. "Now, what would you like to know? Where I buy my flowerth?"

Being a tactful person, regardless of certain people's opinions to the contrary, I decided to let her take the lead so I could approach what would undoubtedly be a painful subject in a roundabout way. "That would be great. Thanks."

"It's a place in Chicago called Thayer

Floral Thupplies. You can find them on the Web."

"Thayer Floral Supplies," I repeated, pulling out my notebook and pen to jot it down.

"No, dear. Not Thayer. *Thay*-er."

I glanced up at her, blinking in confusion until it clicked in. "Oh, right. Got it." I crossed out *Thayer* and wrote *Sayer.*

She daintily selected a deep pink dianthus and held it up for inspection. "These are all edible, of course. Flowerth are rich in nectar and pollen, and even in vitamins and minerals, in thum cases. I use a thupplier I trust because the blooms must be picked fully opened in the cool of the day, after the dew hath evaporated. I'm very particular about my flowers. Take this dianthus, for exthample." With her index finger she pointed out a wilted petal. "See this?" She plucked it off and dropped it in a trash container under her counter. "I won't use anything on my cakes that's the least bit defective."

I indicated the flowers on the tray. "How long will these last?"

"With the crythtallithation protheth they'll latht up to a week, but mine latht longer becauthe I add thomething thpecial."

I started to reach for a rosebud, then saw her mouth open in a silent gasp, so I pulled my hand back. "How do you crystallize them?"

Her eyes shimmered with pride as she lovingly traced a gloved fingertip across a gleaming mint leaf. "It'th my thecret rethipe."

"A secret recipe. Of course."

She moved her hand over the tray, then plucked out a stem of miniature rosebuds. Using tiny snippers, she cut off each bud, then selected one and held it up. "This one will never do. It's flawed. See how ugly it is next to the retht?" She deposited it into the can with the other less-than-perfect blooms.

"I use fresh flowers on my cakes, as well, but those are mostly for thpecial occasions, such as weddings, when I know they'll be used right away. They're harder to process and don't last as long, so I have to make sure I don't order too many flowerth at a time. Of course, when I do have extras, I add them to the special cake I take to Denny every Thaturday."

As soon as the words were out of her mouth she realized her mistake. Struggling to keep her composure, her chin trembling, she added a mint leaf to her design. "He always looked forward to those cakes. His favorite wath banana. He would only allow himthelf one thlice a day tho it would latht all week, until I brought him a new one."

She turned her back to me, her shoulders shaking in silent sobs as she reached for a tissue from a box on the counter behind her. "I'm sorry," she said at last, her voice barely above a whisper. "I'm trying to block it from my mind, but it'th so painful."

"I'm sorry for your loss."

She blew her nose, dropped the tissue into a large waste can, took a moment to compose herself, then pulled off the used gloves and put on a fresh pair. She heaved a tremulous sigh as she resumed her decorating. "I'll be so relieved when the police finish their investigation and I can put this all behind me."

"We all will, believe me. Have the police told you how the case is going?"

She dabbed the corner of her eye with her sleeve. "They're not very talkative. I called yethterday afternoon to thee if they could tell me anything, but Offither — oh, heavens, what was his name? Kensington . . . Kenderman . . ."

"Kellerman?"

"Yes. Kellerman. He wathn't very nithe. He thaid he'd get back to me when he had something to report." She sighed sadly. "It's tho frustrating."

"Maybe I can help you."

"You? How?"

"Believe it or not, I have sort of a sideline business going as a private investigator."

"Really?"

I pulled out the frayed newspaper clipping. I was going to have to get it laminated before it fell apart. "This is one of the cases I solved."

She scanned it, then turned her twinkly gaze on me. "Wath your picture in the newthpaper about a month ago . . . thomething about a profethor who wath thtabbed at the law school?"

"Yep. That was me."

She nodded sagely. "I remember now. You're a very bright young lady, Abby."

"Thank you. I do try. So . . . what do you think?"

She placed another leaf in her design. "I apprethiate your offer, but I can't afford a private invethtigator. It takes a lot of money to run a business, as I'm sure you're finding out, and there's not much to spare. I'm afraid it would be quite out of the quethtion."

"Money won't be a problem. I'll do it pro bono." (Actually, pro Marco.)

"Good graciouth, I couldn't athk you to work for free."

"Then how about throwing in a cake and

210

we'll call it even?"

"Just a cake? Are you sure?"

"Positive. Just one thing I should mention, however. It would be better not to say anything to Officer Kellerman about me. The police can be very territorial about these matters."

"I underthtand."

"Okay, then. Let's get started." I pulled out my notepad and pen. "I understand Dennis moved to town about two months ago. Correct?"

She pondered it as she arranged the last two rosebuds on the icing. "Yes, I believe it has been two months thince he moved back here."

"Did he live here before?"

"For about ten yearth. My huthband and I had a home in the country, a cothy little cottage bethide a brook. I started a catering business there — mostly desserts, you know. That'th my specialty."

Cozy country cottage, I wrote. "Do you still live there?"

"I had to sell the house after my husband died. I have an apartment in town now, so I can walk here. I'm not much of a driver, you see." Her voice caught and she paused, her gaze staring past me. "Besides, there were too many memories in that house."

I couldn't tell by her expression whether they were good or bad memories, so I elected to step around that subject. "Do you know if Dennis had a girlfriend here in town?"

"Not that I knew of."

"Two of the neighbors reported that they saw a young woman visit Dennis right after he moved to town. I thought maybe you'd know who that might be — a friend, a cousin, a coworker maybe? It could be important."

"No, I'm thorry. I don't know who that could be. I wasn't familiar with the people at the motorcycle shop, and Dennis didn't have any cousins. My husband was an only child and so was Dennis."

I jotted the information in my notebook. "I understand Dennis was in a clown troupe."

Eve sighed wistfully as she reached for a rosebud. "As with most children, he loved clowns from the very first time he saw one perform. I'm sure you had a thimilar exthperienthe. Heaventh, did I thay something wrong?"

"Just a sudden chill." I tried to discreetly pat down my hair, which was doing its best to stand on end. Not a pretty sight unless you were fond of red-maned lions.

"But with Denny, hith love of clownth continued. I do believe if he could have made a living at it, he would have quit his mechanic'th job in an inthtant. But he altho loved tinkering with engines, so I thuppose he had the best of both worldth." Her chin started to tremble again, so I switched topics.

"Have you met any of Dennis's neighbors?"

"I've met Mr. Mazella. He was very rude to Denny. He actually threatened to do thomething dreadful if Denny didn't move out of the neighborhood. Thuch a violent man. It'th not thurprithing that hith wife hath mental problems."

"You've met Mrs. Mazella?"

"No, but Denny told me about her. She's a little off her rocker, poor creature. Denny thought she might be a witch because she'd been holding thecret theremonies in her back yard late at night."

"Secret ceremonies?"

Eve selected a stem of dianthus. "Yeth. With candles. Denny thaid it wath thpooky. He thought maybe the was trying to catht a thpell on him."

Hmm. Maybe that spell had worked. "Did Dennis ever mention the name *Lily* to you?"

"Not that I remember."

"How about *Trina?*"

"Trina Vathqueth? Heaventh, yeth. She lived acroth the thtreet from Denny." Eve lowered her voice to a whisper. "I hate to say this, but she's a thtrumpet."

There was something very satisfying about writing the word *strumpet* beside Trina's name. "Really? How so?"

"She was a tease. She'd egg Denny on with those *come hither* glantheth and thkintight clothing; then the'd call the polithe and claim he wath harathing her."

It wasn't my fault; it was hers was a common excuse among stalkers. "Have you ever met Trina?"

"No, but I've theen her." She stepped back to size up her arrangement. "I wouldn't be at all thurprised if she was in on the murder."

"In on the murder with whom?"

"That former policeman. Oh, dear. What was his name? I believe he ownth a bar over on Franklin. Down the Hatch."

My hands suddenly went clammy. "Are you talking about Marco Salvare?"

Her forehead wrinkled for a moment; then she nodded. "Yeth. Salvare was his name. I'm glad the police are investigating him. It was just horrible what he did to my thon two yearth ago. I'm thtill outraged when I

214

think about it."

I swallowed a small lump of dread and managed to say in a calm voice, "I was away at school two years ago. Would you mind telling me what happened?"

"Of courthe not. It'th a matter of public record. Officer Salvare arrested Denny for robbing a convenience store — wrongly so, of course. Denny sued the police force and as a result, Officer Salvare was given his walking papers."

Dennis Ryson was responsible for Marco being off the force? And Marco hadn't told me?

Eve glanced at me over the wire rims of her glasses. "I would think that would make a polithe offither quite bitter, wouldn't you? Bitter enough to want revenge. Would you like a glath of water, dear? Your freckles are as pale ath buttermilk frothting."

CHAPTER FIFTEEN

I accepted the glass of water and sipped it while I collected my thoughts, which at that moment were all over the place.

"Feeling better?" Eve Taylor asked, peering at me in concern.

After hearing that little bomb go off? It would take more than a glass of water to pull me together now. "Thanks. I must have been dehydrated." I set the empty glass on the marble counter, put away my notepad and pen, and took out a business card. "I'll let you get back to work. If I find out anything at all, I'll let you know. And if you think of anyone else who might have had a beef with Dennis, will you call me?"

"Of courthe. Don't forget your cake."

Oops. The cake. I was already at the door and had to turn back. The only way I would leave a cake behind was if my mind was preoccupied, which it was, big-time. I couldn't decide whether I was more angry or more concerned. Why would Marco have with-held such crucial information from me? Had he been carrying a grudge against Ry-son all this time? Was that why the prosecu-tor had zeroed in on him? And, most impor-tant, what else was he not telling me?

Hmm. Angry or concerned? I'd have to go with — angry. Marco and I needed to have a serious talk.

As I cut across the courthouse lawn I checked my watch and saw that it was eight forty-five, too early to catch him at the bar, so I phoned him instead and got his voice mail. He had to be up by now. Why wasn't he answering?

"Hey, Marco. It's me. We need to talk. Call me the moment you get this." I dropped my cell phone into my purse, crossed over to Franklin Street, and headed up the sidewalk toward Bloomers, where Jingles the window washer was cleaning one of our bay windows.

Jingles had been a fixture on the square for as long as I could remember, toting his bucket and squeegee, an old rag hanging out of his back pocket, as he moved from storefront to storefront, making sure every piece of glass on the square was polished to a diamondlike shine. Besides washing win-dows, he also served as a general maintenance man and Mr. Fix-It for minor emergencies.

He was a tall, stoop-shouldered, slow-talking man who had to have been in his early seventies. He had a sparse covering of hair on a freckled pate and a long, thin, droopy face that always sported at least two days' growth of gray stubble. He wore a plaid shirt beneath a faded brown jacket, with navy work pants and worn brown shoes.

He had come by his nickname because of his habit of shaking the coins in his pockets whenever someone stopped to talk to him. It was common knowledge that if you wanted to know what was happening on the square, all you had to do was ask Jingles. And now that I was almost at the shop and could see that he wasn't cleaning the window but staring through it, I did just that.

"Hey, Jingles. What's happening?"

He glanced around at me, then, with a sheepish look, started wiping the glass with his rag. "Morning, Ms. Knight. Seems like you have lots of feathers in there. I didn't know birds came in all those colors."

To think that for fifteen hours I had managed to block out my mother's art projects. "We're having a special sale on feathered items this week, Jingles. Would your wife like a pretty fan? Or how about a frame for that special grandchild's photo? I can let you have one for a real bargain."

He shook his head once to the right and once to the left. "No, ma'am, thank you anyway. My wife's allergic to feathers. That's why we got rid of our chicken coop. I sure do miss those fresh eggs, though."

His shoulders went up, then down, in a silent sigh; then he returned to his task without another word. Jingles was not given to much chatter. I wished him a good day, unlocked the door, turned the CLOSED sign to OPEN (it was almost nine o'clock), and stepped into my rose-scented haven where, no matter how bad things got, I could share my worries with Grace and Lottie and find solace.

But today I didn't feel like sharing, and that made me grumpy. Honestly, what would I tell them? *"Guess what? That hunk I'm crazy about has been keeping secrets from me."* I didn't want two of the most important women in my life to think badly of the most important man in my life. What if the women advised me to cut and run?

I forced a cheerful tone in my voice and called out, "Good morning, ladies." A gust of wind swept in with me, causing various feathered objects to shiver off about a pound of colored particles before I could shut the door. I coughed as I made my way to the parlor, where Grace had my usual cup of coffee with a hearty shot of half-and-half waiting.

"Look. I brought a surprise for you and Lottie." I put the white box on the counter, then accepted the cup and saucer and took a sip as Grace dabbed the corners of her eyes with a white handkerchief. "Are you all right, Grace?"

"I must be coming down with a cold. My eyes keep watering and my throat feels scratchy."

It wasn't a cold. It was the feathers, and I was at a loss as to what to do. Should I promise to get rid of the stuff and run the risk of permanently damaging my mother's psyche, or say nothing and let Grace suffer? And what would I do with all those feathered objects, anyway?

As my conscience deliberated, Grace untied the string and peeked inside the box. "Oh, how lovely."

"The flowers on top are edible."

"Remarkable. Shall we save it for lunch?"

"Works for me." I finished the last drop of java, put my cup in the sink behind the coffee counter and headed for the workroom, where Lottie was filling a wicker cornucopia with artificial fruit and silk flowers in the reds and golds of autumn.

"Morning, sweetie. What's the news from the bakery?"

She smiled at me, and I had to look away on the pretense of putting my purse on my desk and checking the spindle for orders. I simply couldn't bring myself to tell her about Marco's subterfuge. "I bought a cake for you and Grace. You'll have to go take a look. It's decorated with edible flowers."

"Well, isn't that thoughtful? I've seen those cakes but never bought one. My boys would have it devoured before I got the string off the box. Now, you want to tell me what brought about that new wrinkle in your forehead?"

With my back toward her, I pushed against the tattletale crease between my eyes. "I didn't get some information that I'd hoped for."

"Well, like my mama always said, every path has a few puddles. You just gotta pull on your rubber galoshes and wade through them."

If only it were that simple. I eyed the clock, wishing Marco would return my call.

Grace stuck her head through the curtain. "Sgt. Reilly is here to see you, Abby."

For once that was good news. As I followed Grace to the parlor, she whispered, "I tried to seat him near the bay window but he insisted on a corner table."

"It's a cop thing, Grace. They like to keep their backs to the wall and their eyes on the room." Plus, I knew Reilly was skittish anyway about coming to see me and would prefer to keep a low profile.

"Morning, Sarge." I pulled out a chair and sat across from him. He was in his police uniform — a light blue shirt and dark slacks, his belt loaded with the standard police paraphernalia and his badge shiny above his shirt pocket flap. His face was smoothly shaved and, judging by the scent, splashed with a little Old Spice. His hat was hanging on his knee, which was bouncing up and down, probably due to nerves.

As Grace set out a basket of the light butter cookies she called biscuits, I said. "Reilly, what would you like? It's on the house."

"Coffee, please — black."

I asked for an espresso — I was feeling the need for extra caffeine — and when Grace went to fill the orders, I pushed the basket toward Reilly. "Cookie?"

He took one and munched on it. "Very good," he mumbled, brushing crumbs off his mouth. He finished the treat, then glanced around as though he were looking for an escape hatch. "I wish to hell I knew what I was doing here."

The parlor was empty, so I didn't have to lower my voice. "You're here to save your friend's skin, that's what."

"I've already told you I can't get into the file. I don't know what more I can do."

"Come on, Reilly. You didn't stop by here just to tell me you can't help."

He scowled at me until Grace brought our coffees; then he took a sip and his face smoothed out. "This is really good."

"Thank you, Sergeant." Grace beamed proudly as she headed for the shop in response to the jingle of the bell over the door.

Reilly put down his cup, crossed his arms over his chest, and resumed his scowling. "I came here out of courtesy to you, Abby. That's it."

"I appreciate the courtesy, but I need more than that. I found out this morning that Marco has a history with Ryson, and now I understand why he's the focus of the investigation. Would you please tell me about the convenience store robbery and Ryson's arrest?"

He rubbed his eyes with his finger and thumb. "Why don't you ask Marco?"

"I'd like to get your take on it first."

Reilly peered at me over his thumb. "You don't think he'll tell you, do you?"

"Of course he'll tell me. It's not that. I just can't figure out why he didn't level with me right away."

"There could be a number of reasons he didn't want you to know. Marco always plays it close to the chest — you know that."

"Yeah. The strong silent type — not always a plus. Would you please tell me what happened?"

Reilly picked up his cup and sipped his coffee for a moment, as though trying to refresh his memory. "I'm not sure of the details anymore, but this is how I remember it. We got a ten-forty from a store and Marco was the first responder. He called in that he'd sighted a perp in a ski mask run out the door and head east carrying a paper bag. Marco gave chase on foot and finally caught up with him in the woods east of the university campus, where the perp gave him a full confession, even telling him where he dropped the sack of cash."

"The perp was Dennis Ryson?"

"Right."

"Then it wasn't a false arrest?"

"Who told you it was?"

"Ryson's mother."

"His mother is living?"

"Since I don't regularly communicate with the dead, yes. She lives right here in town, as a matter of fact."

"If you say so. I don't remember any family members in that case."

"Who'd lie about being Dennis Ryson's mother? Her name is Eve Taylor — that's her business name. She owns the Icing on the Cake. I just talked to her this morning."

"Like I said, my memory isn't that great. But I can tell you for sure, it wasn't a false arrest. Marco didn't make those kinds of mistakes."

"Was Ryson convicted?"

"It never went to trial. There were no witnesses who could identify him, and since Marco didn't have anything for Ryson to sign to verify his statement at the time of the arrest, the prosecutor wouldn't touch it." Reilly's lips pressed into a hard line; he was obviously still angry about it. I could only imagine how Marco had felt.

"Then that bastard had the nerve to sue," Reilly continued. "He claimed he hadn't confessed to anything or had his rights read to him."

"That's crazy. Marco wouldn't have forgotten to read him his rights."

"Of course it's crazy. So was Ryson —

crazy like a fox."

"Why would the prosecutor take his word over Marco's?"

"Come on, Abby. You know Darnell. He's one of those sticklers for detail who has to have every *i* dotted and *t* crossed. Plus, Ryson claimed that Marco broke his jaw and a few of his ribs, and you know how people react to any hint of police brutality. So they settled with him out of court."

"Did you see Ryson when Marco brought him into the station? Did he look like he'd been beaten?"

"I wasn't on duty that night." Reilly shifted in his chair. "You have to understand, Abby; sometimes it takes a little force to subdue a perp."

"Broken ribs and a broken jaw are not the result of a *little* force. That's not something Marco would do."

Reilly's whole body tensed up as if I had just insulted him. "I didn't say that. All I'm saying is that sometimes extra force is necessary for the perp's protection as well as for ours. You know from hearing your dad's stories that these jerks can get so wacked out they're dangerous. Now, whether the battery charges were valid or not, I can't tell you because I didn't see Ryson until after he'd spent the night in jail. It wasn't his first time there, either, by the way. He could have got into it with his cell mate that night, or maybe he started something with Marco and they both ended up with broken ribs. Remember, the guy was a punk, a troublemaker from day one."

Reilly certainly painted a different picture of Ryson than Eve had. Then again, she was his mother. Her version had Dennis as a sweet boy who liked cakes and clowns. "What was Ryson's defense?"

"That he had walked in on a robbery in progress, and when the alarm went off, the robber shoved the bag at him and fled. Ryson saw the cop car pull up and thought he'd be blamed because of his priors, so he took off."

"How did he explain his ski mask?"

"The mask was never found. So Ryson, who had a rap sheet as long as my arm, walked."

"Unfortunately, that's the way the legal system works, Reilly. Look what happened to my dad."

"Yeah, well, it still sucks."

"I won't argue with you there. But if the arrest was a valid one, why was Marco kicked off the force?"

"Did Ryson's mother tell you that, too? Marco wasn't kicked off . . . but he might as well have been. Kellerman gave him a reprimand and it cut his heart out. Two weeks later, Marco turned in his badge and gun and disappeared for a few months. Next thing I know, he's back in town working as a PI. Then he bought the bar and you know the rest."

Reilly paused for another sip of coffee. "The whole thing is a crying shame. Marco made a damned fine cop. He would've had quite a career ahead of him, but one scumbag ruined it all."

"Are you talking about Ryson or Kellerman?"

Reilly glanced at me but didn't answer.

"Okay, tell me about Chief Kellerman."

"I thought you knew all about him."

"Not about his relationship with Marco."

Reilly leaned back, his leather belt creaking. "Kellerman was Marco's watch commander at the time of the robbery. They were always butting heads. Marco hoped to eventually make detective, but he wasn't one for rules, as you know, and Kellerman seemed to get a lot of enjoyment out of sending Marco on the worst assignments, always trying to push his buttons."

"Why?"

"Could've been some jealousy behind it. Marco was well regarded and Kellerman was an ass. Still is, for that matter. Don't forget, Marco had been a Ranger, and everyone looked up to him. Maybe Kellerman was afraid Marco would make detective before he did. All I know is that there was no love lost between them."

I finished off my espresso and put the cup and saucer to the side. "Do you think one reason Marco is a suspect is because of Kellerman's dislike of him?"

"I can't answer that because I don't know what evidence they have on him."

"According to Dave, it's circumstantial at this point, but there's a lot of it. He was seen at Ryson's house and freely admitted he and Ryson got into it — and has the bruises to show it. Then there's the scuffle they had after the parade."

"That damned scuffle. You know how bad that looks? First thing a detective would think is that Marco went back to finish what he started at the parade."

Another strike against Marco. "Are they looking at any other suspects, Reilly?"

"I don't know." His knee started to bob again.

"Any way you can find out?"

"Not if I want to keep my job."

"Have you been out to Ryson's house?"

"Yeah, I was there when the crime scene

team went through."

"Did you see anything that might point to someone other than Marco being there?"

"That's not my area of expertise." He glanced at his watch, downed the last drop of his coffee, and rose, settling his hat on his head. "I'd suggest checking with your friend in the prosecutor's office."

As much as I disliked the thought, Reilly was right. It was time to bring Greg Morgan onto the team. I just needed to figure out how.

In high school Morgan had been the star quarterback on the football team, endowed with the prerequisite agility and speed, along with dimples, blue eyes, and a cheerleader-girlfriend, while I had been a short, flat-chested, freckle-faced redhead who couldn't have coordinated two pompoms to save my life. Back then he had treated me as if I didn't exist, but now, for some reason, he had developed an interest in me. I wasn't sure why — after all, other than my chest measurements, what had changed? Nevertheless, I milked that interest whenever I needed his help. I figured it was payback for all those snubs I'd gotten from him.

But it wouldn't be easy to get Morgan's help on a sticky case like this one. So what clever ploy could I use?

Lottie's words flashed through my mind. *"Figure out what it will take to get those fellas on your team and go after them."*

I checked the time. Almost noon. Greg always left the courthouse at midday to grab a bite to eat. Hmm. I toyed with a button on the mint green shirt I'd paired with my dark blue jeans. Maybe it was time to bring back the bimbo. In fact, she and I were both feeling like a juicy sandwich at Rosie's Diner would be just the thing.

Chapter Sixteen

To reach the prosecutors' offices on the courthouse's second floor, I had to either take the ancient elevator that groaned and trembled as if a few circus elephants had climbed aboard, or use the wide center staircase (allowing me an extra helping of chocolate yogurt that evening — if I remembered to buy some). So I took the stairs — a no-brainer — then strolled into the prosecutors' outer office as though I didn't have a care in the world. There I encountered Kirby, the snobbish, semi-efficient receptionist-typist shared by all five deputy prosecutors.

Miss Blue Tints, as I liked to call her, was a nasal-voiced, thirty-something woman who favored tight pencil skirts and sweaters, and tiny, titanium-framed glasses with blue lenses, which she had a habit of peering over when she talked to people. She also liked to pretend she didn't recognize me. It was a game we played.

She sat at her desk tapping away at the keyboard with her inch-long, white-tipped fingernails, her gaze fixed on the monitor. I stood facing her on the other side of the desk, a pleasant smile pasted on my face. Let the game begin.

"Hi, Kirby. Is Greg Morgan in?"

Without glancing up she said, "Who shall I tell him is here?"

"Well, let's see. There's you — and there's me — and since you've probably already seen him today, then I guess that leaves me."

Scowling at me, Kirby pushed a button on her phone and spoke into the receiver in a hissy voice, "That florist is here to see you." She listened a moment, then hung up. Turning back to her computer, she said snippily, "Mr. Morgan will see you now."

I didn't even bother to hide the gloat as I sashayed past her and tapped on Morgan's door.

"Come in."

Antiquated and cramped, Morgan's small office had stacks of files everywhere — on filing cabinets, spilling out of boxes, sitting on an old wooden chair in front of a beat-up old desk — and no matter how many cases he disposed of, the stacks never shrank.

"Hi," I said with a little wave, leaning

through the doorway.

"Abby! Great to see you. Come in." He got up and stepped over piles to greet me, his gaze instantly dropping to the open front of my shirt as he took my hand and squeezed it.

I squeezed back, hard. Glimpses of my frontal epidermis did not come cheaply. "How are you, Greg?"

"Totally red-faced with embarrassment. I promised to get back to you Saturday about that clown's arrest and never did. You must think I'm the biggest jerk in the world. Am I right?"

As if I would answer that honestly. I tried to look aggrieved. "You broke my heart, Greg. How will you ever make it up to me?"

He yanked his gaze from my chest to his watch. "Tell you what. It's noon and I was just heading out to lunch, so why don't I treat you to a bite at Rosie's?"

I loved it when men thought they'd come up with an original idea. "I can't think of anything I'd like more, Greg."

Rosie's Diner had been decorated to mimic the styles of the 1950s, with knotty pine wood paneling, high-backed aqua vinyl booths, polka-dotted Formica tables, chrome and orange plastic chairs, and a golden brown linoleum floor. There was a single cash register station facing the door, and a kitchen through a pair of swinging doors in the back.

The menu was classic diner food: the thinnest, crispiest hamburgers in town with a selection of toppings; chicken, turkey, ham, and beef sandwiches; a choice of three soups (one always being French onion); batter-fried fish, meatloaf, fried and mashed potatoes, and homemade pies. Nothing fancy, nothing vegetarian, nothing expensive, no substitutions, and the place was always jammed.

Greg steered me toward his usual booth where, as always, the waitresses fell all over themselves trying to get his attention. They actually drew straws to see who his server would be. Today it was a woman with a heavy dose of garlic on her breath.

"Hello. I'm *Heidi,"* she said gustily, bending to give him a glimpse of her cleavage, which was impressively more ample than mine, yet squeezed into a much smaller space. "I'll be your waitress today. *Having* something to drink?"

Morgan pretended to scratch both sides of his nose at once, using his thumb and index finger. Anyone with half a brain could tell he was actually pinching his nostrils shut to block the offensive odor. "I'll hab ad iced tea, ad a burger with mushroobs ad fries."

Heidi marked it on her little tablet, then tilted her head sympathetically. "You should take something for your cold, Mr. Morgan. Have you ever tried raw garlic?"

"Dough," he replied, shaking his head, his fingers still clamped on his nose.

"One clove a day. You'll have to try it. I haven't had a virus in a year."

Or a date, either, I'd bet. I smiled up at Garlic Girl. "Give me what he had, but hold the fries, please."

"*Happy* to oblige," she said, and scooted away.

Greg removed his hand. "Someone should tell her."

"Don't look at me. I like my food untainted by human spit." Checking to make sure Grace wasn't nearby, I leaned my elbows on the table. "So, how is that investigation going on Snuggles the Clown?"

"You mean the Ryson case?" As if he didn't know.

Trying to appear only mildly interested, I said, "I understand the grand jury is convening Monday. Are you involved?"

"Mel's handling it alone, not that I blame him. If the grand jury comes back with an indictment and this goes to trial, he'll get lots of exposure. As you know, the more exposure, the greater his chance of being reelected. But I wouldn't discount the possibility of him bringing me in as second chair."

"You don't really think the grand jury will indict, do you? It seems awfully soon for that to happen."

"Mel thinks it's a slam dunk."

"How could it be a slam dunk? The investigation has hardly gotten under way."

Morgan paused as Heidi brought our iced teas. "*Here* you go. Your *hamburgers* will be out in a few minutes."

Morgan gave her a fleeting smile, then leaned forward to say quietly, "What are you doing, Abby? Are you on a fishing expedition for Salvare?"

"Do you think I would accept a lunch date with *the* Assistant Deputy Prosecutor Greg Morgan simply to fish for information?"

That was the type of question that could be asked only of someone with Morgan's ego, because he'd never want to believe otherwise. Yet he waited so long to answer that for a moment he had me worried.

"You're right. What was I thinking?"

We both laughed. Then Heidi swooped in with our plates, plunked down a bottle of ketchup, and left before I realized that she'd brought fries with my burger. I lifted a hand to get her attention, then changed my mind and reached for the red bottle instead.

"So why all the questions about Ryson's case?" Morgan asked, suddenly serious. "You know I can't tell you anything."

Here was another game I'd played before. "You know me, Greg, a frustrated law school student. I can't get enough of these fascinating murder cases, and this one particularly intrigues me because of my run-in with Snuggles. So you don't really mind indulging my curiosity a bit, do you? I swear it won't go any farther than here." I pointed to the table — and under the table, on my lap, was my purse, containing my notebook. But he didn't know that.

If I was a sucker for french fries, Morgan was an even bigger sucker for women asking him for favors. He pretended to be put out, but I could see that gleam in his eye that said, *She needs me. I'm somebody important.*

"I suppose I can help."

"Super! Thanks, Greg. I really appreciate this. So tell me about the case — murder weapon, suspects, that kind of thing."

He held up his palms. "Slow down a minute. Haven't you forgotten something?"

Oh, right. The other part of our game: you

scratch my back, I'll scratch yours. "I was thinking along the lines of a big bouquet of roses for your secretary."

He wrinkled his nose, not that I blamed him. Kirby had already benefited once from my largesse. She wasn't nice enough to get two bouquets in the same year. "My mother has a birthday coming up next Monday," he told me.

"Good for her. Does she like roses?"

He looked around, then said out of one side of his mouth, "Just so we're clear, this isn't a bribe."

"*Pffft.* Hey, if your mother happens to get a flower delivery and thinks they're from you, can I help it? Now, about the weapon?"

"Still unknown. The investigators found wood fibers in the victim's scalp that could have come from his coffee table when he landed on it or from something else wooden that would have left a similar imprint, like a two-by-four, for instance. The lab is analyzing the fibers. What we don't know is if the victim was struck or pushed, or fell.

"Whichever it is" — Morgan let out a sigh, as if he regretted what he was about to say — "it's not looking good for Salvare." He ticked the items off on his fingers. "We have witnesses and evidence that put him at the scene, we know about his earlier altercation with the victim at the parade, we know about Salvare's history with Ryson, we have photos of the bruises he suffered in the fight at the victim's house, and we have his admission that he went there to have a chat with Ryson. That adds up to motive and opportunity."

Talk about the odds being stacked against a person. Wow. This called for another french fry. "I agree it seems bad for Marco, but other people had motives and opportunities, too. Be honest with me, Greg. Have the detectives looked at *anyone* else?"

"They've questioned a few people," he said vaguely.

I chewed the fry, studying him. "What you mean is that the detectives went through the motions because they'd already decided on Marco. But why would I expect otherwise? Pin it on the handiest person, give the citizens peace of mind, and life goes back to normal. Meanwhile, a decent guy goes to prison and a murderer gets off scot-free." I picked up my burger and bit off a hunk, letting that guilt trip settle over him.

"What do you want from me, Abby?"

"I want you to have an open mind on this case and at least entertain the idea of other suspects. For instance, I did a little homework on Ryson's next-door neighbor, Ed

Mazella, and found out he had an ongoing beef with Ryson. In fact, at one point it got so heated that Ryson threatened him with a tire iron. After meeting Mr. Mazella, I can tell you he's not the type to take a threat sitting down, and he certainly would have had the opportunity to kill Ryson. So why isn't he a person of interest?"

Morgan shrugged, watching me as he gobbled his sandwich.

"Next we have the neighbor across the street, the woman Ryson had been harassing — Trina Vasquez — who also had motive and opportunity and was heard threatening Ryson."

Morgan gaped at me as if I were out of my mind. "Have you met Trina Vasquez? I sat in on her interview and I have to tell you, she's this" — he paused to describe a figure eight shape with his hands — "little thing. I just don't see her easily subduing a big guy like Ryson."

"Okay, first of all, what you just drew in the air does not mean little; it means shapely. Second, she's not a *little* thing. She's taller than I am. I've seen her toting two kids on her hips without breaking a sweat, so she's not a lightweight, either. And has anyone checked to see where she was at the time of the murder?"

"At her mother's house in Michigan."

He sure spit that answer out quickly. What was it about Trina that so mesmerized men? "Wrong, Greg. She was still at home. She didn't arrive in Michigan until after ten o'clock, which means she didn't leave her house until a little before nine."

"You've done some homework on this, haven't you?"

I stuck another french fry in my mouth. "A little."

"Here's your mistake. You didn't allow for Michigan being on eastern standard time, an hour ahead of us. Going by Central time, Trina arrived at her mother's house a little after nine. It's an hour and fifteen minute drive, so she would have left here before eight o'clock. The victim's time of death was between eight and eight-thirty."

"Back up a minute. If I can make it up there in fifty-five minutes, so can she."

"If she drives like a bat out of hell." Looking smug, Morgan took another bite.

"My point is, Trina could have killed Ryson, then raced up to her mother's house."

"So she left her son home alone, watched for Salvare to leave, snuck into Ryson's house and struck a fatal blow, then ran back across the street to get her son and drive up to Michigan?"

"Why not?"

"When the cops got there, the front and back doors were locked. How did she get in?"

"Maybe she knew where a key was hidden."

He scoffed at me. "Completely implausible, Abby. There's simply no evidence to support her being there."

"I'll just have to get the evidence, then, won't I?"

Morgan had been about to take another bite, but at that, he put down the burger. "I get it now. This isn't about satisfying your curiosity. You're working for Salvare."

It had taken him long enough to figure that out. Then again, no one had ever accused Morgan of being quick. If I'd wanted to, I could charm my way out of it again, but I was tired of making excuses. "You know how strongly I feel about justice, and if there was ever a time I'd fight for it, this is it."

"If I were you, I'd tread carefully, Abby. You know the law."

How many times was I going to hear that? "Marco is innocent, Greg. I'd bet anything on it. He went to Ryson's to have a friendly chat with him because a childhood friend was being harassed. That doesn't make him a killer."

"He might not have intended to kill Ryson, but that doesn't mean he didn't deliver the fatal blow."

"No way. Ryson was alive when Marco left."

"Have you considered that he might have died *after* Salvare left?"

"Of course I've considered it. I'm not stupid. All I'm saying is that the prosecutor can't rule out other suspects. It's too early. Can't you quietly tell the detectives to at least take another look at the next-door neighbor?"

"I can't, Abby."

"Why not?"

"Short answer?" He glanced over his shoulders, then leaned in close. "Martin Kellerman."

"Don't tell me you're afraid of him, too. What kind of hold does this man have on everyone, Greg?"

Morgan turned red in the face. "He doesn't have a hold on me and I'm not afraid of him, but I'm not an idiot, either. Look, if you can bring me some concrete evidence, I'll make sure it gets to Mel, but that's all I can promise. And the sooner you do it, the better."

I jammed one last fry in my mouth,

slapped a ten-dollar bill on the table, and stood up. "Fine. I'll see you in a few days, Greg, *with* the evidence."

CHAPTER SEVENTEEN

Fifteen minutes later, I parked the Vette in front of the Mazellas' tidy, white-frame two-story and got out. From that vantage point I had a clear view of Trina's house, driveway, and garage — and that meant Ed and his wife would have, too. Perfect. Hopefully, one of them had seen Trina leave her house Sunday evening and noted the time. Also perfect was that Ed's black tow truck wasn't in the driveway. As soon as I talked to Trina, I wanted to question Eudora without Ed there to protect her.

With my purse over my shoulder, I got out of the car and headed toward Trina's house. I had barely stepped onto her front porch when the door opened and Miss Split Ends herself stepped out, spitting mad and ready to do battle with me.

"You had the nerve to question my mother?" she hissed in my face, pulling the door shut behind her as tiny tots in the background began to howl. "What the hell were you thinking? Do you have any idea how upsetting that was for her?"

"I didn't say anything to upset her, and she was very gracious. I explained that it was just part of the investigation, nothing personal. She was fine with that."

"Nothing personal? When you harass my mother *I* take it personally. Next time you want to know something, you ask *me*, got it?"

Boy, did she set herself up, or what? "Got it. So how about telling me what time you really left to go to your mother's house Sunday night?"

She drew back, blinking in surprise. "I told you it was around seven thirty."

"*Around* seven thirty?"

"When Marco told me to leave I wasn't exactly thinking about the time. I was thinking about getting my son away before something happened. In case you haven't figured this out already, Ryson was a dangerous, demented freak."

"Okay, let's say it was seven thirty. You didn't arrive in New Buffalo until after ten o'clock, which would be after nine o'clock our time."

"So?"

"It took you an hour and forty minutes to

drive there?"

She blinked again, clearly flustered. "It might have. My engine light came on, and I had to find a gas station that was open on a Sunday evening to have it checked out."

Not very original as far as excuses went. "Do you remember the name of this station and where it was?"

"What is it with you? Are you trying to blame me for Ryson's murder?" She pointed to herself. "*I'm* the victim here. *I* asked Marco to take care of Ryson because I was afraid of the bastard. Do you actually think I'd be stupid enough to try to deal with that creep myself?"

"But you did try, didn't you?"

"What?"

"You went to the motorcycle shop and confronted him. The guys he worked with told me about it."

She folded her arms across her chest. "Yes, I went there — during the day, when lots of people were around. What does that prove?"

"Actually, it was after five o'clock, when most of them were gone for the day."

"I couldn't go earlier," she sneered. "I had to wait until my kids' parents had come for them."

"Did you tell the police about your confrontation?"

"They never asked."

Gee, there was a surprise.

With a furious scowl she stepped back inside and closed the door in my face. Well, tough luck, toots. It would take more than a door to stop me. I turned to walk away, then heard the door open again.

"It was Jake's BP Amoco." This time she not only shut it, but kicked it as well. That was quite a temper she had.

"I'll check it out," I called, pulling out my cell phone.

As I headed across the street I dialed Bloomers and got Grace. "Would you find the phone number and the location of a gas station called Jake's BP Amoco, please, and see if they have any records of servicing a car for a Trina Vasquez on Sunday night? I'm not sure where the station is. Somewhere between here and New Buffalo."

"Certainly, dear. I'll get right on it."

Take that, Trina. I put the phone away and stopped at my car to retrieve the bouquet of white and yellow mums that I'd picked up at Bloomers earlier. Now to see whether the reclusive Eudora would talk to me.

Making sure the flowers were visible, I rang the bell and caught a ripple in the drape at the front window. Was she watching me? I waited a moment, rang again, then rapped the wood with my knuckles. "Mrs. Mazella? I have a flower delivery for you."

Nothing. Maybe she'd be more favorable to visitors at the back door.

I walked around the house and knocked again. "Mrs. Mazella, I'm Abby Knight from Bloomers Flower Shop. I brought you some beautiful mums."

Inside, I heard a soft flutter of cloth, as though someone had shaken a sheet. Then a muffled voice said, "Why?"

"I was hoping you could answer some questions about your neighbor, Trina."

"Is she in trouble?" This was asked more in curiosity than concern.

"No, Trina is fine, but there's some discrepancy about where she was Sunday night. I thought maybe you'd recall what time she left her house."

She muttered something, but I couldn't make out the words.

"I'm sorry, I didn't catch that. Maybe if you'd open the door?"

"Are you clean?"

What did that have to do with anything? I checked my clothing for soil smudges, then my hands, to make sure I didn't have ketchup on my fingers. "Yes. All clean."

The door opened a crack, sending a waft

of sage-scented air my way; then a muted voice said, "Turn around."

I obliged, holding my arms away from my body.

"Step inside," the voice commanded. "Hurry. Before they come." The door opened just enough for me to squeeze through.

Before *they* come? Feeling as though something was about to attack me from behind, I walked into a kitchen that was shuttered from all daylight. Around the room, tall white candle pillars flickered from the sudden movement of air, casting wavering shadows on the walls and filling the room with the scent of hot wax. A long plant light beneath a row of cabinets hummed as it diffused a blue-white glow on clay pots overflowing with herbs. I spotted basil, oregano, parsley, thyme, and sage among them.

Beyond the plants sat a row of small glass jars filled with what appeared to be dried herbs, and a stainless steel mortar and pestle, possibly for pulverizing the herbs. More bundles of herbs hung from the ceiling in various stages of drying. An enormous schefflera stretched over the top of an old white refrigerator, completely filling one corner of the kitchen, and a treelike plant of another sort — maybe an aralia — filled the opposite corner, its big, multifingered leaves trembling from the disturbed stillness in the room.

Hearing the door shut and a bolt slide into place, I spun around and immediately stepped back with a gasp. If this was Eudora Mazella, Trina had been right about her. She was definitely odd, starting with her huge wooden mask painted with a frightening, warriorlike face. If that wasn't eerie enough, she also had on a white, ankle-length, terry cloth bathrobe — worn backward and tied at the waist — with two heavy gold pendants around her neck, one with a Celtic cross on it, the other one the yin-yang symbol. Her feet were protected by soft white shoe covers, such as hospital workers used, the total outfit shielding her from the top of her skull to the bottom of her feet.

At once she tossed something ashy over me. I coughed and blinked, brushing pale green particles from the front of my shirt, then lifted my fingers to sniff them. Sage? She circled around me, chanting something in a language that sounded like Latin as she waved a smoking bundle of herbs in the air over my head.

Maybe I should have stayed outside.

I inched closer to the door. "You know, if this isn't a good time to talk, I can always come back later."

Her incantations halted. She thrust a long index finger toward her kitchen table. "Have a seat."

Figuring I had nothing to gain by running away, I perched on a straight-backed oak chair and pushed the bundle of flowers toward the middle, as though I were offering up a sacrifice. She stretched a robed arm around me, plucked the bouquet from the table, and held it up to the eye holes on her mask. Satisfied, she took the flowers to her sink and began to chant softly as she filled a vase with water.

"Nice selection of herbs you're growing over there," I commented.

She brought the vase to the table and took a seat opposite me, where she watched me silently, making me feel like a bug in a jar.

"Your schefflera is certainly a fine specimen. You must have a green thumb."

Silence.

"Is that other plant an aralia? I'm not familiar with it."

"Castor bean."

"Interesting. I've never seen a castor bean plant up close." I turned for a better look. I'd never heard of a castor bean plant being grown indoors. The shrubby foliage was usually found in a landscape setting, and even then, people tended to remove them because of the danger of a pet ingesting the toxic seeds. The oil from the bean, however, was very useful, although Grace had told me a few horror stories from her childhood about being dosed with castor oil to clean out her insides. The weekly purging, she had called it.

I folded my hands on the table, not sure what to say next. Trying to talk to someone wearing a tribal mask was disconcerting to say the least, and the mask was proving to be the proverbial elephant in the room. Did I pretend it wasn't there or ask why it was?

What the heck. "That's quite a mask you have on. Is it African?"

She said nothing. Maybe I wasn't supposed to notice.

"Anyway, the reason I'm here —"

"You have a healthy aura."

I blinked several times. "I don't get that often, but thanks."

"Not many people have a healthy aura."

"I see. Well, that's good to know." I waited a moment to be sure she was finished. I had a feeling my chances of having a normal conversation with her were remote. "Okay, then. Can you tell me if you saw Trina leave her house Sunday night?"

"Trina has a disruptive aura."

"You know, I sensed that about her."

"She's not good for that little boy, either. Mark would better off with his father, Luis."

"Please correct me if I'm wrong, but isn't Luis, well, dead?"

Through the holes I saw Eudora's eyes crinkle and knew she was smiling. "Luis is here with us right now."

The hairs on my nape rose as I glanced behind me. Was she talking about a ghost?

"Don't be afraid. Raise your hands in welcome." To demonstrate, she held up her palms as if she were pushing away the ceiling and tilted her masked face up.

So as not to offend her I imitated her movements, then closed my eyes, silently counted to ten, and gave her a shrug. "Sorry. I'm not getting anything."

"You're a skeptic. You need to open your mind." She fingered one of the yellow mum petals. "This flower has a spirit, you know. But you must know. You work with them every day. They're what calm you, give you peace. Their spirits enter your body each morning, filling you with purity and light, and that's why you have a healthy aura."

"I'd never thought of it that way, but you're right. They do give me peace."

"You asked about Trina."

It took a moment for me to redirect my thoughts. "Trina, right. Did you see her leave her house Sunday night?"

"Yes."

"Do you remember the time?"

Eudora nodded her head, brushing dried herbs off the table into her hand.

"Was it early evening? Late?"

"Twenty-seven minutes after seven o'clock."

How could she be so precise? Did she keep a clock by her window? "Are you sure it was after *seven* o'clock, not eight o'clock?"

She sat absolutely still for a long moment, giving me the distinct impression that underneath the mask she was glaring at me, as though offended by my question. The problem was, I needed to be sure, because if Eudora was correct, then my theory about Trina was wrong.

She rose suddenly, making me jump, but she was merely taking the crumbs to a white plastic trash can. With her back to me I could see her hair, a drab brown-gray mix hanging below her shoulders, crudely chopped at the ends, as though she'd cut it herself. She brushed the crumbs into the can, then, with her hands folded, mumbled something that sounded like a prayer. Was she praying for the crumbs' spirits?

Silently, Eudora glided back to her chair. "Anything else?"

Obviously she felt she'd said enough about the time issue. I'd have to come back to that later. "Did you see anyone visit Dennis Ryson Sunday evening?"

The mask actually trembled. "You mustn't speak that one's name. He has an evil spirit. Call him Sinned."

"Sinned?"

"That's his name backwards."

That was eerie. "Okay, did you see anyone visit Sinned on Sunday evening?"

"Many visited him."

"Can you describe them?"

"It would be dangerous to do so."

"Dangerous how?"

"They might visit me."

"I'm not clear on this. Are you talking about real people or spirits?"

"The two are one. They cannot be divided."

Oh, brother. This wasn't going well. "Okay, then can you tell me anything about Den— Sinned's — activities on Sunday? For instance —"

Her arms went skyward and she resumed her chanting, drowning out the rest of my sentence. At first her words seemed unintelligible; then I caught, "Ob-la-di, ob-la-da," which I was pretty sure came from an old Beatles tune.

Okay, so she didn't want to tell me about Ryson's activities. But why was that? Had Ryson done something to frighten her?

I waited until she paused for a breath; then I said, "Mrs. Mazella, I understand the subject makes you uncomfortable, but if you could just answer one more question? Did Sinned ever harm you or threaten to do so?"

The mask trembled again. "Evil spirits do great harm and must be dealt with."

I decided to take that as a yes. "I'm not really up on these things, so can you tell me how one would deal with an evil spirit?"

She stared at me for a long moment, making me wonder whether she'd dozed off. Then she whispered, "You must purify the spirit."

"How do you do that?"

Her shoulders rose in an elegant shrug, as if the answer was so simple, it was staring me in the face. "By cleansing."

"How does one cleanse?"

"By purging."

We were going in circles. "Okay, and to purge an evil spirit, what tools are needed?"

"Purity of heart. If one has that, the key

258

lies within reach."

Either she was talking nonsense or I was getting dizzy from the smoking herbs that clouded the air. I glanced at the white clock on her wall. It was one thirty and I had work to do back at Bloomers, so I decided to just come out with it.

"Mrs. Mazella, I'm trying to find out who killed Den— Sinned. If you know anything at all about what happened at his house Sunday evening —"

"Stop!" she shrieked. "You'll bring him here!" She shot out of her chair, grabbed the bundle of herbs from their holder, and began to wave them around her as she turned in circles.

"Who, Mrs. Mazella? Who will I bring here?"

"Sinned!" She resumed her chanting, her movements growing frantic, making me fear that she was going to have a nervous breakdown. When she went to sprinkle more ash on me, I ran for the door, slid back the bolt, and got the hell out of there.

No wonder Ed hadn't wanted me to visit her. The woman was a fruitcake. But was she a harmless fruitcake or a fruitcake with information about Ryson's death?

CHAPTER EIGHTEEN

I was still shaking when I got to the car. That was definitely an encounter I wasn't eager to experience again. Perhaps I'd better stick with questioning Ed.

I started the engine, fastened the seat belt, then got out my phone to check my voice mail. Still no call from Marco. Was he ignoring my calls or hadn't he received my messages? I phoned Down the Hatch, but he wasn't there, so I tried his cell phone again. It rang three times, and then I heard a woman say, "Hello?"

A woman was answering Marco's private cell phone line?

"Hello?" the voice repeated. "Who is this?"

"Abby. Who is this?"

"Francesca Salvare."

An Italian accent, a throaty, mature voice . . . Omigod. It was Marco's mother. I cleared my throat to say in as pleasant a voice as possible, "Mrs. Salvare, hi, I'm Abby Knight from Bloomers Flower Shop. Maybe Marco has mentioned me? Anyway, is Marco there by any chance?"

"Abby who?"

"Knight."

"My son is away, Abby, but if you tell me what you want, I will let him know as soon as he comes home."

Suddenly, I heard the growl of a male voice in the background; then Mrs. Salvare said, "I think he just came in. Hold the line, please."

Marco came on and he didn't sound happy. "Hey. What's up?"

Was he kidding? I had to unlock my jaw to speak. "Lots of things are up. We need to talk. Are you going to be at the bar tonight?"

"I'll be there. How's five o'clock?"

I noticed he didn't ask me to go into detail about our forthcoming meeting. Either he was afraid his mother would overhear or he'd heard my teeth grinding. "Five o'clock is fine."

In the background I heard his mother whisper, "Invite her over. I want to meet her."

He shushed her, then said to me, "I'll see you at the bar."

I tossed my phone onto the seat. Okay, so

261

Marco didn't want me to meet his mom. I wasn't exactly in the mood to schmooze with her, either. Having steam coming out of your ears tended to make a bad first impression, and I was fried that he hadn't told me about his history with Ryson. Add to that the problem he seemed to be having returning my phone calls, and I couldn't help but wonder what was next. Would I find out he actually *did* kill Ryson?

I clapped a hand over my mouth as though I'd spoke those traitorous thoughts out loud. *Take that back this instant, you doofus. You don't believe for a moment that Marco had anything to do with Ryson's death. You're just angry.*

Yes. That was absolutely it. I was so angry I wasn't thinking rationally. I started up the engine and headed back to Bloomers, trying to convince myself that once Marco explained everything, the anger would go away and we'd be fine.

I got back at one forty-five to find Grace alone in the parlor, blowing her nose, and Lottie behind the counter in the shop, apologizing profusely as she rang up purchases for two women, both of whom were having sneezing fits. I saw a dust mop behind the counter sitting beside a pile of colored down. What I didn't see were the feathered frames and fans. Had a windstorm blown them away, or had someone bought them all? Did I dare hope?

"Grace?"

She balled up the tissue and dropped it in the trash container behind the coffee counter. "Hello, dear," she said in a nasal tone.

"What happened to my mother's stuff?"

There was a long pause. "Perhaps you should ask Lottie."

Passing the buck wasn't like Grace, and that made me nervous. Before I could probe further, she pulled a piece of paper from her sweater pocket. "I was able to get the information you wanted on Trina Vasquez. Jake's BP Amoco is located on Route 20 in Michigan City. The owner — his name actually is Jake — verified that a blue minivan was serviced for a Trina Vasquez at 8:10 Sunday evening. I asked him to describe her, and I must say, she left quite an impression on him."

"She has that effect on men." I cast a disparaging look at my short body. What was it about Trina? My hair was just as silky as hers — a little too red and not nearly as long — but still, it was thick and natural. And I had curves — lots of curves. It had to be her long legs.

Grace handed me the note. "Jake said to call if you wanted a written statement."

There went my Trina theory. At least Marco would be happy that I'd crossed her off my list of suspects. But what did that leave me with? A very weak Ed Mazella and a mystery girlfriend.

"How is your investigation going, dear?"

"I don't have one solid suspect, Grace."

"Something will come up. Be diligent and have faith in your abilities."

"And there we have it, Grace, the crux of the problem." I plunked down on a chair. "My abilities are arranging flowers and growing plants, not finding murderers."

Grace clucked her tongue. "This is not the Abby I know. Give yourself some credit, dear. Not only are you a whiz with flowers, but you're also a marvelous busybody, and that makes for an excellent private investigator. Something else is bothering you, isn't it? Would you like to talk about it?"

The bell jingled as customers left the shop, and Lottie quickly hustled into the parlor, rubbing her hands together, saving me from giving Grace a lame excuse. "Goody, we're all alone. Tell us about your lunch date with Mr. Gorgeous."

Who'd have thought Greg Morgan would

become my bargaining chip? "Not until you tell me what happened to the frames and fans."

Lottie glanced at Grace, and they both heaved guilty sighs. "Not to hurt your feelings, sweetie, but I couldn't take those feathers one more minute. I swear the fans were waving at me every time I passed by, and poor Grace, with her sneezing and blowing . . ."

On cue, Grace pulled a fresh tissue from her sleeve and sneezed into it.

I rubbed a spot above my right eye, feeling a tension headache coming on. "Okay, what did you do with them — or do I want to know?"

"I packed everything into two big boxes and set them by the basement door." Lottie shrugged, palms up, as if to say, *What else could I do?* They watched me expectantly, waiting for my reaction.

"You want to store my mother's art in the basement?"

Both women nodded.

"Okay, then. Let's get those suckers downstairs."

The plants in the next room quivered as the two sighed in relief.

"And if there are no customers when you return," Grace called as Lottie and I headed toward the kitchen, "we shall have a tea break and sample some of that lovely cake you brought in this morning."

I'd completely forgotten about Eve Taylor's cake. "You've got it," I called back.

We stowed the boxes against the rear basement wall beside stacks of terra-cotta pots, then joined Grace at a table in the parlor where she'd already poured cups of tea and distributed forks, napkins, and cake on dessert plates.

"What are you going to tell your mom about the feathers?" Lottie asked, her mouth full of chocolate.

I licked creamy frosting from the tip of my fork. "I don't know. I need a really convincing story, though."

Grace cleared her throat. "As Mark Twain once said, 'When in doubt, tell the truth.' "

Sure, the truth was one way to go, but I was thinking more along the lines of a little white lie. I decided to keep that to myself, however. One quote per slice of cake was enough.

"Yummy," Lottie said, diving in for another forkful, while Grace picked the crystalized flower petals from her icing before trying her first bite.

"The blossoms are edible, Grace. Eve assured me she wouldn't use them if there was any risk of harming customers."

"I prefer my flowers brewed into a tea, thank you." Grace took a tentative bite, swallowed, and smiled. "Outstanding. Shall you tell us about the wonderful lady who created this masterpiece?"

"And *then* tell us about Mr. Gorgeous," Lottie said.

Over the rest of the cake and several cups of tea, I filled them in on my busy morning, making them chuckle at my description of Santa Claus's wife, making Lottie sigh wistfully as I described lunch with Morgan, and leaving them as frustrated with my lack of progress as I was. But I still couldn't bring myself to tell them about Marco's deception. It hurt too much.

I watched the clock all afternoon, impatiently awaiting closing time, eager to have Marco answer my questions and put my mind to rest so I could dispose of my anger. I didn't like being angry, especially with Marco, but he'd hidden information from me, and that wasn't something I could ignore. And although there were orders to fill and customers to wait on, I also couldn't stop my brain from reviewing every conversation I'd had and every scrap of information I'd learned on the case, like a clip show of annoying movie trailers that played continuously.

Three items stood out. Eve Taylor's revelation about Marco's history with Ryson; the mysterious white Mustang; and Eudora's cryptic behavior — although the idea of flowers having spirits still escaped me. What about thorns? Did they scream in silent protest when I stripped them off a stem? It wasn't a comforting thought.

At fifteen minutes before five o'clock the bell over the door tinkled, signaling an incoming customer. Since Lottie was up to her knuckles in planting soil — did a bag of dirt have a spirit? — and Grace had just left for a hair appointment, I quickly slipped through the curtain to find a tall, thin woman standing at the counter, one elbow resting on top, impatiently tapping her long, glossy fingernails (painted a shade I'd have to call "exceedingly violet").

She had a narrow face, sharp cheekbones, a hawkish nose, and a long jawline, all covered with a heavy coating of makeup. Her lips were lumpy, as though they'd been plumped with collagen in random locations. Her hair was long, curly, and as shiny as doll's tresses. Her knee-length jade green sweater was belted at the waist, hiding most of her skinny jeans, below which I could see jade green, pointy-toed high heels.

"May I help you?" I asked cheerfully, hoping she'd be quick.

She peered at me over the rims of her jade green sunglasses, taking me all in before pulling them off to reveal enough black eyeliner to startle a raccoon. She shook back her hair — at least she tried, but those curls weren't budging — then pointed to the refrigerated display case and, in a voice that sounded reedy and strained, said, "I want all of your bright pink roses. *Bright* pink. No pale ones. No white. No peach. No two-toned."

I liked a woman who knew what she wanted, especially when I was in a hurry. There was only one problem. "I'm afraid we have only two bright pinks left. If you want to come back in the morning —"

"Just give them to me."

I opened the case and removed the pair so she could inspect them — fine specimens of the bright pink tea rose called Fragrant Cloud. "Are these okay?"

"They'll do. I want to take them with me. They're a gift. For someone special." She looked down her nose at me as though daring me to contradict.

"No problem." I added several fern stems, wrapped them in pretty floral paper, and gave her one of my Bloomers pens and a

269

small gift card to sign.

She waved them away as if I'd slobbered on them. "You write the card for me."

Fine. Anything to get her out of the shop fast. "What would you like to say?"

She walked over to the small wicker settee we used for display and made herself comfortable, crossing one long leg over the other. "Ready? Okay. To the sweetest friend in the world, for all that you've done."

In my best penmanship, I wrote it down. "There you go. Do you want to sign your name?"

"I'm not finished."

"Sorry. Go ahead."

"Now, where was I? You made me forget where I was."

I repeated what she'd dictated; then she continued, "For sitting up with me all night and holding my hand, for helping me work through my shame, for putting up with my . . ."

I flipped the card over and squeezed in as many words as possible. And still she talked, until I had to hold up a hand to interrupt her. "Sorry. I ran out of room." I grabbed another card. "Okay. I'm ready."

She sighed, clearly annoyed with me. "You'll have to read that last line again."

"For putting up with my . . . ?"

"Oh, yes. With my temper tantrums, and my ravings . . ."

Whoever this friend was, he or she needed more than two roses. I filled a second card, and the woman kept going, pausing every so often to gather her thoughts. Lottie came through with her purse, ready to go home. I glanced at her and she rolled her eyes. Obviously she'd been listening from the other room.

"Now, let me see what you've written." The woman held out a hand, empresslike, waiting for me to walk them over to her.

I had a feeling that whoever came up with that motto about the customer always being right had never actually worked in a retail shop. I glanced at the clock as the woman read over the cards, her lips moving with each word. When she'd finished, she sighed and held them to her heart, a single tear forging a canal through her makeup as it rolled down her cheek.

"Isn't that just too beautiful?"

"Lovely."

"You're mocking me."

"No. I mean it. Beautiful words. You must be a writer." It was a white lie, but again, much kinder than the truth. Plus, it was good practice for the upcoming confrontation with my mother.

"I should be a writer, I know, but alas, I'm not." She glanced at me, clearly expecting me to respond, then gave up and volunteered the information. "I'm an actress." She raised her wrist to her forehead and sighed dramatically. "Yes, an actress on this funny little stage we call life."

An actress. Gee, there was a surprise.

Her wrist came down. "Perhaps you've seen me."

"I don't get out much."

"Oh, come now. Surely you've seen me. At the New Chapel Opera House?"

I shrugged.

"In *Waiting for Godot*? It's playing right now."

"Oh, sure. Now I remember you. Brilliant acting." Those little lies were coming more easily now. Was that a good thing? I darted a quick glance at the clock. Yikes. It was five! Time to get her out of there. "So, was there anything else you wanted to say?"

She studied the cards again, then handed them back. "Yes."

Ten minutes later, I was on the eighth card and she was still on the settee. When she paused I said, "I really hate to interrupt, but I'm going to have to close up shop. I have an appointment — actually, I'm late."

"Well, then." She rose in a graceful, swanlike move and swayed over to me. "Give me your pen."

I handed her the pen and a fresh card, tamping down the urge to snap, "Would you get on with this?" She nibbled the cap — I had to remember to throw that baby away — then started to write, changed her mind, started again, and finally scribbled something that looked like *Love, Videt,* and handed the card back. The pen, I noticed, went into the pocket of her sweater.

"What do I owe you?"

I stuffed her cards into envelopes — it took three — then did a tally. "Two roses and, let me see . . . nine cards will be ten dollars even." It should have been more, but I couldn't wait to get rid of her.

Videt, or whatever her name was, pulled out a ten and tossed it onto the counter with a sniff. "Much too expensive." Snatching the wrapped flowers and the stack of cards, she swayed out the door.

I grabbed my purse, set the alarm, locked the shop, and dashed up the sidewalk to Down the Hatch, only to find that Videt had beaten me there. She stood just inside, trying to get one of the waitresses to seat her, probably so she could make a dramatic entrance. But it was Gert who noticed her first, and no one, not even a poodle-headed actress, could make Gert behave like a hostess.

"Over here, doll." She motioned Videt into a booth as though she were a plane taxiing into the hangar, set a plastic-coated menu in front of her, and said, "I'll be back for your order."

Then Gert saw me, and a smile lifted her sagging jowls. "Hi, doll. The boss is in his office. Have a seat and I'll send him out."

"Thanks anyway, but I need to talk to him privately."

"Uh-oh. Sounds like he's in the doghouse."

I made my way past the customers lined up at the bar and up the short hallway to Marco's door. I rapped twice; then, hearing a quick "Come in," I peeked inside and saw that he was on the phone. He motioned for me to come in, so I shut the door, took a seat on one of the sling-back chairs, and pretended to be captivated by my overgrown cuticles, but totally unaware of what he was saying. *"You were having a telephone conversation? No way!"*

"Yes, I will." He checked his watch. "In an hour. Because I have something to do first. Okay, Ma, forty-five minutes. No, I don't want your lasagna to get cold. I promise I'll be there at six." He hung up, rubbed his eyes, and gave me a long-suffering look. "If I can survive my mother's visit, I can survive anything."

"How long is she staying?"

"She hasn't decided. A week — an eternity."

"Doesn't your sister live in town? Maybe your mother could stay with her." Why was I trying to solve another problem for him? I couldn't even get a handle on the first one.

"Gina is camping out at my place now, too. She says she has the stomach flu and needs mothering, but I think she and my brother-in-law are on the outs again. So, anything new turn up on the case?"

"Oh, yeah. Something turned up all right."

He sat forward expectantly. "Tell me."

"For starters, I found out that you arrested Dennis Ryson for a convenience store robbery a few years back."

Marco leaned back in his chair but said nothing.

"I also learned that you got a reprimand from Kellerman because of that arrest, and then you quit the force."

"Wait. Time out. I quit the force because I was fed up with all their Mickey Mouse bureaucracy. The reprimand over Ryson's arrest was just the last straw. It was a good arrest, yet they chose to believe some thief's word over mine."

"You asked me to help you, Marco; then you purposefully withheld critical information from me. Does that make sense in anyone's world? No wonder the prosecutor targeted you. You have an honest-to-goodness motive."

He pressed his fingertips against his eyebrows. "All right. I should have brought it up, but my concern was that if you knew about my history with Ryson, your judgment would be clouded."

"So you don't trust my judgment. Didn't it occur to you that I might uncover the information by other means? I mean, if my detective skills are so bad, why did you ask me to help?"

His palms came down on the desk. "Hold on a minute. Before you get completely bent out of shape, what about trusting *my* judgment? Have you stopped to consider that I might have a reason for not telling you about my history with Ryson? Where is your trust in me?"

I hadn't seen that one coming. And since I couldn't think of a good answer, we sat there glaring at each other, obviously at a stalemate. I saw him glance at his watch and knew it was time to go. Maybe we both needed some distance, anyway, to sort things out. I pushed myself out of the chair and headed for the door.

"Hold up a minute, Abby."

"That's okay. Your lasagna is waiting. I wouldn't want you to get in trouble with your mother."

He caught up with me at the door (only because I let him). "The food will keep, and so will Mom. Come on. Look at me, Sunshine."

I raised my gaze to his, drinking in those soulful, earnest eyes as he ran a fingertip along my jawline. Then his hands gently cupped my face and his penetrating gaze searched mine, as though trying to peer deep into my heart. I tried not to blink because I knew that scratchy feeling behind my eyelids was angry tears just looking for a reason to escape.

"I was wrong, Abby, and I'm sorry. You have to believe me when I say that I trust you more than anyone I know. I should have been up front with you about Ryson."

"Damn right you should have. So why weren't you?"

He thought about it for a moment. "Pride. Shame. I don't know. It was a bad time for me. I didn't want you to know, is all."

"That's your reason for nearly sabotaging your case? Marco, you know all about my failures. Why didn't you want to share that with me?"

"Vanity. Male ego. Stupidity. I'm sure you'll come up with a better name for it."

"Stupidity works for me."

A tiny grin lifted one corner of his mouth. He reached out for a lock of my hair, giving it a playful tug. "Are we good again?"

"Not so fast, bud. What about in the future?"

He studied me, looking for cues as to how he should answer. Then he got it. "I'll be up front with you in the future, too."

"About everything?"

His lips pressed together, and I knew there was a battle of wills going on inside his head. As Reilly had pointed out, Marco played things close to the chest. To be completely open with me wasn't an easy place for him to be. But he gave a nod, and for Marco, a man of few words, that said a lot.

Could I stay angry with him after that? Bruised around the edges, yes, but not angry. It was all I could do not to throw my arms around his neck and rain kisses on his face, but I pretended to be cool about it. "Good. Then I promise to trust your judgment, too."

He slipped his arms all the way around

me and pulled me into his safe, warm embrace. I pressed the side of my face against his T-shirt, breathing in the male essence of him, feeling the steady thud of his heart. After a full minute of hugging, though, we were zooming past the warm feelings and heading into the hot zone.

"Um, Abby?"

"Hmm?"

"The lasagna?"

"Oh, right," I murmured into the soft cotton front of his shirt. "I don't want to hold up your dinner." I also didn't want to let him loose.

"I have an idea."

About time.

He unwrapped my arms, walked to his desk, and picked up his phone. After punching in a number he said, "Ma? Set another place. I'm bringing a guest."

CHAPTER NINETEEN

Marco opened the door of his office and waited for me to exit, but I couldn't move because my legs had turned to ice. He wanted me to meet his mother *now?* I glanced down at the jeans and green shirt I'd worn all day, an outfit that had seen me through a visit to a bakery, a lunch at Rosie's with accompanying onion odors, a shower of ashes, and probably some brightly colored down in my hair. Was that any way to meet the woman who might someday be my mother-in-law?

"Maybe we should do this some other time."

"No time like the present." He smiled that little Marco smile that tugged at my heart but did little to settle my nervous stomach. "You'll be fine. She'll love you."

"In this outfit? She'll think I'm a slob . . . or that you've picked up a stray . . . or that you've lost your mind."

He tugged my elbow. "Come on. It'll be painless. Don't be one of those flighty females who thinks appearance is every-thing."

"What does that mean? Is my appearance that bad?"

I allowed him to coax me out the door and down the hallway toward the bar as doubts crowded my mind. Did I have lip gloss in my purse? A comb? A breath mint? Was my blouse unbuttoned too far? Should I close it up to my neck? Were my feet clean? I hadn't painted my toenails in weeks — no, months. Oh, wait. I had on my Adidas . . . my *scruffy* Adidas with a hole in the sole. How could I possibly meet his mother now?

When we entered the bar area I saw Videt still seated in the second booth with her back to me, but now there was a woman across from her. As we approached, I got a look at her companion's face and made a quick grab for Marco's arm, dragging him backward until we were hidden by five guys crowded around one girl on a barstool. (What was that about?)

"Look at the second booth, Marco. See that woman facing us? That's Lily, a clown in Ryson's troupe. The woman with her just bought flowers from me, and I think they're for Lily."

"So?"

"Just watch for a moment."

Videt slid the cone-shaped bundle across the table toward Lily, who seemed pleasantly surprised, her mouth forming the words, "You shouldn't have." She unwrapped the flowers and lifted a blossom to her nose to inhale its fragrance.

"Why are we watching them?" Marco asked.

"I can't put my finger on it, but something about those two bothers me. It's that gut feeling I get. Do you have your little spy camera handy?"

"In my office."

"Super. Go get it. I'll chat them up while you take photos."

I waited until he'd gone for the camera — a sleek, small, high-tech device that produced fast, clear prints on demand. Then, as he positioned himself at the far end of the bar, I made my way toward the front until I was almost past the second booth; then I glanced at them and pretended to be surprised. "Well, hello again."

Videt tilted her curly head to study me through her thick black lashes, as though trying to place me. "Hello," she said with an unfriendly sniff.

I ignored the snub and turned toward Lily.

"And hello again to you, too, Lily. We met yesterday evening at the funeral home. I'm Abby Knight from Bloomers."

"Of course Ah remember you, Abby. Always nice to see you."

"How do you like your flowers?"

"Ah adore them." She selected one of the long stems, then brushed a velvety rose across her cheek. "Violet is such a sweet thing."

"They're roses," I said.

Lily gazed at me as if I had sprouted some of my mother's neon feathers. "Yes, darlin', Ah know it's a rose. *She's* Violet." She pointed to her companion, who batted those lashes again.

Violet? Violet? Well, I'd been close. "Lily and Violet — both flower names. That's quite a coincidence."

"Lily is mah clown name," Lily said. "Ah never cared for mah real name — Gertrude — after mah great aunt of the same name."

"Horrid," Violet said to her, wrinkling her nose.

"Are you both clowns, then?" I asked.

Violet slipped on her sunglasses just so she could push them down her nose and peer haughtily over the rims. "As I said before, I'm an *actress.* I do the clown gigs only on occasion."

"Sorry. My mistake. You're with Clowns-on-Call?"

"Yes, we are," Lily said with a smile. "A clown for any occasion, as the ad goes."

"Then you must have known Dennis Ryson, too," I said to Violet.

"Yes," Lily said with a sad sigh. "Wasn't that a shame about his death?"

She was studying her purple fingernails as though the subject bored her. "*Some* people might say he *deserved* it," she sang under her breath.

"Violet, hush now," Lily said quietly. "You shouldn't speak ill of the dead."

They exchanged a quick glance, but I couldn't tell what it meant. Did they know something more about Ryson's death, or was it simply that Violet had disliked him? I had to get her to say more.

"Were you in the parade Saturday, too, Violet?"

She gave a sharp huff. "I *believe* I was one of the *stilt* walkers."

A stilt walker. Hmm. Wasn't that interesting? Stilts were made from long pieces of wood. What a handy weapon.

I thought back to what she'd written to Lily on her card, thanking her for *"sitting up with me all night Sunday and holding my hand, for helping me work through my shame,*

284

for putting up with my temper tantrums, and my ravings . . ."

A remorseful, bad-tempered, raving stilt walker. Was there any worse kind? Well, yes, there was, because apparently *this* one had to be consoled all Sunday night, conveniently just after Ryson's murder. Was it a coincidence?

I suddenly remembered that Marco was supposed to be taking photos. I darted a quick glance over my shoulder and saw him standing behind the bar. He made a circling motion with his hand, then pointed to Violet. Ah. He needed her to turn toward him. How could I get her to do that?

I focused on an unsuspecting male seated on a far stool, then pointed to myself as if he were flirting with me. "Me? Now?" Both women craned their necks for a look, providing a perfect, full-faced mug shot.

When they turned back, I shrugged. "I guess he wasn't interested after all."

"What a surprise," Violet muttered.

My thoughts exactly, only for a different reason. It seemed that Violet's swiveling had caused her sweater to gape open half an inch, revealing a patch of dark curly hair. She saw my gaze and, with a look of horror, quickly adjusted the sweater, cinching the belt tighter at the waist.

Chest hair?

Her eyes narrowed, as though daring me to mention it. And now that I took a closer look at her, was that stubble showing through her makeup? And weren't her curly tresses a bit too glossy to be real? Okay, then. Violet was a man.

"Was there anything else?" she said with obvious contempt.

I glanced back at Marco and he gave me a victory sign. Mission accomplished. "No, I think that will do it," I said to them. "Nice chatting with you, um, girls. Enjoy your evening."

As though I didn't have a care in the world I strolled casually outside and started up the block. In a few moments, Marco came striding up behind me. He took my hand and placed the photos on my palm. "I don't know if your gut feeling is right or not, but that was quick thinking on your part. I got four solid shots."

I couldn't help but beam. I loved hearing his praise, and there sure had been a lack of it lately. I shuffled through the stack, pleased to see that he'd managed to capture clear images of Violet and Lily. I wasn't too pleased that I was in two of them, with my mouth open, but then my mouth was usually open.

I showed Marco one of the photos. "Take a closer look at this woman."

"What am I looking for?"

"Try a wig and a five-o'clock shadow. Violet is a *man,* Marco. She — or he — is in the same clown troupe that Ryson was in — *and* she's a stilt walker. A stilt walker!" I glanced at the cars parked along the street. "And just maybe she owns the white Mustang, too."

"Where are you going with this?"

Boy, was he slow today. "Stilts are made from pieces of wood, right? Going by what Greg Morgan told me at lunch —"

"You had lunch with Motormouth?"

"Motormouth. Good one. Yes, I did have lunch with him. It was on my list of things to tell you. Anyway, Morgan said there were wood fibers in Ryson's head wound, so as soon as Violet said she was a stilt walker, I made the connection. One of her stilts could have been the murder weapon. Think about it, Marco. She could be the mystery girl in the Mustang."

"Way too many leaps there, Sunshine. First of all, does she have a motive? Second, even if she owns the Mustang, none of Ryson's neighbors reported seeing it there Sunday. And third, Violet is a male, and I don't think Ryson swung that way."

Three valid points. But I had one of my own. "What if Violet came on to Ryson and he rebuffed her? Wouldn't that be a motive? You know Grace's saying: 'Hell hath no fury like a woman — or guy in drag — scorned.' It could be purely coincidental, but it's worth investigating. What do we have to lose?" (Precious time, if I was wrong.) "Sometimes you have to think outside the box, Marco."

"*I* have to think outside the box?"

I tucked the photos in my purse. "Tomorrow I'll show these snapshots to Ryson's neighbors to see if anyone recognizes either woman. I'd bet good money that Violet is the mystery girlfriend." I craned my neck for another look at the cars. "I don't see a Mustang here, but it could be in one of the public lots."

All at once, I saw my excuse for missing his mother's dinner. "You know what I should do? I should drive through all the parking lots around the square to see if the Mustang is there. Even better, I can do a stakeout of the bar and follow both women when they leave. So you go on home and I'll hang out on the bench across the street."

"Nice try, Sunshine, but you're not getting out of dinner that easily. My mother is expecting a guest. You don't want to disappoint her, do you?"

"I think your mother would understand that finding a killer to save your backside is a little more important than her lasagna."

"You don't know my mother."

He also didn't know how sexy his backside was. "I can't just leave Violet and Lily here, Marco. Who knows when this opportunity will come up again?"

He pulled out his cell phone and made a call. "Chris? Hey, man, do you see the two women in booth two? I need to know what make of vehicles they're driving. Will you take care of it? Great."

He shut his phone and looked at me. "*Now* are you ready?"

Would I ever be ready to meet his mother?

With his hand on the small of my back, Marco guided me toward Lincoln. We had just rounded the corner and were ready to step off the curb when Marco tugged me to a quick stop and pointed up the block. "There's your white Mustang."

I followed the direction of his index finger. Pay dirt! Quickly, I took off toward the rusty Ford, with Marco right behind. While he walked around to the rear of the car to get the license plate number, I peered through a dirty glass window on the passenger's side, glimpsing about a week's worth of fast-food containers, disposable cups, and crumpled napkins. And was that the end of a stilt poking through the litter in the backseat?

"Marco, take a look inside. Do you see a piece of wood with a metal foot plate on the end? That has to be one of Violet's stilts."

He cupped his hands around his eyes for a better view through the window. "I see it. It looks broken."

I wiped the grimy glass with my hand, then took another peek. Sure enough, the wood appeared to have splintered about two feet up from the foot plate. But what caused the break? Had it been used on Ryson's head? I yanked on the door handle but it didn't budge. "Can you pop the lock?"

"Forget it. Just my luck a cop would see me."

"But I need to have the wood tested. Wait. I know. I'll call Reilly and have him get a search warrant." I started to dig in my purse, but Marco stopped me.

"On what grounds?"

"Suspicion of murder."

"How do you know Violet didn't fall during a performance and damage the stilt?"

He took the wind so far out of my sails that my boat sank. But he was right. I should have known better. Then again, there was a reason I'd flunked those law classes.

Marco tore a piece of paper off his note-pad and handed it to me. "Here's the license plate number. Have Eileen trace it. Then call Dave to see if he's heard anything more about the cause of that blow to Ryson's head. The crime scene team should be able to determine if the coffee table was the culprit. *Then* we'll know if you should investigate Violet. And *now* we'll go to dinner."

CHAPTER TWENTY

"Tell me what else you found out," Marco said as we buckled ourselves into his Prius. "I'm guessing you had a chat with Reilly."

"I did?" My thoughts were so wrapped up in the forthcoming dinner with his mother that I had totally spaced out. "Oh, right, about that. I know you told me to leave him out, but I ran into him at the Pickle Polka and somehow the subject of Snuggles the Clown just sort of, well, came up. Not that it put his job on the line or anything. He's way too smart for that. But he did mention something I'd meant to ask you about before. Remember that scuffle you had with Snuggles at the end of the parade? What was that about?"

"It was about him being paranoid, that's all. He spotted me in the crowd and came at me, raving something about me following him and being out for his blood. Luckily, one of the parade cops witnessed it and had him taken in."

"Was he drunk?"

Marco glanced at me with one of his *get real* looks. "It *was* the Pickle Fest."

"But you *were* following him."

"I was looking for an opportunity to talk to him."

"And you thought that opportunity would be at the end of a parade?"

"Do you always know when an opportunity will present itself?"

"You're right. Okay, one more question, just so I can clarify this in my mind. Why did you end up confronting Ryson at his house?"

"It sure as hell wasn't my idea. I'd hoped to catch him at a bar or a pool hall, or wherever he usually hung out. But for some reason, he hunkered down in that house the rest of the weekend. He came out only one time, and that was Sunday evening when he saw me talking to Trina."

"Do you think he knew you were tailing him?"

"No way."

"So you watched him from the time you saw him at the parade on Saturday morning until you left his house Sunday evening?"

"Except for about an hour Saturday afternoon, when I saw you and Nikki."

We were two blocks from his apartment. I rolled my shoulders to ease the tension. Why had I agreed to this dinner again?

"What else did Ryson's mother tell you?" Marco asked.

"That her son was a sweet boy who loved being a clown and always looked forward to the special cakes she brought him. I couldn't believe we were talking about the same person. And here's something else. She said Trina led Ryson on, as if she were asking for the harassment, and that she wouldn't be surprised if Trina was in on the murder."

"You're kidding me. In on it with whom?"

"You. That was when she told me about her son's so-called false arrest."

"Do you know how long Mrs. Ryson has owned the bakery?"

"She goes by the name Eve Taylor. She's owned the bakery less than a year, but she did some catering from the house she had out in the country."

"Taylor. Hmm. Okay, anything else to report?"

"Let's see. I also paid a visit to Eudora Mazella, Ryson's next-door neighbor, a woman who is heavily into the paranormal. She tossed ashes on me, did a lot of chanting, and told me Dennis Ryson had an evil spirit. Did you know that Dennis is *Sinned* backward? Anyway, when I asked her if she knew who killed him, she freaked out. It wasn't pretty."

"What's your take on her?"

"Eudora is a strange woman, but is she a killer? I suppose she could have gone off the deep end. Then there's her husband, who *really* hated Ryson. Both of them had the opportunity to get into the house after you left, do the dirty deed, *then* call the cops. But I'm not sure she's sane enough or he's clever enough to pull that off."

"It had to be someone Ryson knew," Marco said. "According to Dave, the cops didn't find any evidence of a break-in, which means that Ryson opened the door for his killer."

"Unless someone had his house key — like a former girlfriend or his mother. I'll check it out."

We were moments away from his apartment, and I was starting to perspire. Why had I worn this shirt today? It looked horrible with my hair color and probably had ash on it. Oh, no! Was there ash on my face? I pulled down the visor to check the mirror. Okay, no ash, and my coloring wasn't too high if I squinted to block out the freckles. Lip gloss would definitely be an improvement. I opened my purse and dug through it.

"You want to tell me about your lunch with Morgan now?"

I glossed my lips, pressed them together, then dropped the tube back in my purse. "Are you jealous?"

Marco made a little grunting noise. Obviously, he was burning up with jealousy.

"I finagled that lunch invitation to see what information I could get out of him. But I suffered for nothing. He didn't have anything new to offer." I couldn't bring myself to tell Marco that Morgan had confirmed that they had stopped looking for suspects.

We turned another corner and there was the big, white two-story house. My hands grew so clammy I had to wipe them on my pants. "Maybe you should take me home so I can change into something nicer."

"We're here, and you look fine."

Marco parked the car along the curb, then came around to open my door. My insides shook as I followed him up the driveway. This was just his mother, for pity's sake. I had a mother, didn't I? Nothing scary about that.

Way to kid yourself, Abby.

Marco unlocked the door on the far side

of the screened porch, then stepped back so I could enter. I glanced up the flight of stairs and swallowed. "You go first."

"Abby, she won't bite you."

"Please?"

"Fine." He jogged up the steps ahead of me, while I took them one at a time. Why did I feel like a prisoner on her way to an execution?

The staircase opened onto one corner of a large, airy, carpeted room that ran the width of the house, with double-hung windows at each end covered by white wooden blinds. There was a poker table and five club chairs in front of one set of windows to my right, then a hallway that lead toward the rear of the apartment, then the living room that contained a flat screen television, two recliners, and an overstuffed tan sofa. A door in the center of the front wall was ajar, and inside I could see a double bed covered by a blue comforter, a row of windows over-looking the street and — were those African violets on the window ledge? Surely not.

"Ah, here you are, Marco!" I heard a woman say, rolling the *r* in his name. "The lasagna just came out of the oven. Where is your guest?"

Hiding.

Marco suddenly noticed I wasn't standing

beside him and stepped aside to allow her full view of me. "Mama, this is Abby Knight."

I gave a little wave. "Hello."

"The little flower bambina?" She opened her arms wide. "Welcome, Abby!"

Wow. She wasn't at all what I'd expected. Francesca Salvare was a tall, beautiful, vibrant woman with an hourglass shape — how did she keep her narrow waist? — bouncy, shoulder-length hair in a rich walnut brown highlighted by natural silver strands, high, prominent cheekbones, the same soulful brown eyes Marco had (only covered by oversized, tortoise shell–framed glasses), a wide, full mouth, and a generous, warm smile.

She had on a black print silk blouse and black trousers, with classy black flats, not an old-fashioned dress with an apron, as I'd pictured. In fact, she reminded me very much of a younger version of the actress Sophia Loren.

"It's a pleasure to meet you, Mrs. Salvare," I managed as she folded her arms around me. She even smelled good — like oregano and basil and Parmesan cheese.

She held me at arm's length so she could survey my face and body, turning me as though I were on a spit. "Bella, Abby. You have a womanly figure. Not so skinny like a twig, eh, Marco?"

Umm . . . was that a compliment?

"How much do you weigh, Abby?"

My face flooded with heat. She didn't really expect me to answer that, did she?

"Ma," Marco said sharply, giving her a warning glance, "time for dinner."

"In a moment. Do you like Italian wine, Abby?"

"I *love* Italian wine." Had I said that too eagerly?

A toilet flushed somewhere in the apartment. Marco glanced around. "Is Gina still here?"

"Yes, and she has a surprise for you after dinner."

His sister was eating with us, too. Great. Two Salvare women to size me up. A moment later, a younger, slimmer version of Francesca strolled into the room, looking just as chic as I remembered. Gina and I had never actually been introduced, but I had seen her before . . . well, okay, spied on her, but only because I thought she was Marco's girlfriend.

She held out her hand with a friendly smile even as she checked me out. "You must be Abby."

"My sister, Gina," Marco said belatedly.

"Nice to meet you at last," I said.

"Same here."

"Let us eat," Francesca said, and shooed us toward the hallway.

Gina linked arms with me as we headed for the kitchen. "I've heard a lot about you."

I knew I was blushing. "I hope Marco was kind."

"Actually, it was Trina."

"Then I hope *she* was kind."

Gina gave a light laugh, as if to say, *"Like that's a possibility."* She leaned her head close to whisper, "You knew that Trina and Marco dated a few times in high school, right?"

"I'd heard something to that effect. How did that go?"

"It didn't go anywhere. The sparks never happened for Marco. Trina was too much of a kid sister to him. Besides, she wanted to get married and have babies — the last thing my brother wanted." Gina gave me a calculating glance. "So what are *your* future plans, Abby?"

Let the inquisition begin. "I bought a flower shop about six months ago, and that's my main focus."

"Do you plan to be a career woman, then?"

"Gina," Marco said from behind us,

"shouldn't you be home with Christopher?"

"He's with his father," she replied over her shoulder, then in a quiet voice asked, "Have you thought about having children someday, Abby?"

Marco put his arms around us both. "Doesn't that food smell good?" Then I heard him whisper to his sister, "Knock off the questions." He must have pinched her neck, because she jumped.

"Get bent," she said.

The kitchen was all the way at the back, past a bathroom and small guest bedroom. It was divided by the hallway into two spaces — a tiny cooking area on the left and a dining nook on the right. Inside the nook was a picnic table covered with a blue vinyl tablecloth and two cedar benches. In the kitchen was a small black refrigerator, an apartment-sized stove in black, an old white porcelain sink, and two feet of counter space. There were pots and pans everywhere, and a big baking dish full of golden lasagna on top of the range.

"Sit. Sit," Francesca commanded, pointing me toward the picnic table.

I followed Marco onto a bench as his mother set out the lasagna along with a long basket of crusty bread, already sliced. Gina took a seat directly opposite me, where she watched me as her mother poured red wine into our glasses and dished out the lasagna — big, hearty slabs dripping with tomato sauce and melted cheese. Francesca took a piece for herself, then sat down, bowing her head for a moment to say a silent prayer. We followed suit; then she raised her glass and we did that, too.

"Buon appetito," she said merrily.

Marco, Gina, and I repeated her toast; then I put down my glass and reached for my fork, so eager to taste the lasagna that I was nearly drooling in anticipation.

"And here's to you clearing my son's good name, eh, Abby?"

My hand halted in midair. They *knew?* I'd thought the pressure was high before. Now it was ten times worse. The lasagna suddenly didn't look so appetizing.

"Let's not spoil the meal, Mama," Marco said, giving her a frown. *Too late,* I thought.

"I can't wish her good luck? What kind of world is this?"

As she and Gina raised their glasses to me, I quickly ditched the utensil and raised mine, too. I could feel Marco tense beside me, so I said, "Thank you for sharing your dinner with me, Mrs. Salvare. Everything smells wonderful."

"Wait till you taste it. *Mangia!* Eat, eat."

Before I'd wanted to shovel in that pasta. Now I had to force myself to take a small mouthful. But as the taste sensations melted over my tongue — tomato, basil, oregano, onion, garlic, and, oh, those Italian cheeses — my appetite came back. "Oh, wow. This is" — I swallowed the first bite and readied another — "heavenly."

"I'm so pleased you like it, Abby," she said.

"Like it? I love it. I've never had lasagna this delicious."

"I'll give you the recipe. It's easy once you know how."

"Maybe she doesn't cook, Mama," Gina said. "Not everyone is like us, you know. Do you cook, Abby?"

"When I have time." Which was never.

"Have some more wine," Francesca said, filling my glass to the brim. "It's a Barolo, my favorite."

I had no problem with that, especially given the pressure I was under.

Suddenly Gina's eyes got wide and her skin turned ashen. She nudged her mother, who immediately slid off the bench and let her dash to the bathroom.

Without missing a beat Marco said, "She'd better not be contagious."

"Your sister is not sick," Francesca said. "We were going to wait until after dessert, but I'd better tell you now so you don't worry. Gina went to the doctor today. She's going to have a baby!"

Thank heavens *that* wasn't contagious.

"Is she happy about it?" Marco asked, probably because of the marital trouble Gina had been having.

"What kind of question is that? Of course she's happy," Francesca said, ignoring the sound of Gina being sick in the background. "Now little Christopher will have a brother or sister." With a wink, she leaned toward her son. "You'll have to hurry if you're going to catch up with her, eh, Marco?"

He didn't answer, but he did look slightly green around the gills.

Francesca reached for the wine bottle to top off our glasses. "I've decided to throw Gina a baby shower before I go back home. We can have it a week from Sunday, at your bar. Just a small, family affair. It is her second baby. Abby, we should have table decorations from your flower shop. You and I will have to meet soon and decide what to use, eh?"

Poor Marco. If he turned any greener, he'd croak.

CHAPTER
TWENTY-ONE

An hour and a half later, with my stomach pouched out from all the food and my mind a bit on the fuzzy side from the wine, I stumbled out to Marco's car and let him help me tackle that door handle, which was proving difficult to work.

"I'll take you home," he told me, buckling the seat belt, elusive devil that it was. "You're in no condition to drive."

"And you, kind sir? What condition are you in?" I lifted my eyebrows suggestively. At least I think I did, but they seemed to be moving independently of my wishes.

"That wine really got to you, didn't it?"

"You can't take me all the way home. What about my car? I don't want to leave it in the public parking lot all night."

"I'll take care of it."

Aw. My fearless knight, coming to my rescue, just like old times. I giggled as it occurred to me that both of us were knights, only mine was spelled with a big *K*.

"What's so funny?"

"You have a small *k*." I dissolved into a puddle of laughter.

"I don't even want to know what that means."

I wiped the moisture from my eyes, growing pensive. "I'm glad you invited me tonight. I was beginning to think you didn't want me to meet your mother."

"She can come on a little strong. Thanks for being a good sport."

"I loved her lasagna, and her bread, and the wine." With a contented sigh, I leaned my head against the headrest. "Wasn't that sweet of her to ask me to do the flowers for Gina's baby shower? She could have asked anybody, but she asked me. I feel so honored. I really love your mom."

"You don't have a clue what you're getting yourself into, do you?"

"Don't be such a stick-in-the-mud. It'll be fun."

"Have you ever seen the movie *My Big Fat Greek Wedding*?"

"I loved that movie." At that moment I loved the world. I was feeling quite expansive.

"Sunshine, my family could *be* that movie — the Italian American version."

I pointed a finger at Marco — the Marco on the left. I didn't like the way his twin on the right was leering at me. "The way I see it, if you can handle my family, I can handle yours."

"Now I know you're blitzed."

My eyes kept closing on the ride home, so we seemed to get there with amazing speed. Marco helped me out of the car and into the apartment building; then we stood in front of the old elevator until I remembered it was out of order. Nice of the superintendent to put up a sign. We took the stairs — even though they were leaning dangerously to one side and I had to brace a hand against the wall to keep from falling against it. Eventually, though, we made it to the second floor. I'd have to call the super about those steps in the morning. Someone could get hurt.

Though it tried to elude me by hiding under my wallet, I found my key but couldn't manage to slip it into the lock. "You know, they just don't make things like they used to."

"There's nothing wrong with your lock." Marco opened the door, then stood back to let me enter. Simon sat just inside, his long white tail sweeping the floor, his pointed ears forward in a *hello, how are you? Now feed me* pose.

I stooped to give him a pat on the head, but he sniffed the air, then backed away from me as though I were a rancid dish of cat food. "Fine. Be that way." I rose unsteadily. "So what are you saying, Marco? That I can't work a simple lock because of a mere two glasses of wine?"

He laughed. "Two? My mother refilled your glass at least three times. She probably would have given you more, but I cut you off."

"Why would she want to get me sloshed?"

"She was testing you to see how good you are at holding your liquor. The more you can hold, the lower your score."

"Marco, I stink at tests. Did I ever tell you how many tests I flunked in law school?"

"Don't worry about it. You passed this one."

"That's a first." My knees began to go numb, so I leaned against the nearest source of support, which, happily, turned out to be Marco. I gazed up into his incredibly handsome face and felt my heart expand twofold. "Did I tell you how much I love your mother?"

"Yes, Sunshine, you did."

"And did I tell you how much I love *you?*" *Whoa. Had I said that out loud?*

He swept me into his arms just as the floor began to suck me down. "Good timing," I said, laying my head on his shoulder as he carried me into my bedroom and deposited me gently on the bed. I lifted my head and patted the spot next to me. "Room for two, mister."

He covered me with the bottom half of the bedspread. "I think I'll take a rain check on that."

"Why? The night is young."

"You need to sleep off that buzz, and I need to check on things at Down the Hatch anyway. Want anything before I go? Water? Antacid? A bucket?"

I tried to form my lips into a pucker, but they'd obviously been talking to my eyebrows. "How about a kiss . . . and maybe a glass of water?"

"I'll be right back with the water."

"Don't forget the kiss." I closed my eyes and smiled. A kiss from my knight. What else could a maiden ask for?

Then my stomach did a full rotation, followed by a somersault, then a few lurches, and suddenly that bucket sounded mighty good. I rolled off the bed and stumbled toward the hallway, using the door jamb for support as I catapulted myself into the bathroom. I gave the door a shove and just made it to my knees in front of the commode before my gut heaved. Then I sat back on my knees while the room swam around me.

"Abby?" Marco rapped on the door. "You okay?"

My voice came out as a croak. "I'll be fine." In a few weeks, perhaps — if I was lucky.

"Need any help?"

And have him see me like this? "No, thanks. I'm just going to rest here a while."

"I put your water on the nightstand. Call me tomorrow, okay?"

"Okay." I crawled to the sink, felt for the faucet, got a palm full of cold water, and splashed it over my face. Then I curled up next to the tub, regretting every sip of wine I'd ever had, and finally fell asleep with the terry cloth bath mat rolled under my head.

Only a moment later, or so it felt, Nikki shook my shoulder. "Abby, are you sick or drunk?"

"Neither. Well, maybe both."

"Tell me you didn't drive home."

"Marco brought me. He's my knight with a small *k*."

"How did your car get back to the parking lot?"

"Marco said he'd bring it. Guess what,

Nik? He finally invited me over to his apartment. And I got to meet his mother and eat her lasagna, and meet his sister Gina and be interrogated. She made this big Italian meal, Nikki. His mother, not his sister, because Gina was sick. Well, not sick so much as pregnant. Anyway, this lasagna was the best I've ever had in my life, with lots of crusty bread and wine and . . . Okay, I can't think about it anymore or I'll puke."

"Want me to help you back to bed?"

I closed my eyes and felt myself drifting off to sleep. "No need. I'm comfortable right where I am."

"You're going to regret that decision in the morning."

"I have few regrets in this life, Nikki."

"Now you sound like Grace. Good night."

The morning sun was streaming through the tiny bathroom window when I opened my eyes again. I squinted and saw Nikki's pointy blond head peering down at me. "Are you still here?" I croaked.

"No. I was in bed, sound asleep, but Lottie called and woke me up. She wants you to phone her at the shop right away."

I tried to bring Nikki's face into focus but the bright light hurt my eyes. In fact, blinking hurt my eyes, and every muscle in my body hurt, but maybe that was from sleeping on a hard floor. "Did she say why she wanted me to call?"

"No."

"What time is it?"

"Nine o'clock in the morning." Nikki perched on the toilet as I pushed myself to a sitting position. "You had quite an evening, didn't you?"

"You'll never guess what Mrs. Salvare was like. A sixty-year-old Sophia Loren."

"Honest?"

I leaned my back against the tub, holding my aching skull between my hands. "She was gorgeous and friendly and the best cook ever — and she liked my womanly figure."

"Ew. She didn't really say that, did she?"

"Yes, she really did. She also asked how much I weighed."

"You didn't tell her, did you?"

"Of course not. But she seemed to like me anyway."

"I'm sure that made Marco happy."

"I guess so, although he wasn't too pleased that she kept refilling my wineglass. He said she was testing me. The good news is that I passed her test. You want to know why? Because I can't hold my liquor. How great is that?"

"Wonderful." She rolled her eyes. "I hope

you didn't puke in front of her."

"I was fine until the ride home. I have a vague recollection of being carried to my bedroom . . ." I gasped as I remembered more details of the evening. "Oh, no! I think I told Marco I loved him."

"So?"

"You know that's the kiss of death to a budding relationship. What should I do?"

"Nothing. He'll know it was the wine talking."

"Will he, Nikki?" I clasped her wrist. "Will he?"

She peeled off my fingers and gave me a glass of ginger ale to sip. "You'd better call Lottie."

I took one sniff of the contents and set the glass on the floor as my stomach threatened a revolt. "I have a feeling this is going to be a bad, bad day."

I called Bloomers, and Lottie answered on the first ring. As soon as she heard my voice she said, "Now, there's nothing to panic about, sweetie. We've got a water leak. A pipe burst under the kitchen floor and ran down into the basement. I've got a plumber on the way."

I sagged in relief "Okay. That's not so bad."

"Well . . ."

Whenever someone started a sentence with *Well . . .*, there was no way the rest of it could be good. "There's more?"

"You know the boxes we put in the basement yesterday?"

I swallowed. "The frames and fans?"

"They're soaking wet."

I fell back on the bed with a moan. I should have known I'd be punished for putting those things in the basement. "Okay, Lottie. I'll be in as soon as I shower and have breakfast — wait, never mind the breakfast. I'll figure out something to do in the meantime."

"You'd better think fast. Today is Thursday, and you know what that means."

Yikes. On Thursdays, Mom usually dropped by the flower shop. My day of reckoning had arrived. I let the phone fall onto the bedspread.

"What happened?" Nikki asked.

"A water pipe burst and what was left of Mom's feathered artwork got soaked. What kind of daughter hides her mother's art in a basement? What was I thinking? And she's due to stop by the shop today. Do me a favor. Hold the pillow over my face and end my misery."

"Can't you dry everything before she gets

there? Here's an idea. Put them on the roof. It's so hot you could bake a cake up there."

I lay still a moment, considering her suggestion. We did have a flat roof, and the sun was out . . . "That might work. I can spread everything out and let the sun do the job for me. Nikki, you're a genius. I love you."

"I think you've maxed out that expression, don't you?"

As Marco had promised, my Corvette was parked in its reserved space in the apartment's lot. I phoned to thank him and got his cell, so I left a message that I was alive and would talk to him when I felt human again. I phoned Dave Hammond next, but he wasn't in his office, so I left a message asking whether he had any more information, anything at all. I had to get moving on the investigation. It was Thursday already, and I hadn't made any real progress. Luckily, I had a license plate number and the photos of Violet and Lily, so at least I had something to work on.

I made it to the shop a little after ten o'clock to find a plumber's van parked out front and Grace in the parlor making coffee. I held up a hand in greeting and kept going, not wanting her to see my bloodshot eyes and start asking questions. I made my way down the old wooden steps, trying not to put my hand on the crumbling cement wall or breathe stale, damp air for fear of upsetting my stomach even more. At the bottom I found Lottie mopping the floor while the plumber repaired the pipe from his ladder.

"He's almost done," she told me, then came toward me for a closer look and shook her head. "You took on a snoot full last night, didn't you?"

I felt my stomach prepare to launch a new attack, so I said quickly, "Marco's mother made dinner for us and she was a little too free with the wine. I can't think about it or I'll puke. Where are the boxes?"

Lottie led me toward the opposite end of the basement. I opened the nearest box and removed one of the frames, holding it up to the bare yellow lightbulb dangling overhead. The feathers were shriveled and damp, their dye leached into the cloth that covered the wood beneath. The fans had simply disintegrated.

Lottie held up another frame. "It's not too bad, is it?"

"You've got to be kidding."

She put it back in the box and pushed up her sleeves with a sigh. "Well, there's always the Dumpster in the alley."

"I have a better idea. The fans are a total loss, but let's take the frames up to the roof and put them in the sun. With any luck, they'll dry back to their original fluffiness and be fine."

"It can't hurt to try."

We lugged the box upstairs, through the shop, and to a door that led up a stairwell to the second-floor apartments. At the end of that hallway another set of stairs led to the unused third floor, where a door at the back opened onto a flat, rubber roofed area.

"This used to be the patio of the penthouse apartment," Lottie told me.

A penthouse apartment overlooking an alley in downtown New Chapel. Not exactly a Central Park view. We spread the frames over the warm rubber coating, then shut the door on the whole ugly mess and hoped for the best.

Back in the shop, I made myself a cold compress and held it to my forehead, which felt as though someone had pumped about two hundred pounds of pillow stuffing into it. Then I sat down at my desk, dug out the piece of paper with the license plate number on it, and was just about to pick up the phone to call Eileen at the DMV when Grace sailed in with a phone order for the spindle.

"Headache, dear?"

I nodded.

She tilted my face toward hers. "Good heavens. Lottie, you shouldn't have made Abby carry that big box all the way to the roof. Now she's burst blood vessels in her eyes." She bent closer. "That *is* what caused the redness, isn't it?"

Why had I thought I could slip my hangover past her? "I had too much wine last night."

"Wait. I want to hear this again," Lottie said, hurrying in from the kitchen.

With a resigned sigh, I told them all about Marco's mother and her little test and his sister and her cross-examination. I braced myself for Grace's lecture, but instead she merely said, "Lottie, do we have eggs in the refrigerator?"

"Last time I checked," Lottie replied.

I felt my stomach shift. "Eggs?"

"Yes, dear. It's the perfect antidote. Three raw eggs stirred into —"

"Stop! Don't say another word. I just need to let my stomach settle; then I'll be fine. Now, if you don't mind, I have a phone call to make."

"Perhaps some ginger tea, then," Grace said, and sailed out of the room. Lottie rolled her eyes and went back to the kitchen.

I dialed the DMV and patiently punched my way through the menu. This time it took only two minutes to reach a live person, who connected me to Eileen without a problem.

"Hi, Eileen, this is Abby Knight again. Remember that white Mustang I asked you about? I was able to get a license plate number on it. Can I trouble you to run it for me?"

"Sure. Go ahead."

I read the numbers and waited while she checked. In a sympathetic tone she asked, "How is Marco doing?"

Oh, right. She was the president of his fan club. "Well, Eileen, to be truthful, he's hoping you'll be able to get this information for me quickly." That was called a subtle hint.

"The computers here are really slow. Okay, here it comes. Hmm. This is odd. The car is registered to a person named Violet. No last name. Who does she think she is, Cher?"

Eileen chortled at her joke, so I had to laugh with her just to be polite. "Can you give me the address, too?"

"I'm not allowed to do that."

"But," I prompted, "since it's for Marco?"

There was a long pause, then a sigh. "Okay, since it's for Marco."

I wrote as she whispered it to me. "Bless you, Eileen. He'll be so grateful."

"Give him a big hug from me, okay?"

I'd gladly hug Marco — but I might not tell him where it came from.

The business line rang and I heard Lottie answer it from the front. In a moment, she stuck her head through the curtain to tell me Eve Taylor was on the line. I punched the flashing button and answered as cheerfully as my throbbing head would allow. "Hello, Mrs. Taylor."

"I hope I'm not bothering you, Abby, but I wath wondering if you'd learned anything."

"No, but I have a new lead I'm going to follow up on today, so maybe I'll have some news for you later." Not to mention a few questions for her, such as whether she had a key to Ryson's house. I leaned down to pull the photos from my purse, lining them up in front of me. "By the way, did Dennis ever mention a woman named Violet?"

"That doethn't thound familiar at all."

"How about Lily?"

"Thorry. Not that one either."

Lottie came through the curtain again, signaling that she needed to talk to me, so I promised Eve I'd get back to her and hung up. "Sweetie, there's a cop here to see you and he sure as heck isn't what you'd call the warm, fuzzy type."

"Did you get a name?"

"Martin Kellerman."

CHAPTER
TWENTY-TWO

Yikes! Had Kellerman gotten wind of my investigation? *Calm down, Abby. Don't jump to conclusions. Maybe he came to order flowers for his wife.* Right. So why was I stuffing the photos in my desk drawer?

I *knew* this was going to be a bad day.

"Are you all right, sweetie?" Lottie asked. "You're shaking like a leaf. Is it because of that cop out there? You want me to tell him to take a flying leap off the nearest cliff?"

We didn't have any cliffs in New Chapel, but even if we did, I couldn't have Lottie tossing people off them to protect me. I had to think of Kellerman as just another bully to be faced. "Thanks, Lottie, but I'll be fine."

"You just say the word, and I'll knock him from here to tomorrow."

We did have tomorrows, but my answer was still no. I explained why.

"Abby," Grace said, coming through the

curtain, "that bobby up front is becoming quite tiresome. Shall I send him away, then?"

I glanced at Lottie. "A little help here?"

Lottie motioned for Grace to come closer so she could fill her in, while I straightened my shoulders and strode through the curtain like a woman of purpose. Kellerman was standing stiffly by the bay window in his police uniform, watching me with cold, calculating eyes. He was sturdily built, with thinning brown hair combed straight back, small, bland features, a weak chin, and a face that was as rigid as a block of wood. Until I was face to face with the man — well, actually face to somewhere just above his belt buckle — I hadn't realized how tall he was.

You can do this, Abby. He's just a very tall bully. Face him bravely and he'll back off. I walked around behind the counter, putting some distance between us. "What can I do for you, Officer?"

He tapped the two bars on his shoulder. "Captain."

"Captain. Sorry." I tamped down a tiny spark of irritation and pasted on a polite smile.

He nodded toward the coffee parlor. "Let's have a seat inside."

"Good idea." It always helped to act like I was in control. I started to lead the way to a table by the window, but he passed me and headed for the corner, as Reilly had done. He pulled out a chair for me, then one for himself across from me.

"I'm a busy man, so I'll get straight to the point. I understand you've been snooping around in the Ryson case."

My face instantly grew warm. I tried to look amused by the whole idea. "I wouldn't call it snooping. I might have asked around a bit, but —"

He pointed an index finger at my nose. "Don't fence with me, Miss Knight. You were in law school long enough to know what the terms *obstruction* and *interfering in police business* mean."

In school *long enough?* Ouch. So he'd checked my background. And now he was making threats, too. Was I supposed to be frightened? Because that's not the effect he was having on me. In fact, I was so ready to let loose with a sharp retort that I had to take a deep breath and go to a happy place in my mind. The last thing I wanted was to enrage this man and make it even worse for Marco.

"I promise you, Captain, I haven't obstructed anything. All I've done is ask a few questions. A few harmless questions."

He leaned toward me, his mouth a line of steel, his eyes like flint. "You listen carefully because I don't want to have to come back. You just hunker down in your shop here and let the police do the investigating. Got it?"

I *so* wanted to tell him what to do with it. "Yes, sir. I have it," I said crisply. "So I take that to mean you're still investigating? Because I had the impression that the investigation was closed."

His eyes bored into mine. "Don't get cute with me. I'll be watching you." He marched out without another word. As soon as I heard the bell jingle, I sagged onto the tabletop, my alcohol-induced headache hammering away at my temples.

"I'll get tea," Grace said, and hurried to the back counter, while Lottie parked herself in the chair Kellerman had just vacated.

"What a jackass!" she said, then patted my arm. "You said the right things, Abby. You did yourself proud."

"You were wise not to attempt to argue with him," Grace said, placing a cup and saucer and a steaming teapot in front of me. "If I may share a quote from William G. McAdoo . . ."

As if there was any way to stop her.

She cleared her throat, holding her cardigan as if it had lapels. " 'It is impossible to defeat an ignorant man in argument.' "

Lottie clapped, but I refrained. My head couldn't handle the motion. "Thanks, Grace."

The phone rang, and Lottie jumped up to answer it in the shop while Grace filled my cup with fragrant ginger tea. "This should calm you."

I took a long, slow sip and felt the soothing brew slide down my throat. How dare Kellerman threaten me! If I wanted to pay a visit to certain people and happened to ask a few questions while I was there, what harm was that? I had my rights. Sure I knew the law, but I wasn't obstructing anyone or interfering with the police. I was just being, well, nosy. There was no law against nosiness.

I took another drink of tea. How about that? It was working. I could feel my energy returning, and that little drummer boy in my head had finally packed up his tom-toms.

Lottie came to the doorway. "Marco's on the line."

The tom-toms started up again. I finished the tea and pushed to my feet. "I'll take it at my desk."

"Are you going to tell him about Kellerman's visit?"

"Not on your life. He's worried enough as it is." I went to the workroom and picked up the phone, trying to put on a cheerful voice for the second time that morning. "Good morning."

"Hey, Sunshine, how are you feeling?"

"Don't ever let me drink more than a glass of wine at one meal, okay? Well, maybe one and a half. Okay, two. But no more than two. And thanks for bringing me and my Vette home. We both appreciate it."

"It was the least I could do. Not many guys can say their mothers got their girlfriends drunk."

I couldn't say I felt really special about that.

"Any word from Dave?" he asked hopefully.

"I haven't had a chance to call him."

"You sound tense."

I hated keeping things from him, especially when I'd just scolded him about doing it to me. "A pipe burst in the basement this morning, but we got it fixed. Listen, Marco, I'm sorry to cut this short but I need to get back to work. We're totally swamped this morning. I'll check in later."

I riffled the orders on the spindle and counted a whopping five. At least now I had time to work on the case. I took the photos out of my desk drawer and set them beside my purse so I wouldn't forget them.

"Anyone I know?" Lottie asked, peering over my shoulder. Grace came hurrying in to see them, too.

"Violet and Lily, two clowns from Ryson's troupe. I'm hoping his neighbors can identify one of them as the mystery girlfriend. It's a very thin lead, but at this point I'll try anything. Would either of you mind if I left for about an hour?"

"Of course not, dear," Grace said. "But please be careful. You don't want that nasty police captain to see you snooping."

"And be back by noon," Lottie added as I stepped into the cooler to gather a bouquet of purple lilies and yellow button mums. "I'm not facing your mother alone."

With the photos in my purse and the wrapped bouquet under my arm, I headed out the back door, in case Kellerman was watching. Ten minutes later, after circling the block several times to make sure I wasn't being followed, I parked a few doors down from Ryson's house and hurried up the street to knock on Trina's door. While I waited, I turned to glance at the Mazella house and at once the drape in the front window rippled. I knew Eudora was watching, so I lifted my hand in a friendly greeting. No sense pretending I hadn't seen her.

The door opened behind me and I turned to find Trina carrying the same curly-headed tot on her hip as the first time I met her. His nose was still running, too.

"What do you want now?" Trina snapped.

I waved the photos in front of me. "I'd like you to look at these to see if you recognize either of the women in them."

With a sharp sigh, she put the toddler down, then stepped outside. I handed her the photos; she studied them for a moment, then tapped a long fingernail against one of them. "That's the woman I saw getting into that rusty white car."

"Are you sure it's the same woman?"

Trina rolled her eyes as if I were an idiot. "Yes, I'm sure. I saw her coming out of Ryson's house at least twice."

"Did you see that car in the neighborhood Sunday evening?"

"No. But if you'll remember, I was gone by seven thirty. Why don't you ask Eudora? She sees everything. Now, if you don't mind, I have a houseful of sick kids." She opened the door to go inside and the toddler waiting there sneezed, showering her with slime.

"Gross," I said with a shudder.

"Welcome to my world." Scowling at me, Trina shut the door.

Yet another reason I was happy being single. "Thanks for your help," I called.

Checking to make sure there was no sign of a squad car or Ed's tow truck in sight, I crossed the street and slipped up the Mazellas' driveway to the back of the house, where I noticed that their big, wooden garage door was open. Wide open. As in, an *open* invitation to look inside.

The garage was tidy and organized, with big boxes labeled with their contents, a rack of tools hanging along the back wall, and a stack of lumber underneath — two-by-fours, two-by-twos, and one-by-threes. Hmm. Any one of those would make a handy weapon.

"Mrs. Mazella?" I called, knocking on the back door. "It's Abby Knight from Bloomers. I brought photos for you to see. I'd really appreciate it if you'd take a look at them."

"Are they clean?" came her muffled voice.

Not that again. "They're clean."

"Hold them up to the glass in the door."

I selected one photo of Lily and one of

Violet, then pressed them against the pane.

After a moment she said, "Yin, yang."

"Excuse me?"

"Yin, yang."

Whatever. "Have you seen either of these women before?"

"Yin."

"You saw Yin? Which one is Yin?"

"His aura is confused."

His aura? She had to mean Violet, but how did she know Violet was a man? Was that what she'd meant by *yin, yang?* I took the photos down and looked at them. They were clear pictures, but still, would I have picked up on Violet's disguise? No way.

Maybe there *was* something to this spirit stuff. "Did you see Yin visit Dennis — I mean Sinned?" I called.

"Yes."

We were off to a good start. "Did you see him Sunday evening?"

"No."

"Did you see a rusty white Ford Mustang?"

"Not on Sunday."

That didn't mean Violet couldn't have parked around the corner. "Mrs. Mazella, was that pile of lumber in your garage on Sunday?"

Silence.

"Mrs. Mazella?"

"You must leave now."

"Okay, but first can you answer my question?"

"Now!" she cried. "Go!"

What was the rush? "I'm going. I'm sorry if I upset you."

At once she began chanting, and I could hear her stomping her feet as though she were performing a dance. A moment later Ed's black truck came roaring up the driveway.

It wasn't even close to five o'clock. What was Ed doing home?

CHAPTER
TWENTY-THREE

He got out of his truck, slammed his door, stuck a cigar in his mouth, and barreled toward me, his thick hands curled into fists at his sides. I froze, not sure whether to face him or run. Gazing at those huge hands, I was leaning in favor of running.

"What the hell are you doing here?" he bellowed.

Holding the photos out for him to see, I took a step backward, forcing myself to say through chattering teeth, "I c-came to see if your w-wife recognized the women in these pictures."

He slapped the photos out of my hand, and I drew back, fearing I'd be next. "This is the second time you've come to my house and, damn it, I told you to see me at work if you had any questions. Now, what part of that didn't you understand?"

"The thing is, Mr. Mazella, I had to talk to Trina anyway, and since I was right here in the neighborhood, I thought I'd just pop over to see if your wife could help me out."

"Pop yourself back in yer damn car and get yer ass off my property or I'll call the cops and have you hauled outta here."

He would, too, and I surely didn't want another visit from Kellerman. I swept up the pictures and stuffed them in my purse. "Okay. No need to call the cops. I'm very sorry for bothering your wife."

Then I fled.

Once I was safely inside the Vette with the doors locked, I thought over Eudora's frantic reaction when I asked about the wood. Had she freaked out because she knew it was the murder weapon, or because she knew Ed was about to arrive home? Hmm. Maybe I needed to get a piece of that wood. Maybe I could wait until Ed left, then sneak back and . . .

Suddenly, I heard a diesel engine rev and glanced in my rearview mirror just as the big truck came roaring up behind the Vette, yellow emergency lights flashing, headlights blinking on and off. I scrunched my eyes shut and held my breath, waiting for the crash. When I opened my eyes again, his truck completely filled the mirror and he was standing beside my window. He made a circling motion with his hand.

Roll down the window? I shook my head and gave him a scowl. "No way."

He glanced around as if to make sure no one was watching, then he bent down. "I ain't gonna hurt you. I just wanna talk to you."

"Talk through the glass."

"I just wanna explain somethin' " — he glanced around again — "about my wife."

I pulled out my cell phone, flipped it open, and showed it to him. "If you try anything, I've got my finger on the button to call the cops."

"I ain't gonna do nothin' but talk."

I rolled down the glass two inches. "Go ahead."

Ed rubbed his balding scalp, as though searching for the right thing to say. "Look here, I shouldn't have scared you like I did, but you gotta understand something about Eudora. She's — well — she ain't right in the head these days. She hears voices and sees ghosts . . ."

"Why are you telling me this?"

"Because you gotta understand that she makes up stories. You can't believe what she tells you. She's okay when she takes her nerve pills, see, but she stopped about a month ago because she said they made her feel dizzy. Trouble is, when she don't take them, she acts —" He made a circling motion with his index finger, pointing at his brain. "So I don't know what she told you, but you shouldn't pay no attention to it. It's crazy talk."

"She told me Dennis Ryson had an evil spirit that needed to be purged."

"That's what I mean. Crazy talk."

"But why would she say that unless he provoked her?"

"Because she's off her meds, like I said before."

I wasn't buying it. "I asked you this before, Mr. Mazella, but I don't think you told me the truth. Did Ryson ever threaten your wife or hurt her in any way?"

Ed's fists clenched at his sides again. "You calling me a liar?"

I checked to make sure my thumb was still on the Send button. "Why won't you answer my question?"

Waving me off like a bad smell, he turned and started for the truck.

"Mr. Mazella," I called. "I understand you're trying to protect your wife, but I'm trying to protect someone I care about, too."

Ed had his hand on the truck's door handle. He shifted the cigar to the other side of his mouth, as if he were considering what to do, then he came back. "You want to know about Ryson? Okay. He killed our little dog, that's what that sumbitch did. He had antifreeze sitting open in his garage and the little mutt got into it."

"When was this?"

"About a month ago. Eudora hasn't been the same since. My wife loved that dog — Daisy was her name. Cute little thing, too, a Boston terrier. We had her nine years. When we found her dead on the back stoop, Eudora grieved her like she'd lost a baby. And that pile of trash next door never even said he was sorry."

"Was that when she stopped her meds?"

"Yup, and then she started hearing the voices, and wearing that mask and bathrobe. We got those wooden masks twenty years ago, as souvenirs. Now she wears them to protect herself from ghosts. I tried to get her to go back to her doctor but she claims he's working for the devil, or some such nonsense. So I just leave her be. She wants to believe in her spirits? Fine by me. I go to work, I go to the VFW, I have some beers, I bowl, same as always."

"Maybe she needs to be hospitalized, Mr. Mazella."

"She was a good wife to me for thirty years. I can't lock her away with a bunch of loonies. I can't do that. So you leave her alone and don't come back here again. Eudora ain't up to no more questions. It's too upsettin' for her."

Ed stamped back to his truck, put it in gear, and pulled around the Vette, stopping next to my window. "You remember what I said, now. I'm tellin' you this for your own good. Stay away from her."

That sounded like a challenge to me.

My next stop was the Dunes Inn, a motel half an hour north of New Chapel on Route 20. I'd passed it many times on my way to Michigan but hadn't really paid attention to it. Now, as I pulled into the crumbling parking lot and looked around, I rechecked the address Eileen had given me.

The motel dated back to the 1950s, when the road was a major thoroughfare to Chicago. It consisted of a string of ten small rooms, with an office on the near end that had an ice machine and a soda dispenser out front. Each room had a dark green door with a brass number on it, and a picture window covered on the inside by a vinyl-backed drape.

Violet actually lived in this dump? Obviously she did, because there, in front of the door marked with a brass *3,* was the white Mustang.

I parked the car, tucked the wrapped bouquet under my arm, put my purse strap over my shoulder, then got out, wrinkling my nose at the odor of mildew and sour beer that greeted me. If Violet had told the truth about acting in a play, then she wouldn't have left for the theater yet. The New Chapel Opera House didn't open until one o'clock. (I knew this because a year ago, Grace had starred as Marian the Librarian in *The Music Man.*)

I paused outside the door and heard the drone of a television through the thin wall. Good. She was home. I lifted my hand to knock and suddenly heard a scream.

I rapped on the door. "Violet? Is everything okay?"

I heard another scream, long and agonized, so I tried to open the door, but it was locked. "I'll get help!" I cried, and dashed to the manager's office, where an overweight, middle-aged man in a red checked shirt and gray sweatpants sat behind an old wooden counter with his feet propped on a stool and his eyes glued to a small television.

"Someone is in trouble in room three," I panted, digging for my cell phone with my free hand.

His feet swung down, he grabbed a ring

of keys from a back wall, and he followed me as I sprinted for Violet's room, still hunting for my cell phone. Where was the darn thing?

I found the phone and flipped it open just as the manager inserted a key in the lock. I stopped to punch in 911, then followed him inside, where I saw a double bed, a ratty wooden table and two chairs, and a small TV on a Formica-topped credenza opposite the bed, but no Violet.

The manager glared at me, clearly perturbed. "There ain't no one here."

Then the scream came again and he bolted for the bathroom. I dropped the bouquet on the bed and followed as he swung open the door.

Inside, a naked man jerked around to gape at us. "What do you think you're doing?" he shrieked, grabbing a purple towel to cover himself.

He was so skinny his ribs stuck out, and his head was as bald as a lightbulb. He had one foot perched on the side of the small, rust-stained bathtub, and inside the tub, just visible over the rim, was Violet — or at least the top of her curly head.

"Perverts!" the man raged, turning toward us. "Get out of my bathroom this instant!"

His bathroom? Wait. Was he wearing eye

shadow? My gaze dropped to his hand, where I saw a long strip of hair-coated wax. On the floor beside the bathtub were several more. He was waxing his legs?

"This is nine-one-one," the operator said in my ear.

"Just a minute." I peered over the rim of the tub and there, at the bottom, on a white stand shaped like a human head, was a brown wig. I turned to gape at the man. "*You're* Violet?"

"You're on your own, toots," the manager said, and fled.

The naked man, who apparently *was* Violet — a very *angry* Violet — stamped a bare foot on the cracked linoleum floor. "I said *get out!*"

"I'm so sorry. I heard a scream and thought someone was hurt. I'll leave now." I backed through the doorway and pulled the door shut.

"This is nine-one-one. Hello?" the phone squawked in my ear.

"Never mind. False alarm." I gave the dispatch operator my cell phone number, explained the situation, and apologized profusely. Then, as I shut the phone and dropped it back in my purse, I glanced around the cheesy room and spotted the bouquet I'd dropped on the bedspread.

"Um, Violet? I have a flower delivery for you."

There was a long stretch of silence; then she said with reluctance, "Fine. Just a minute."

A few moments later she appeared in her wig and a purple satin bathrobe, looking exasperated yet curious. I held out the bouquet.

"Purple lilies — oh, they're my absolute favorites." She took them from me and immediately ripped away the paper. "I don't see a gift card."

"They're from Bloomers. From me, actually. I was hoping you'd answer some questions about Dennis Ryson."

"You have some nerve." She shoved the bouquet at me and fled back to the bathroom. "Go to hell."

"Wait, Violet," I said before she slammed the door. "I really think you should talk to me."

"What I should do is call the cops."

"You know what? That works for me. And when they get here, you can explain that broken stilt in your car."

"What are you talking about?"

"That piece of wood in your backseat. Did you know the police are looking for a murder weapon, possibly a long piece of wood?"

"And you think that broken stilt is it? Honey, you're crazier than I thought. I broke that stilt months ago. I use titanium now. They don't break." She sashayed to a narrow door against the back wall and opened it, where I could see dresses hanging on wire hangers, and shoe boxes on the floor. She reached inside, fished around in the back, and brought out a pair of long, brushed metal stilts. "This is what I use now."

"So you wouldn't mind giving me that broken end in your car to have the fibers tested?"

"I'll do better than that." She dug through the boxes again and produced the other end of the stilt. "I'll give you both pieces." She thrust it at me, then picked up a set of car keys and headed outside.

As I followed her to the Mustang I said, "What about your relationship with Dennis? Are you going to deny that you were seeing him?"

"What relationship are you talking about? We did a few clown gigs together."

"But you were seen visiting his house several times. His neighbors described your car and even identified you from a photo."

She laughed as she shoved away a mound of trash on her backseat and found the broken end. "I was at his house to teach Dennis how to ride a unicycle. We used his basement to practice. You want to call that a relationship? Honey, be my guest."

"Can you account for your whereabouts on Sunday night?"

"Who are you, Nancy Drew? I was at the theater. Check with the director if you don't believe me." She handed me the jagged piece, snatched the flowers from my hand, and flounced back into the motel.

Fine. I'd check with the director, but I wasn't going to believe her story until those stilt pieces had been analyzed. I placed the two ends in the trunk of my car, then got into the driver's seat and dug out my cell phone to call Dave Hammond.

"Hey, Dave," I said a moment later, "I have samples of wood that need to be tested for traces of blood and scalp. Who should I take them to?"

"It's too late for that, Abby," he replied dejectedly. "I got a lab report about an hour ago. The wood fibers in Ryson's scalp came from his coffee table."

"So no weapon was involved?"

"He was either pushed onto or fell onto the end of the table — and that may or may not have been the cause of his death. Ryson could have been dead before he *hit* the table. In any case, you've probably guessed what that means."

I rested my forehead on the steering wheel. Marco was still their man.

CHAPTER
TWENTY-FOUR

"We've got three and a half days before the grand jury meets, Dave, and the only suspects I have now are the couple who lived next door to Ryson — but I don't have a single way to link either one to the murder scene. Is there anything at all in that report that I can check out? Time of death? Ryson's health? Something?"

I heard him shuffle papers. "No, it's pretty much what I told you before, Abby."

I closed my eyes, wishing I was on a tropical island with an umbrella drink in my hand, sand under my feet, and Marco on the lounge beside me, instead of in my car in the parking lot of a seedy motel. What was I going to tell him? That he never should have trusted me? That I'd told him so? A lot of good that would do him. At the end of the day, I could go back to my flower shop. Marco was the one who would pay for my failure.

"Wait a minute," Dave said.

My head came up with a jerk. I pressed the phone tighter against my ear. "You found something?"

"This report says Ryson vomited shortly before he died. But here's the interesting part. It mentions pieces of undigested flower petals stuck to the front of his T-shirt."

"He vomited flower petals? What kind of flower petals?"

"Dark purple is all it says. We'll need the toxicology report for details."

I had a sudden vision of a cake with dark purple violets on it. Violets weren't toxic for most people, but for someone who was highly allergic and didn't know, they'd find out when it was too late. Could that have happened to Dennis Ryson?

I immediately saw a problem with that theory. Ryson had been eating Eve's cakes on a regular basis. Surely he'd encountered violets before . . . unless she'd added something to those particular flowers. What had she told me? *"With the crythtallithation protheth they'll latht up to a week, but mine latht longer becauthe I add thomething thpecial."*

Could that something have been poison? Did I have any reason to believe Eve would want to harm him? No, I didn't. But then something Reilly said popped into my mind. *"I don't remember any family members in that case."* Marco, too, had seemed surprised to learn about her existence. Where had she been when Ryson was arrested for robbery? Wouldn't an outraged mother have been somewhere in the picture? My antennae were up and quivering.

"Okay, Dave, bear with me a moment. The prosecutor is claiming that Ryson's death came as a result of a blow to the head that triggered his fall onto the coffee table, or that he was pushed against the table and hit his head, causing his death. Now the report says he vomited purple flowers. What if he fell because of what he ate, not from a blow to the head?"

"Are you talking about an allergic reaction?"

"Or a poisoning."

"Where did you come up with the poison angle?"

"It's a hunch. I'll tell you about it after I check it out. Do we know what Ryson ate before he died?"

"I don't see that on the inventory, so probably not."

"The detectives noticed that he vomited but didn't think to check his food supply?"

"They must have been satisfied that he

became nauseated as a result of the blow, but you're right. It should have been investigated."

"How long before you get the toxicology results?"

"Not soon enough to help our case. Two weeks, at least."

"Can you ask Darnell to stall the grand jury vote until we get the lab reports back?"

"Abby, come on. You know a grand jury is a prosecutor's tool. He convenes it when he wants an indictment, and right now Darnell has his sites set on Marco. The only way to get him to delay the vote is to have something credible to show him. A hunch isn't going to do it."

Damn. My forehead went back against the steering wheel. How else could I find out whether those flowers were toxic?

Wait a minute. Grace had been a nurse. She might know. I promised Dave I'd get back to him; then I quickly dialed Bloomers and told Grace the situation.

"We could always ring the hospital to see if they've admitted anyone for food poisoning in the past week," she said. "I'd be happy to make that call for you."

"Super. And would you also use your librarian skills to find out everything you can about Eve Ryson, aka Eve Taylor?"

"I'll get right on it."

Yes! The investigation was moving again, and I even had a plan. First up was a call to the Icing on the Cake bakery, where Sharona was kind enough to put me straight through to Eve.

"Hello, Abby," Eve said, as though pleasantly surprised. "Do you have newth for me?"

"Actually, there are a few things I'd like to review with you. Would you have time later this afternoon?"

"Oh, my heaventh, I have *tho* many caketh to do today. If you don't mind me working while you're here, why don't you thtop by at three o'clock?"

"I'll be there." I parked the Vette just off the town square and punched in Reilly's cell phone number as I headed toward the police station. "Hey, Reilly! How's the ultimate police sergeant doing today?"

"What do you want, Abby?" he said impatiently.

"I have to talk to you. I'm almost at the door of the station now, so if you can get away for just a few minutes —"

"I can't do that right now. Just tell me."

A squad car pulled up in front and a cop got out and strode toward the door, so I moved several yards away. "I have to get inside Ryson's house to check his refrigerator."

He laughed.

"I'm serious, Reilly. The grand jury convenes *Monday.* Will you at least hear me out?"

There was a pause. "Go ahead."

I glanced around to be sure no one was listening. "I've got this strong hunch that it wasn't the fight Ryson had with Marco that killed him. It was something he ate that caused him to black out and hit the table. If I'm correct, there should be a partially eaten cake in Ryson's refrigerator that has toxic flowers on it. And if that's true, Marco is off the hook. *That's* why I need to get inside Ryson's house."

In a whispered voice he said, "What do you expect me to do? Steal the key from the evidence box? What don't you understand about the word *illegal? Pension? Rules?* Give me a break."

"No, give *Marco* a break, Reilly — your buddy Marco, whose life is hanging in the balance." I paused, hoping that would trigger something, but all I heard was silence. "Okay, fine. Forget I asked. I don't need your help."

"What are you going to do?" he asked warily.

"Figure out a way to get inside. Of course, I could always use a helpful hint, such as if the screens are loose, or if there's a broken basement window, a spare key under the mat . . . I mean, you *have* been out to Ryson's house, after all."

I heard a muffled groan. "You're determined to do this, aren't you?"

"Like you really need to ask."

There was a long moment of silence, followed by a heavy sigh. "I knew I shouldn't have answered my phone. All right, listen carefully. I want you to *think* about what's in your purse."

He was giving me a hint. I used my free hand to grope inside my leather bag. "I have a set of keys . . . a pack of tissues . . . lip gloss . . . my wallet."

"Stop."

"My wallet?" I pulled it out and unzipped it. Nothing inside but a ten and a few singles, a Gap card, and my Mastercard. Hmm. A credit card? Was Reilly telling me to use the old plastic-card-in-the-latch trick? "If I'm *thinking* that Ryson's door locks are the cheap, flimsy kind, would I be right?"

"Now, how would I know that?"

That was a yes. "Okay, Sarge. I've got it. And just in case you want to help me *think* some more, I'll be using my *head* about nine o'clock this evening."

I snapped the phone shut, dropped it in my purse, and glanced around to see Captain Kellerman walk out the door. Talk about good timing. I gave him a polite nod and walked away, feeling his cold, snake-eyed glare on my back.

Who cared? My luck was finally on the upswing.

When I got back to the shop, Lottie gave me a phone message from my mother saying that she wouldn't be able to make it to the shop after all, but might be able to stop by before school on Friday. Whew! That would give me more time to dry the frames.

Even better, Grace had already completed her research and was waiting in the workroom to share it with me. "Not one person has been admitted to the hospital for food poisoning of any kind in the past two weeks," she reported. "I even added an extra week just to be on the safe side."

"So if Eve used something poisonous on Ryson's cake," I said, "we could safely say it wasn't used on her other cakes."

"Unless he was the only one to have a reaction to it," Lottie pointed out as she snipped stems for an arrangement.

"If the substance were that toxic, someone

else would have fallen gravely ill," Grace said. "It would be more likely that she used it on Dennis's cake alone."

"Then she must have done it by accident," Lottie said. "It just isn't natural for a mother to poison her own child."

"Ah, but Dennis *wasn't* her child," Grace said, arching her eyebrow. "Eve's husband had Dennis by his first wife. Interesting that she didn't mention she was his stepmother, isn't it?"

That was more than interesting. That was suspicious.

"She could have thought of him as her own child," Lottie said.

"I don't believe that feeling was reciprocated," Grace said. "A week ago Dennis filed a suit contesting his father's will. It seems the entirety of the considerable estate went to Eve. Dennis received nothing."

"Talk about someone having a motive," Lottie said, voicing my own thoughts.

"Wow," was all I could come up with.

"I, for one, can't begin to fathom why she isn't a suspect," Grace said. "The information was readily available if the detectives had bothered to check."

"It's all about votes, Grace," I said. "Melvin Darnell's not a fool. He went after a sure bet — Marco, who had a history with

Ryson *and* was at the murder scene. It doesn't get much easier than that. Can you imagine the public's reaction if the chief prosecutor had targeted a senior citizen who creates lovely cakes and looks like Mrs. Claus?"

Grace sniffed. "Mrs. Claus indeed. Lucrezia Borgia would be more like it."

"Lucrezia who?" Lottie asked.

"Borgia," Grace answered. "She was a devious, scheming woman."

Lottie clipped another stem. "Was she from New Chapel?"

Grace rolled her eyes and went for tea.

CHAPTER
TWENTY-FIVE

Marco called twice during the afternoon, once to my cell phone and once to the shop, but I didn't take either call. As I had explained to Lottie and Grace, the whole case now hinged on my poisoned-cake theory, but I couldn't bring myself to tell Marco for fear that I'd be proven wrong and his hopes would be dashed yet again.

Besides, if I told Marco how I planned to go about proving my theory, he'd try to stop me, or at the very least, he'd lecture me on the risks involved. I knew I could get caught and be charged with a crime. But I wasn't going to get caught. I was going to be Abby Knight, cat burglar — without the burgle part. So for today my motto had to be "What Marco didn't know wouldn't hurt him." In fact, as far as Lottie and Grace knew, I was going to meet Reilly at the house and he was going to get us inside legally.

The third time Marco called, he left a message on my voice mail. "Where the hell are you? Kellerman was just in the bar, nosing around like he suspects something is up. *Is* something up? Call me, damn it."

It rattled me that Kellerman was snooping around, but I was determined not to cave. So I erased the message and went back to the fall arrangement I had just begun. Using a hollowed-out gourd as the container, I filled it with reindeer moss, crocosmia, red hypericum berries, goldenrod (solidago), and an apricot rose variety called Rosemary Harkness. Quite fetching, I decided, after turning it around to inspect it from all angles.

The fourth time Marco called, Lottie answered the phone.

"Tell him I'm making deliveries," I whispered.

After she hung up she said, "You can't stall that man forever. He'll be heading down this way before long to see what's cooking."

"If he comes, I'll just dash out the back door."

I finished the arrangement, wrapped it, and set it in the cooler, then glanced at the clock on my desk. It was almost three o'clock — nearly time for my appointment with Eve, and a mere six hours before I made my cat burglar debut. I made sure Lottie and Grace were occupied up front, then got my credit card, slipped to the back, and tried to open the bathroom door with it.

"What are you doing?" Lottie asked, startling me. Grace was right behind her. How did they always know when I was trying to be sneaky?

"Um, just attempting to open a door with a credit card."

They came to peer over my shoulders. "Why?"

"Because I thought it would be a handy skill to have, you know, in case I ever forget my key."

"Good luck," Lottie said. "I tried it once when one of the boys locked us out. Herman ended up having to break a window. Now we just keep a key hidden outside."

"Let me have a go at it." Grace took the card from my hand, slid it expertly between the brass latch and the wood trim, and pushed open the door. I didn't even want to know how she had learned that. She handed me the card. "Why don't you try it now, dear?"

After two unsuccessful tries and a little

more help from Grace, I got the door to open.

"Bear in mind that it doesn't work with all locks. Let's try it on our back door." She led the way through the kitchen to the heavy fire escape door and showed me how the card wouldn't fit. "In this instance there's simply no way to get the card between the metal and the door frame. You'll have to try it on your door at home tonight. But why would you need to know this anyway? We have keys to Bloomers, and your roommate has a key to your apartment."

"But Nikki isn't always available. You know how it is being on duty at the hospital. I'd hate to sit around waiting for her to show up."

"Well, then, why not give your cousin Jillian a spare key. She lives just down the hall from you, doesn't she?"

"Grace, I just got my key *away* from her."

I could see her formulating more arguments, and since I was getting tired of making up excuses, I finally said, "I want to know how to do it for the fun of it, Grace. In fact, maybe I should learn how to pick a lock, too. I don't suppose you know how to do that, do you?"

"I absolutely draw the line at lock picking, dear."

It had been worth a shot.

At three o'clock I stepped inside the Icing on the Cake just as Sharona finished ringing up a customer. "Hey, sugar. What brings you down here? You after another of Evie's little cakes?"

"Actually, I came to see Mrs. Taylor."

"I don't know, baby. She's pretty swamped today."

"It'th all right, Sharona. I invited her." Eve Taylor stood in the doorway at the far end of the counter, smiling her warm Mrs. Claus smile, which I no longer found quite so charming. "Come, Abby, dear. Let's talk in the back. Sharona, is there any coffee left?"

"Sure is, Evie. Half a pot, only twenty minutes old."

"Good. Bring two cupth, pleathe."

I followed Eve through her spotless kitchen to her marble work counter, where she was putting finishing touches on a nine-layer wedding cake covered with pink frosting. The layers had been carefully sculpted to look like a spiral staircase winding to the top, with each step sprinkled with miniature rose petals and clover leaves, as though a tiny flower girl had tossed them from a basket on her way up. On the topmost layer, plastic figures of the bride and groom stood under an arbor of miniature rosebuds, their faces frozen into smiles of eternal bliss.

She placed a leaf on the frosting, then turned to beam at me as I settled onto a stool to watch. "What do you think of my latest creation?"

"Remarkable. I've never seen anything like it."

"Here you go, ladies," Sharona called, setting a small tray on the counter. On it were two cups of coffee, two demitasse spoons, a pitcher of cream, and a ceramic dish containing packages of sugar and sugar substitute.

"Thank you, Sharona," Eve called as her assistant left the kitchen. "Abby, you enjoy the coffee while I finish this wedding cake. My he019th, we've been busy today. Wouldn't you know Maxthine would have to leave early for a doctor'th appointment?"

Hmm. That left us conveniently alone in the kitchen, the perfect setup if someone wanted to slip poison into someone else's cup. I glanced at her pink-cheeked face as she poured cream into her coffee and stuffed in a packet of sugar. Was I sitting with a devious, scheming woman or a sweet little baker? To be on the safe side, I decided not to drink or eat anything unless she did first.

Eve glanced up at me with a hopeful smile. "You thaid on the phone you had new information?"

I doused my coffee with cream and added sugar, just as she'd done, debating on how best to get her to confess her crime. "Yes, I do have new information. First of all, Trina has a solid alibi for Sunday evening."

"Oh." She seemed disappointed.

"Also, I located the woman who I thought was Dennis's former girlfriend, but as it turns out, she had only been helping him with his clown act, and her alibi checked out, too."

"And Dennis's neighbors? The Mazellas?"

"Other than that they didn't get along with him, there's nothing to tie them to his death."

She looked smug as she sipped her coffee. "That leaves Mister Salvare, as I'd originally suspected." Smug was good. It was a sign of confidence, and when a person felt confident, she was more apt to give up information.

"By the way," I said casually, "did Dennis have any food allergies that you knew of?"

"I don't think so. Why?"

"I noticed something odd in a report from

the prosecutor's office. But before I go any further, are you okay discussing this? I know it must be painful — he was your *son,* after all."

"Painful doethn't begin to dethcribe my agony, but I need to clothe the door on thith. Tho, pleathe, go ahead."

Aha! Her deception continued. I knew I was on the right track now.

Eve held up a hand. "Wait. Before you go any further, I must clear up a mithunderthtanding. Dennis wasn't my son. He was my stepson."

I didn't have to try to look astonished. I *was* astonished. What did this sudden confession mean? That she knew I was suspicious?

She gave me a chagrined glance. "I'm thorry I didn't tell you earlier, Abby. I called him my thon becauthe I tried to think of him ath my own. And believe me, that wasn't easy. Dennis was always causing trouble, in and out of juvenile detention from the age of thirteen. He couldn't theem to help himself."

"Then how could you believe he was innocent of robbing the convenience store?"

"Dennith made hith thare of mithtaketh, but he wathn't a felon." Eve spotted a misshapen petal on one of the steps and plucked it off, dropping it in the waste can beside the counter with a look of disgust. "I detetht imperfections in my work, don't you?"

If she detested imperfections, how had she ever tolerated Dennis? Yet she seemed to have cared about him, bringing him cakes every week and clucking over his accomplishments as if he were a little boy. However, I still couldn't picture the bald, tattooed, pockmarked, snarling bully I'd seen in the newspaper photo as the *boy* she kept referring to.

"What wath in that report that made you athk about hith allergieth?" she asked.

Was that quick, sharp gleam in her eyes merely curiosity — or uneasiness? "It appears Dennis ate something that disagreed with him, causing nausea and possibly bringing about his death."

"Oh, heaventh!" She put down the tiny leaf in her hand.

"Did the cake you took Dennis on Saturday have purple flowers on it?"

There was a subtle change in her expression, almost like that of an animal that sensed it was about to be cornered. "I may have uthed a few violeth on the ithing — I uthe them all the time, ath you know — but they're perfectly harmless. Besides, Dennis was never bothered by the flowerth before."

"Did you use anything different in processing the flowers?"

"Abtholutely not. I've uthed the thame formula from day one."

"Then I guess we'll have to wait for the lab tests. By the way, do you have a key to Dennis's house?"

"No, why?"

"What did you do with the cake if he wasn't at home?"

Her eyes weren't twinkling now. "I took it back later, of courthe. You know, I find it puzzling that Captain Kellerman hathn't called to tell me about thith new development. Perhapth I should call *him*."

Yikes. That wouldn't be a good idea. "He's probably waiting for the lab results before he contacts you. After all, why would he bother you with something that hasn't been verified?" I held my breath, hoping she'd buy it.

She considered it for a moment. "I thuppothe you have a point. And now that I think back, Dennith *did* complain of a headache and queathy sthomach on Thaturday. Maybe it wath juth a cathe of the flu." She added another leaf to the cake, then stepped back to study it. "There. All done."

Whew. "Just one more question, Mrs. Taylor. Did Dennis file a lawsuit against you recently over his father's estate?"

She went utterly still. "How did you find out?"

"Word gets around. This *is* a small town." I didn't mention that the suit was also a matter of public record — if anyone cared to look.

Tears flooded her eyes. "He filed it juth latht week. I think he'd been planning to do it thince he wath releathed from prithon." She twisted around for a tissue to dab her eyes. "I thtill can't believe he turned againtht me. I wath a good mother to him and a devoted wife to hith father."

She balled up the tissue in one hand, her anger surfacing. "Douglath and I tried every way we knew to thtraighten him out, but Dennith alwayth got into more trouble. The latht thtraw wath when Dennith went to prison. Douglath wath tho furioth he cut the boy out of the will. I'm sure all that dithtreth brought about hith early death. And what gallth me ith that even though Dennith broke Douglath'th heart many times over, he refuthed to give up on hith thon. Even on hith deathbed he made me promith to alwayth be there for Dennith. And I tried; believe me, I tried."

She also got all of her husband's estate.

That must have made her pain easier to bear.

Eve raised red-rimmed eyes to mine. "When Dennith thowed up here two monthth ago, found a job, and got involved with that clown troupe, I truly believed that he'd changed. Then I received those papers stating he was going after the entire ethtate — the *entire* ethtate — claiming I had extherthithed undue influenthe on hith father! I had to hire a lawyer to fight him, and I don't have that kind of money.

"Do you know what lawyers charge these days, Abby? Do you know what it takes to start a business from scratch? I have two mortgages, and three employees to pay, and thupplies to buy. But what choice did I have? If I were to lose all of the estate, I'd have to sell my business."

That was one whopper of a motive. I wondered what else I could get her to reveal. "If someone tried to take Bloomers from me, I'd fight for it, too. But I don't think I would take him a bouquet of flowers."

"I don't thee your point."

"Dennis filed that lawsuit last week, yet you still took him a cake on Saturday."

She blushed uncomfortably. "I know it thoundth foolith, but I thought if I just kept treating him the thame ath I alwayth did, maybe he'd feel bad about hith actionth."

"You really believed Dennis would dismiss the suit because you brought him a cake?"

"There wath no harm in trying, wath there?"

Would a savvy businesswoman like Eve Taylor be that naive, or did she think I was?

She gazed straight at me, blinking innocently, yet behind that pale gaze I caught a glimpse of something hard and fiercely determined. This woman was prepared to fight tooth and nail to keep her bakery. The question was, would she kill for it? I crossed my fingers and hoped the answer was sitting in Ryson's refrigerator.

Out on the sidewalk, I turned my mobile phone back on — I'd shut it off so it wouldn't ring and disturb my conversation with Eve — and saw that Marco had tried to reach me again. I listened to his terse message and decided I should probably call him before he popped a blood vessel.

At his quick hello I said, "Hi, it's me. Sorry I didn't get back to you sooner. What a busy day. You know how that goes." *Yeah, like when you don't return* my *phone calls.*

Silence. Or was that faint staccato sound

him counting to ten? "Marco? Are you there?"

"I'm here — where I've been all day long."

"Like I said, I've been busy, busy."

A pause, then, "Anything new to report?"

Despite his annoyance, the hope in his voice rang loud and clear. I hated to disappoint him, but I was afraid to say anything that might jinx the case. All I could do was hint. "Nothing yet, but I have a strong hunch we're going to get a break soon. I'll keep you posted. Gotta go."

I glanced at the display on my phone before I closed the case. It was only three thirty. Nine o'clock couldn't come soon enough for me.

By four o'clock the shop had emptied out, all the pending orders had been finished, Lottie had gone on a delivery run, and Grace was on the computer at my desk, checking the availability of a new type of rose. I had just slipped into the parlor to get a cup of coffee when the bell over the door jingled and Francesca Salvare strolled into Bloomers.

"Mrs. Salvare," I called, hurrying to greet her. "What a nice surprise."

She was dressed in a white silk blouse and black slacks, with a yellow and black silk scarf at her neck and a black leather clutch under her arm. She took off her sunglasses and gazed around in delight. "I'd forgotten what a lovely flower shop this is. *Bella,* Abby."

She fingered the petals of an apricot-colored rose. "So you liked my lasagna?"

"It was the best I've ever eaten."

"And the wine?" She peered at me, probably to check the condition of my eyes. I'd kill Marco if he told her about the hangover.

As if on cue, Grace came through the curtain, hand extended in greeting. "Haloo! You must be Francesca Salvare. How nice to meet you. My name is Grace Bingham. Do come into the parlor for a cup of tea — or coffee, if you would prefer."

"Do you have espresso? Yes? *Bellisimo.* Abby, perhaps we can discuss flowers for Gina's baby shower, eh?"

Five minutes later, Francesca and I were seated at one of the white wrought-iron tables with cups of espresso and an album of baby shower arrangements.

"Very nice," she said, flipping through the pages. "Now, what is your plan to help my son?"

I nearly spilled my coffee. "My plan?"

"Marco told me you offered to help find the killer, and you know how a mother worries. So tell me, how are you going to help him?"

I gazed into those intelligent, deep-set eyes and knew she wouldn't be satisfied until she had answers. "Will you promise not to say a word to Marco?"

"If it will help my son, then yes. He will not hear it from my lips." She leaned forward on her elbows. "Now tell me everything."

So I did, over two cups of espresso. Then the bell jingled and suddenly I heard Grace exclaim, "Maureen! How nice to see you. Is school out already?"

Oh, no! My mom had come today after all — and her feathered frames were still on the roof.

CHAPTER
TWENTY-SIX

"I thought I'd drop by to see how everything is going," my mother said to Grace. "Is Abigail here? Oh, there she is. Hello, honey."

She waved at me through the doorway, so I lifted my hand to wave back.

Francesca turned for a look. "Is that your mama? Of course it is. You look just like her."

Right. Just like her — except for my eyes, hair, freckles, age, and height.

"You must be Abby's mother," Francesca said, jumping up and heading toward her. "What a pleasure to meet you."

By the time I got there — maybe ten seconds later? — the two mothers were chatting as though they had known each other forever.

"Now, Maureen," Francesca said, "you must help us decide on the flowers for my daughter's baby shower. And maybe you can recommend favors, as well."

"You need favors?" my mom exclaimed in delight. "I have just the thing. Abigail, would you get one of my picture frames?"

I cast a desperate glance at Grace, but she only shook her head at me as if say, *"The jig is up, kid,"* not that Grace would ever talk that way. With her, it would be more like, *"I do believe your goose is cooked."* Either way, I was toast.

"Abigail, the frames."

I took a deep breath. "Mom, there's something you should know. A pipe burst under the floor this morning and leaked into the basement —"

"Here we go!" Lottie called, scurrying into the room carrying a frame in each hand. Whereas before they were fluffy and shockingly bright, now the down was plastered onto the cloth beneath, and the bright dye had run, giving the frames the appearance of being covered in a textured, feather-patterned, watered silk. And they didn't look half bad.

My mother took one look at the frames and gasped in horror. "What happened?"

"Now, Mom, stay calm. They got a little wet, but they look good, don't they? Different — but good." I smiled hopefully, waiting for the obvious question of what the frames were doing in the basement in the first place.

Francesca held out a hand. "Let me see."

Lottie gave her a frame, then wiped perspiration from her upper lip. She must have come back from her delivery, seen my mom, and rushed up to the roof. I gave her a thumbs-up.

"You have more of these, yes?" Francesca asked.

My mother perked up. "Yes, we do . . . don't we, Abigail?"

"How many would you like?" I asked Marco's mom.

"Twenty would be a nice number."

"Done," I said.

Francesca smiled, which made my mother smile, which made Grace and Lottie and me smile. At least until she added, "And all of you must come to the shower."

"Won't that be fun, Abigail?" Mom said, linking arms with me.

My mind reeled at the thought of all that fun.

"Now I must leave you because there is much work to do," Francesca said. "Thank you for the coffee, and *ciao* to you all."

"I'll walk out with you," my mom said. "Abigail, we'll talk later." She gave me a look that told me I wasn't off the hook yet.

As soon as they were gone I hugged Lottie. "Thank you for getting those frames. I'm forever in your debt."

"Phooey," Lottie said. "It's not like I pulled you from a burning building."

I shuddered. "Please don't mention burning buildings."

At Grace's puzzled look, Lottie said to her, "When Abby was a little girl, her brothers volunteered her to be in a clown act at the circus." She held a hand to the side of her mouth to whisper, "It left scars."

"You're all grown up now, dear," Grace said. "It's time to move on."

That was exactly what I intended to do. I had an important evening ahead that I hadn't spent much time planning for and, frankly, breaking into someone's house was scary enough, without having to call up memories of being terrorized by freaky faces and burning buildings.

"Abby," Lottie said before I could get away, "that wrinkle in your forehead is back."

"Are you hiding something from us?" Grace asked, peering at me.

As if I could hide anything from those two for very long. Well, why not be honest? "Okay, I'll admit it. I have been keeping something from you. I'm going to become a cat burglar."

They glanced at each other. Then Grace said, "When you're ready to tell us the truth, dear, we'll be in the back."

Dressed in a long-sleeved black T-shirt, black jeans, black boots, and a black stocking cap, I parked my car a block away from Ryson's house, grabbed my black flashlight, and stole up the sidewalk, trying to stay away from the streetlights. The half-moon winked at me between passing clouds, the wind was still — and Reilly was nowhere in sight. I checked my watch. It was already ten minutes past nine. Damn. I was really hoping he'd show up.

The neighborhood was quiet, as though everyone had settled in for the night. Only a dog barked somewhere down the street. As I crept alongside the house I glanced at the Mazellas' and saw a sliver of light glimmering feebly from between the edges of a closed drape. Nothing rippled in the window. No sign of Eudora. I doubted she could have seen me anyway.

A lone maple shaded the back of Ryson's house. There were no shrubs along the foundation or near the garage, just a mixture of weeds scattered across hard, bare ground. The back door still had yellow crime scene tape across it, so I picked at a corner and slowly lifted it away from the wood, trying not to make a sound. I aimed my flashlight at the worn brass knob, relieved to see it was the kind sold at the local Ace Hardware for about ten bucks. On the off chance it was unlocked, I gave it a twist; then when that failed, I tapped softly on the door. Hollow and thin, just what I'd hoped to find. Cheap doors usually had cheap locks.

I reached into my pocket for my credit card and eased it in above the lock, between the latch and the flimsy wood frame. I slid it down until it pressed against the metal latch, then tried to maneuver the card over the latch.

It popped out. I rolled my shoulders to ease the growing knot of tension, then tried again, but it wouldn't budge. I glanced around. Where was Reilly?

Patience, Abby. I put the flashlight between my thighs, clamped my knees together to hold it steady, then guided the card along the front of the latch. Damn! It still wouldn't budge. My hands were perspiring, so I gripped the card with my teeth and wiped my palms down the front of my jeans.

Okay, here we go. Third time's the charm. I refocused the beam, inserted the card, and tried again. The plastic began to bend under the force of the pressure. "Please don't snap," I whispered to it.

Something moved behind me. I jerked my head around and lost my grip on the flashlight, and it fell to the cement stoop with a loud *thwack* and rolled away. I held my breath and listened, searching for shapes in the darkness. Was someone there?

Then came the scamper of feet across dry ground and a scrabble up rough bark. A tree branch rustled above me. The clouds parted, and the moonlight revealed the outline of a raccoon, its eyes shining as it watched me. I let out my breath. Just a raccoon. No reason to be afraid.

I picked up the flashlight and once again clamped it between my legs. Then I slid the card in and tried again. The latch moved inward ever so slightly. *Steady as she goes.* I rolled my shoulders again. My scalp itched beneath the hot knit cap, but I forced myself to ignore it. Then I pressed harder against the card and felt more movement. Yes!

Suddenly something bumped against the back of my legs. With a gasp I spun around, catching the flashlight before it slipped to the cement. A pair of golden cat eyes blinked up at me, head tilted as if to say, *"Oh, did I scare you?"*

"Go away," I whispered, but the cat only meowed and rubbed against my legs again.

"No, don't do that. Go away."

Being a cat, he interpreted my *no* to mean *try again.* I gave him a nudge with my shoe, and the cat pulled back with a hiss. Down the street, a porch light went on and a woman called, "Here, Tinkums! Here, boy!" The cat scampered off

Tinkums? No wonder he was ill-tempered. I wiped my hands, readjusted the flashlight, and tried again. This time I knew just how to wiggle the card around the latch, and a moment later I felt it give. A little more pressure . . . and . . . it opened.

I paused to glance behind me, just to make sure Tinkums hadn't returned, then slipped inside the house and eased the door shut. The house smelled of moldy food, sour beer, and odors I didn't even want to guess at. I stood motionless until I was satisfied that the house was deserted, but even then I was spooked. Boy, did I wish Reilly was there.

I locked the door, then clicked on the flashlight and shined the beam around the room, keeping it away from the window, which was covered only by a thin curtain on each side. In the dim light I could see a bag of newspapers sitting beside the door, a sink piled high with dishes, a row of cabinets above and below a countertop, a steel-legged table and two chairs, an oven with a crooked door, and — there it was — a mustard gold refrigerator.

"Bingo," I whispered. The prize was a mere three yards away.

I tiptoed across the room and opened the refrigerator only a few inches to make sure the light wouldn't be seen through the window. Inside I saw a six-pack of Budweiser, a carton of eggs, half a loaf of white bread, a partially eaten salami log, jars of pickles, mustard, and mayonnaise, a bottle of ketchup . . . but no white cake box.

Oh, no. Where was the cake?

Letting the door close with a soft *whoosh,* I hunkered low to the ground and cast the beam around the room. Surely he hadn't consumed an entire cake in one day. He must have put the box somewhere else. It wasn't on the table or countertop. Would he have stowed it in a cabinet?

I opened the lower cabinet closest to the refrigerator and peered inside, then made my way along the row to the sink. I got to my feet and worked my way through the high cabinets. In the last one I found what amounted to a pantry. The lowest shelf was stocked with canned soups, tuna, and more jars of pickles. The second held bags of chips and corn puffs and a half-eaten bag of popcorn. I stood on my toes to see the top shelf. Was that a white box way up there?

I put the flashlight on the counter, hoisted myself up, twisted to my knees, and rose. Yes! A white box. I stretched my arms up and carefully lowered it to the counter. Then I turned to slide off and my hand hit the flashlight, sending it skittering down the Formica, into the sink, where it hit an aluminum pot with a loud *clang.*

"Okay, *that* was a stupid move," I whispered.

I retrieved the flashlight, then propped the light on the counter. I freed the side flaps and pulled back the lid, releasing the sweet scent of vanilla. There sat a creamy white frosted cake topped with crystallized yellow roses, green mint leaves and — ha! — dark purple violets. Best of all, one huge slice was missing.

You did it, you clever, multitalented cat woman! Take that, Reilly. Who needs you?

A scrape of metal on metal brought my head around. I listened intently. Was someone trying to get in the front door? Had Reilly come after all?

Then I heard a soft flutter, like someone shaking a sheet, and caught a whiff of something acrid. Burned sage maybe?

Eudora?

CHAPTER
TWENTY-SEVEN

I turned just as a white-robed figure came rushing toward me, crying, "Evil spirits must be purged!"

A scratchy blanket heavy with the cloying odor of smoked herbs was thrown over my head and twisted noose-like around my neck. Before I could even draw a breath I was yanked off my feet and dragged backward across the floor.

"I'm not an evil sprit," I rasped, my voice muffled by the thick fabric. "I'm Abby — from the flower shop."

At once we stopped, sending me scrabbling to loosen the material around my throat only to have her jerk it away with such force that my head hit the floor with a hard thud and my mind spun. Then I felt myself float upward like a giant bubble. Up, up, and away.

Ouch. The back of my head hurt. I tried to

rub it but I couldn't lift my hand . . . or my arm . . . or my other arm. Were they tied behind me? Was I dreaming? I wiggled my fingers and felt linoleum beneath me — gritty, unwashed linoleum. That wasn't a dream.

My eyes flew open and I blinked to bring the light into focus, but it wavered and darted in front of my face. I turned my head and discovered that I had been propped against a cabinet next to the refrigerator. A slim white taper in a brass candlestick appeared in front of me. Behind it stood Eudora, a ghostly, white-robed figure wearing a wooden mask with round eye holes. Why had she tied me? And why was she staring at me as though I had grown horns?

Trying not to appear as nervous as I suddenly felt, I said, "You gave me quite a scare, Eudora. How did you get into the house?"

She jabbed a hand between folds in the robe and produced a key. "If one has purity of heart, the key is always within reach."

Right. More like a spare key under the mat. Ryson must have kept one outside for emergencies, and Eudora had probably seen him hide it. I tugged on the rough cord that dug into my wrists. "There's no reason to tie me. I'm not dangerous. I'm harmless little Abby, the florist from Bloomers. I came to get that cake in the box on the counter."

The mask tilted to one side. "The cake can't leave here," she said, as though explaining to a child.

"It's evidence, Eudora. You can always get another cake. And would you *please* untie my hands? The cord is cutting my wrists."

"You can't have the cake," she said firmly, floating toward the white box. "It has been anointed to kill evil spirits. You shouldn't have removed it from the cabinet."

She anointed the cake? Eudora's cylinders were really misfiring today. I wiggled my wrists back and forth, trying to loosen the binding. Damn, she'd tied it tight. "It's just a cake, Eudora. It can't protect against evil. Besides, Dennis — I mean Sinned — is dead. No evil spirits left. So why don't you let me loose and we can both get out of here?" I swiveled my torso so she could see my hands.

Her voice shook with anger as she swung around to glare at me. "Don't talk to me as if I'm crazy. I know what I'm doing." She set the candlestick on the counter, then began to chant as she produced a small glass jar from her robe. Inside I could see a pale ashy substance.

I tugged harder on the binding, sliding my wrists farther apart as she removed the lid, took a pinch of the contents, and sprinkled it over the frosting and flowers. "What is that, Eudora? Sage?"

"Ohm-m-m-m-castor-ohm-m-m." The mask muffled her words, making them indistinct.

"Castor oil? It looks more like a powder to me."

She shook her head as she continued her ritualistic sprinkling and chanting. "Ohm-m-m-m-casper seeds-ohm-m."

I worked the cord back and forth as I tried to decipher her cryptic drones. Casper seeds? What the heck were casper seeds? Wait. Did she mean *castor* seeds? "Eudora, please tell me you didn't grind up seeds from your castor bean plant."

She nodded.

She *had* ground them. At once my skin began to crawl. Castor bean seeds contained ricin, a deadly substance that would cause an immediate, powerful reaction if even a tiny bit got into the body — headaches, asthma, vomiting, diarrhea, even hallucinations. As a florist, I'd had to educate myself on plant toxins, and I knew this was one of the deadliest.

"Eudora, that powder is poisonous. If

someone were to get some on her fingers, then touched food —" I stopped with a gasp. Dear God. That was exactly what she'd done. She'd snuck into the house and sprinkled poison on the cake. Ryson wouldn't have noticed the taste amidst all that sugary frosting. It would have been sweet revenge for the death of her dog.

No wonder Ryson had complained of feeling ill. It hadn't been the flu at all. That would also explain why he had reacted violently when Marco went to talk to him. He'd just eaten a piece of cake and was out of his mind.

But even with all those symptoms, the seeds wouldn't have killed him instantly, or even a day later, not from eating one slice of cake. It would have taken three or four slices over as many days before the toxins built up in his system enough to kill him. Eudora must have slipped into his house several times over the course of a week. The piece of cake Ryson ate Sunday evening must have been the one that finally did the trick.

"Sinned had to atone for his wicked ways," she said in that eerie monotone. "He was a murderer, and murderers must pay."

"Eudora, listen to me," I said, frantically working the cord behind my back. "I understand how painful it is to lose a pet, but sometimes accidents happen. Sinned probably didn't realize he left that antifreeze out. I'm sure he didn't mean to kill your dog."

At that the chanting stopped and she swung to face me, stamping the white bootie that covered her foot, her hands balled into fists. "Yes, he did mean to kill Daisy. It wasn't an accident. He said he'd do something to her if she didn't stop barking. I *know* he put that pan of antifreeze out for her. I saw him do it!"

Beneath the mask, her voice broke, sounding human for the first time. "That devil lured my Daisy over here and let her drink from the pan. How could he have been so evil? She was a dear little animal, never hurt a soul. She was my baby."

She leaned against the counter, head bowed, weeping softly. I couldn't help but feel sorry for her. I had lost pets, too, and knew the grief could be as devastating as the loss of a family member. But I also didn't trust that Eudora had suddenly become reasonable, either. I had to get that cake out of the house.

My wrists were burning from my efforts to free myself, and I knew the skin had been rubbed raw, but the binding was stretching at last, so I gritted my teeth and pulled my hands as far apart as I could. "I'm so sorry about Daisy," I said, trying to keep her distracted, "but there's nothing we can do about that here. Why don't we go look for another dog? There are so many animals at the humane society that need loving homes."

"I don't want another dog," she said tersely. She closed the box, placed it back on the top shelf, and shut the cabinet door, then turned to face me, her moment of lucidity gone. "You shouldn't have entered this unholy place. You've become tainted." She dangled the jar in front of me. "And now you must be purged."

My heart lurched in terror as Eudora knelt down at my side, her wooden mask with its fierce grimace very near mine, her breath shallow. She was too close for me to use my feet against her. I had to try to talk my way out.

"Eudora, please! I'm not tainted. I have a healthy aura, remember? I can shrug off those evil spirits anytime. Poisoning me won't solve anything. It's just wrong, Eudora. Besides, Sgt. Reilly from the New Chapel Police Department will be here any minute, and if you poison me, you'll be punished. You'll go to jail. No more masks or robes to protect you."

Beads of perspiration gathered between my breasts as she placed the open jar beside me, then dipped her fingertip inside and coated it with the powder. "This won't poison you. It will only cleanse you." She began to chant again, this time invoking ancient deities, immortals, goddesses, and even the ghost of Christmas past.

My heart beat frantically as she drew a cross on my forehead, traced circles around my eyes, then drew a line down the center of my nose to my upper lip. I shook my head, pressing my lips together to keep the powder out of my mouth. There was no way I was going to reason with her now. She was too far gone. I had to act.

When she dipped her finger into the jar a second time, I rolled onto my side away from her, pivoting on one hip, jerking back my knee and driving my shoe against her as hard as I could. I landed a strong kick against her side, knocking her onto her back and upsetting the jar.

"No!" she screeched, scrambling to her knees to sweep up the powder with her hands. "You don't know what you've done! Now *everything* must be purged!"

I scooted toward the doorway that led to the living room but made it only as far as the kitchen table before she came after me.

I tried to swing my legs around in time to fend her off, but she was swifter, grabbing my head from behind and slamming it against the floor. I fought back a wave of nausea and gulped air so I wouldn't black out again, only to have her snatch my knit cap and force a fistful of it into my mouth. Then she hauled me upright, lifted a leg of the table, and inserted it between my back and my bound hands.

Dazed and gagged, I watched helplessly as she pulled newspapers from the bag near the door, balled them up, and placed them around the perimeter of the kitchen. She put more on the counter and even on top of the pots in the sink. Then she held the candle flame to the window curtain and watched as it caught fire. Ryson's old house was a tinderbox. If I didn't act swiftly I'd be burned alive.

Focus, Abby. Don't panic!

I pushed my tongue against the wool in my mouth until I could shake my head and make the cap fall out. "Eudora, please, stop what you're doing and put out that fire. Listen to me. You can't bring back your dog, or make your pain go away, or chase away the evil spirits by burning down this house. But I can help you. Just untie me, please, before we both die."

As though in a trance, Eudora stared at the burning curtain until the fire reached the top of the window and the frame began to smolder. Then she moved to the first ball of paper on the floor and knelt to light it.

My breath was coming in short, frightened gasps as Eudora continued around the room, lighting wads of paper that flared quickly, then curled and turned to ash, filling the room with a thin gray haze. I cast a panicky glance at the paint on the wall and saw it start to blister. It wouldn't take long before the walls themselves caught fire.

"Eudora, stop!" I yelled at the top of my lungs.

She wasn't listening. I had to get help before the whole house was ablaze. Where was my cell phone? In my pocket?

I ducked my head under the table, then pushed up against the underside, raising it until the table leg was in the air, then I slid my hands down and under the plastic tip at the bottom, releasing my arms. As Eudora worked her way toward the sink with her candle, I pulled against the binding at my wrists with so much force that I peeled away the skin on the back of one hand. But my hands were free! I nearly cried in relief.

Suddenly, with a loud *whoosh,* the wood trim around the window burst into flame, lighting up the kitchen and sending plumes of thick, black smoke to the ceiling, where it hovered like a storm cloud. There wasn't time to use my phone. I had to get that cake out.

Afraid to breathe the hot, smoky air, I pulled my T-shirt over my nose and mouth and darted toward the cabinet. Eudora saw me and ran at me with a scream of fury, holding the candle like a shield in front of her, making the flame sputter and go out. I struck out with my right foot and sent it straight into her middle, doubling her over with a grunt of pain.

As she fell to her knees I grabbed her mask and tossed it aside. "Get out, Eudora!"

Stunned, she rolled onto her back and lay gazing up at me with blank eyes. Without her mask Eudora was merely a plain, middle-aged woman with sagging skin at her throat and dark hollows under her eyes. The only sign of her madness was a thick, red, ropelike scar in the shape of a perfect cross on her forehead.

I nudged her with my shoe. "Eudora, hurry. We have to get out of here." But she continued to lie there, so I pulled my shirt over my face and dashed for the cabinet. I'd have to get the cake, then come back for her. I opened the cabinet door and rose onto tiptoe, stretching over the smoldering newspaper on the counter, as though I'd somehow grown three inches in the past ten minutes. Damn! I'd forgotten how high that top shelf was.

Loud pops brought my head up with a jerk. The ceiling over the window was ablaze and a line of fire was spreading rapidly across the room. I blinked burning ash from my eyes and dropped to my knees. I could barely see or draw a breath. How was I going to get the cake? Was there time to drag over a kitchen chair?

The back door burst open with a crash, sending a gust of air into the room that momentarily cleared away the haze, then made the fire rage harder. Two dim figures appeared in the doorway, and in the distance I could bear sirens.

"Abby!" came a shout. It was Marco. Dear Marco, my knight in shining armor. Thank God. He'd be able to reach the top shelf.

Eudora struggled to her knees as powerful flashlight beams lit up the foggy room. "Help me," she rasped, stretching out an arm.

The figures moved into the room. "Abby!" Marco called again.

"I'm over here — to your left. I need help,

Marco. There's a cake in here that will clear you, but I can't reach it."

"The ceiling is going to collapse," Reilly shouted. "You need to get out now!"

"Not without the cake. Hurry, Marco." I crouched near the floor as the smoke grew thicker. My eyes watered and even through the cotton shirt over my face I could feel my nose stinging with each inhaled breath.

Long legs appeared through the haze and suddenly Marco's face was in front of mine, a white mask over his nose. "Get out now!" he shouted over the roar of the flames.

I pointed to the open cabinet. "White box. Top shelf."

"I'll get it. Crawl to the door. Go!"

Then other arms reached for me and I was pulled across the floor and out into the backyard, where medics whisked me across the yard and put me on a portable gurney. I raised my head from the makeshift bed, anxiously watching the back door as firefighters ran past, pulling heavy hoses, until at last Marco came out carrying the singed white box.

I cried hoarsely, "Marco, be careful. The cake is poisoned. It's in the frosting." My voice gave out and all I could do was gesture. But Marco got it. He turned the box over to Reilly and the two held a hurried conversation. The medics gave me something cool to drink, then fastened an oxygen mask over my nose. I eased my aching head against the paper-covered pillow and let them bandage my hands and wrists.

Then at once Marco was there, his white mask dangling around his neck. He gathered me in his arms, oxygen line and all, and whispered fiercely, "Thank God you're all right."

Tears misted my blurry gaze and my throat hurt when I spoke, but I needed to make him understand. "Eudora was poisoning Ryson with castor bean seeds. She ground them up and sprinkled them in the cake frosting. The plant is in her kitchen. Now we can prove you didn't kill Ryson."

"You risked your life for a cake?"

My throat tightened and tears spilled down my face. "Not for a cake, you idiot. For you."

"I know," he whispered, and although my vision was clouded, I thought there were tears in his eyes, too.

"We're going to take you to the hospital to check you out," one of the EMTs told me.

I nodded. My throat felt as though it was on fire, and my eyes hurt so much I could barely keep them open.

"Is she okay?" I heard a familiar voice growl.

I lifted the plastic cup to croak, "You're late, Reilly."

He showed me his watch, but I couldn't bring it into focus. "It's nine o'clock," he said. "I'm right on time."

I blinked up at him in astonishment. How could that have happened? I tried to check my own watch but couldn't make out the numbers.

Marco leaned over for a look, tapped the front, then put his ear against it. "Looks like you've got a dead battery."

It was my fault, not Reilly's. All I could do was shake my head in disbelief. If it hadn't been so frightening, it might have been funny. "Sorry," I whispered, feeling like an idiot.

Reilly patted my shoulder. "Don't worry about it. We've got the cake and we have Eudora. She's being taken to the psych ward."

"Her husband," I rasped. "Is he here?"

"From what we can make of Eudora's rambling, he's bowling. Get to the hospital now. I'll be there shortly to get a statement from you."

I caught Reilly's shirtsleeve and motioned for him to bend close. "Why did you bring

Marco here? What if Captain You-Know-Who shows up?"

"Would you stop worrying? We knew what we were doing." He patted the gurney. "Okay, boys, take her away."

Marco walked alongside me as I was wheeled to the street, where I could see a line of flashing red and blue lights, hulking fire trucks, and yellow-jacketed figures running toward the house, which was now fully ablaze. As the medic settled me in for the ride to the hospital and the driver prepared to shut the back door, Marco took a seat on the bench beside me, a smudge of dark hair and tanned skin to my burning eyes.

His hand stroked the side of my face as the ambulance pulled away, siren blaring. "How are you doing, Sunshine?" he asked tenderly.

I whispered through the plastic, "Glad to see you."

"Believe me, I can't tell you how glad I was to see you, too — alive. What I'd like to know is why you didn't tell me what you were planning this evening. You're damn lucky you mentioned it to Reilly."

"I *couldn't* tell you. This was too important — my last chance to prove your innocence. Besides, you would have insisted on coming with me, and I didn't want to put you at risk. Anyway, I was afraid I might not pull it off. I didn't want to let you down."

"Let me down?" He gazed at me with eyes full of gratitude. "You would never let me down, Abby. I'm a lucky man to have you on my side."

Those words were music to my ears. And with that music playing in my head and settling deep into my heart, I surrendered to the overwhelming urge to sleep.

CHAPTER
TWENTY-EIGHT

For a short while my curtained cubicle in the emergency room teemed with people in white coats whose faces were blobs to me because of the ointment in my eyes. Now, finally I was alone, lying in a bed and covered by a thin blanket, wearing a blue gown that tied in the back. Luckily, I no longer needed the oxygen mask, although the doctor was still awaiting results from the chest X-ray that had been taken upon my arrival.

Then two big shapes came through the curtain, one in dark blue with a shiny silver badge on his front, and the other a figure I would know anywhere, even with goo-coated eyeballs.

Marco leaned down to press a kiss on my cheek, which had been washed free of soot and castor bean powder. "Are you okay?"

I tried to clear my throat, not that it helped any. "My head aches, my hands sting, my nose burns, and I can't see or smell, but other than that I'm peachy. Would you raise my bed, please?"

He pressed a button and the top half of the bed brought my head up. "Sean wants to get your statement, if you're up to it."

"Water first," I rasped.

Marco picked up the plastic cup from the portable stand beside the bed and held it to my lips. I swallowed a few soothing sips, then cleared my throat again. "Let's do it."

"I'm going to record you," Reilly said. "All you have to do is answer my questions and speak slowly. Take your time. I'll guide you through it." He started the recorder, then stated his name and rank, the date and time, and our location. Then he said, "I'm here with Abigail Knight, owner of Bloomers Flower Shop in New Chapel, Indiana. Ms. Knight, would you tell me what happened this evening, starting with your reason for being at the property owned by Dennis Ryson?"

"First of all, let me state for the record that I knew right from the start that Marco — that's Marco Salvare, owner of the Down the Hatch Bar and Grill — was not the person who killed Dennis Ryson. Marco is a good man. If he says he didn't kill someone, he means it. Look at his face. There's integrity written all over it. And how the prosecutor could think otherwise —"

Reilly stopped the tape. "Abby, you're not trying to convince a jury. That's the lawyer's job. Just tell us what happened."

"Don't get testy, Reilly. I was getting to it."

He threw me a skeptical glance as he pressed Record.

I reached for the cup to take another drink, then launched into my story, trying to make it as concise as possible. "I went to the Ryson home because I had good reason to suspect that the violets on a cake in that house had been coated with a toxin. I thought Ryson's mother had poisoned the cake — well, actually she's his stepmother, but what's important is that I was totally mistaken about her. She really is the most naive person I've ever met. Anyway, I was certain the cake would prove Marco's innocence, and since I had determined that it was most likely in Ryson's refrigerator, I had to get inside —"

Instantly, Reilly hit the Pause button.

"What?" I asked.

Marco handed me the cup. "Have some more water. You sound hoarse." He leaned close to whisper, "Skip the part where you break in, okay?"

"Did you really think I would put that on the record?"

After a sip I continued. "I found the cake but it wasn't in the refrigerator after all. It was on the top shelf of a cabinet, which I thought was an odd place to put it."

I saw Reilly's hand motion for me to get on with it.

"Anyway, I'd just managed to get the cake down when Eudora Mazella attacked me and knocked me out. When I came to, my hands were tied and she was ranting about how the cake couldn't leave the house because it kept away the evil spirits. That's when she showed me the ground castor bean seeds she'd been adding to the frosting. You'll find a castor bean plant in Eudora's kitchen, by the way. The seeds contain a poisonous chemical called ricin, which would have caused Ryson — Wait. Ricin and Ryson? Is that cosmic, or what?"

Marco nudged me.

"Well, it *is* cosmic! Anyway, the ricin would have caused him to be seriously ill, and he'd never notice it in all that sugary icing." I paused for another drink. The talking was making my throat worse.

"Eudora had been sprinkling powder on his cakes for days, so each time he ate a slice he got sicker, until the toxins built up enough to kill him. The poison would have given him terrible headaches and even hallucinations. And that's why he acted so crazy on Sunday, Marco. He'd just had a piece of cake. He would have died whether you were there or not."

Reilly paused the recorder again. "Talk to the tape, Abby, not to Marco."

"Sorry." I waited until he hit Record; then I continued. "What amazes me about this whole situation is that even with all her delusions, Eudora was shrewd enough to figure out that those cakes Ryson's mother brought each week would be the perfect vehicle for his so-called cleansing and purging. She also showed me the key she used to get in. I'm guessing it was a spare she saw Ryson hide outside. She was always watching from her window.

"And because I removed the cake from the cabinet, she had to purge my evil spirits, too. This woman is seriously mental." My voice cracked again. I knew it wouldn't last much longer so I ended it with a quick wrap-up. "She started the kitchen on fire, I got my hands loose, and then you arrived. And you know the rest."

"Is there a chance her husband knew what she was up to?" Reilly asked.

"He knew something was wrong because

he warned me to stay away."

"Did Eudora admit to killing Ryson?"

"Not in those words. She blamed him for her dog's death and said he had to pay for his sins. But the tox report will prove she poisoned him."

Reilly turned off the tape. "Okay, that should do it for now. I'll take this down to the station and have it transcribed, and then tomorrow you'll have to read and sign it. You know the drill." He patted my foot. "Take it easy."

A moment after he'd gone I heard Nikki call, "Abby? Where are you?" Then a white blob came through the curtain. I'd forgotten Nikki was still at the hospital. Her shift didn't end until midnight.

"I just heard what happened from the X-ray tech. Omigod, Abs, look at you! Your eyes, your hands, your wrists . . . Are you in pain? Stupid question. How could you not be in pain? Did they give you something? Wait! Don't answer. Just nod."

"Nikki, you're giving me a headache," I rasped. "I'll tell you about it tomorrow."

"She's had a rough day," Marco said, putting his hand on my shoulder.

"I'm sorry. I just got so scared when I heard the news that I freaked." Nikki burst into tears. "I mean, she's my best friend. We grew up together. I'm not normally like this, you know. Ask Abby. Wait. Never mind. That was dumb. Don't ask."

Her beeper went off, so she grabbed a tissue from the box beside my bed, blew her nose, then was all business again. "Are they keeping her here overnight?"

"Depends on the X-ray," Marco said.

"I'll go check it out. Oh, I almost forgot. Be expecting some visitors."

"Now?" Marco asked.

Nikki checked her watch. "Yeah, pretty much."

I lifted my head. "Nikki, what did you do?"

She was back at my side immediately. "Abby, don't hate me. Your mother made me swear that if anything ever happened to you I'd call her at once. I'm sorry, but I had no choice."

I laid my head back with a groan.

"I called Lottie and Grace, too," she added.

"I'm out of here," Marco said.

I clutched his arm. "Don't you dare leave me now."

From outside the curtain I suddenly heard a woman call, "Where is she? Where is the little bambina who saved my son's life? Stand back. Let me through, do you hear?

My son's girlfriend is here and she needs me."

I turned my head toward the smudge that was Marco. "You called *your* mother?"

"She was there when Reilly came to get me. I had to let her know what happened."

The curtain was swept back and a dark blur bustled toward my bed. At once I was engulfed in a cloud of Italian seasoning, which was a big improvement over sage and smoke.

"Oh, my poor bambina! What a brave thing you have done. How will I ever thank you?" She peppered my cheeks with noisy kisses. "Look how pale you are. Have they fed you? Marco, hand me my bag. Mama Francesca will take care of everything."

She took a shopping bag from him and produced something wrapped in shiny foil. "There's nothing my cannoli cannot fix, eh, Marco?" She swept a plate under my nose, but I couldn't smell a thing. My nose hairs were singed.

There was more commotion outside, then Mom rushed in, Dad in his wheelchair right behind her. On their heels were Lottie and Grace, and suddenly everyone was chattering away and hugging one another and me. Behind them came the nurses, shushing their loud voices and trying to shoo them all out, but no one paid the least bit of attention. Marco whispered good-bye in my ear, then disappeared. The rat. He braved a fire to save me but cowered before a few hyperventilating middle-agers?

"My poor baby!" Mom cried, and I was hugged again. She pulled back to examine me, decided I wasn't in any grave danger, then began to scold. "Do you have any idea the fright you've given us? Just wait, young lady. One of these days you'll have a daughter who'll scare you half to death."

"It is always so with children, yes?" Francesca said to my parents, shaking her head at me. "They'll rip your heart to pieces every time. Have a cannoli."

"Don't listen to those clucking mother hens," my dad said. "You've made us proud, honey. You're a brave woman. I hope Marco appreciates what you did for him."

Right. He appreciated it so much, he deserted me.

"Yes, you are brave, sweetie," Lottie said, patting my foot. "You said you were going to find the killer and you did. You hung in there even when there was nothing left to hang on to. I'm so proud I could burst my buttons . . . Why, thanks, Mrs. Salvare. I *will* have one of your cannolis."

Grace stepped up to the end of the bed.

"What's important is that you persevered, dear. As John Quincy Adams said, 'Courage and perseverance have a magical talisman, before which difficulties disappear and obstacles vanish into air.' "

I clapped my hands over my ears. "I never want to hear about magical talismans or ghost or spirits or any other kind of supernatural gobbledygook again."

Everyone stopped talking and stared at me. So naturally I had to explain about Eudora, which left me once again with no voice. In the half hour that followed, I was coddled and cuddled and stuffed with sweets, surrounded by everyone near and dear to me. Almost everyone, that was. Nikki was back on duty in the X-ray department, and Marco, well, I'd deal with him tomorrow for abandoning me in my true hour of need.

Still, although I loved each one of them and normally wouldn't mind being the center of attention, after having my hands tied and my skin ripped, and then nearly suffocating in a smoke-filled kitchen, well . . . being trapped in that tiny cubicle and smothered with all that love and attention, not to mention cannoli, was enough to make anyone feel claustrophobic.

At last the curtain parted and a nurse in

blue scrubs pushed a wheelchair up to the bed, scattering the clucking women. "Excuse me. We need to take her down for another X-ray."

That was the first time in my life I actually looked forward to being zapped.

Another nurse helped shift me to the chair; then I was wheeled out of the cubicle.

"We'll be here when you get back, Abigail," my mother called.

Maybe I could talk a doctor into sedating me.

Down the hallway we went, into a deep elevator. Another figure in blue scrubs joined us for the ride to the ground floor. The elevator door opened and I was whisked up a hallway. But instead of stopping at the X-ray department, we moved past it, all the way to the end, where a set of automatic doors let us outside.

I sat up, blinking ointment out of my eyes so I could see. "What's going on?"

A deep, familiar voice off to the side said, "You didn't really think I'd abandon you, did you?"

I turned my head and there stood Marco, leaning against the hood of his car. Although he wasn't much more than an outline to me, he couldn't have looked sexier even viewed in high definition.

My heart expanded several times over as he uncrossed his arms and sauntered over. He gave a nod to the nurses, who slipped back inside; then he scooped me out of the chair into his arms. "Ready to go?"

"You bet I am. But what do we do about our parents? And Lottie and Grace?"

"Nikki is on her way there right now to tell them about a celebration party at my bar, and that you've been sent home to rest under strict orders by your physician, not to be disturbed until tomorrow morning at the earliest."

"My physician?"

"Your *personal* physician." Marco lifted a dark eyebrow, setting off tingles in places I didn't even know *could* tingle. "Doctor Salvare, at your service."

Whoo, boy. Personal physician, knight in shining armor, all around great guy — what more could a girl ask for? Hmm. Well . . .

"So tell me, Dr. Salvare, do you make house calls?"

"Depends on the problem." He slid me onto the passenger seat, then pulled my seal belt across my lap. "Want to tell the doctor about it?"

I walked two fingers up his arm as he clicked the belt into place. "Well, Doc, my symptoms started Saturday at the Pickle

Fest, when this incredibly sexy guy gave me an ice cream cone. Now, whenever I think about that moment, my pulse races, my stomach flutters, and my skin becomes acutely sensitive to the touch of certain males, resulting in a disturbing sensation of melting, and I don't mean the ice cream."

"Sounds serious."

"Oh, it is." My fingers reached his jaw, covered now by a trace of stubble. "And that's not the worst of it. I also get this uncontrollable urge for something tall, dark, and — sweet."

"An uncontrollable urge?" Marco's mouth curved up in that wicked little way of his; then he leaned closer to kiss me, his lips making featherlight contact with mine, temptingly, playfully hinting at more tingles to come. "That's my specialty."

ABOUT THE AUTHOR

Kate Collins, a former teacher, lives with her husband in Northwest Indiana during the mild months, then high-tails it down to Key West for as much of the winter as possible. She's also the author of several romance novels under various pseudonyms. Visit her Web site at www.katecollinsbooks .com.

We hope you have enjoyed this Large Print book. Other Thorndike, Wheeler, and Chivers Press Large Print books are available at your library or directly from the publishers.

For information about current and upcoming titles, please call or write, without obligation, to:

Publisher
Thorndike Press
295 Kennedy Memorial Drive
Waterville, ME 04901
Tel. (800) 223-1244

or visit our Web site at:

www.gale.com/thorndike
www.gale.com/wheeler

OR

Chivers Large Print
published by BBC Audiobooks Ltd
St James House, The Square
Lower Bristol Road
Bath BA2 3SB
England
Tel. +44(0) 800 136919
email: bbcaudiobooks@bbc.co.uk
www.bbcaudiobooks.co.uk

All our Large Print titles are designed for easy reading, and all our books are made to last.